The

LUNCHTIME CLUB
DETECTIVE AGENCY
and the Mystery of
STRANGWAY
TOWER

MICHAEL A. GILBY

authorHOUSE®

AuthorHouse™ UK
1663 Liberty Drive
Bloomington, IN 47403 USA
www.authorhouse.co.uk
Phone: 0800.197.4150

Published by AuthorHouse 09/21/2018

ISBN: 978-1-5462-9772-7 (sc)
ISBN: 978-1-5462-9773-4 (hc)
ISBN: 978-1-5462-9799-4 (e)

Cover image: by kind permission of Pixabay (Braxmeier & Steinberger GbR, eu-Ulm, Germany)
http://www.pixabay.com

Character realisation and original designs: David Gregory, Motion Studio
http://www.motionstudiojersey.com

5% of sales from this book are being donated by the author to Autism Jersey, The Hot Bananas' chosen charity.

A LIMITLESS, CLEAN, RENEWABLE SOURCE OF ENERGY HAS BEEN DISCOVERED.

There are no emissions. No nuclear waste that needs storing for centuries. There is no sickness or disease due to the illegal dumping of waste, or because of polluted air and water sources. This is a dream come true for governments and environmental protection and interest groups alike. It is the stuff of nightmares for the giant conglomerates controlling our lives through their hold over the world's energy resources and infrastructures.

The new energy is free to the consumer - but it comes at a great cost to us all.

OUR FREEDOM.

Access to this life-giving power is controlled by one man and his ruthless empire. He will stop at nothing to maintain his hold over us and our hunger for his energy. He has aggressively taken over oil giants, utility companies, power infrastructures, manufacturing giants, food suppliers and manufacturers, and world-wide providers renewable energy sources.

This powerful man has toppled governments, manipulated armies and infiltrated the very organisations and institutions in place to protect us. He destroys the lives of those who stand in his way. He will dispose of those who dare speak out against him. He wants one thing and one thing only from us:

OUR TOTAL OBEDIENCE.

ONE GROUP IS ALL THAT STANDS BETWEEN US
AND THIS AWFUL DYSTOPIA:

PROFESSOR WEISS AND HIS LUNCHTIME CLUB DETECTIVE AGENCY

DEDICATION

For Morgan:	My son. My inspiration.
Dad:	Sorely missed.
Gabi:	My love, my passion, my soulmate.
The Hot Bananas:	Well, there simply aren't the words...
Silkworth Lodge:	For my life.

EPIGRAPH

Truth is stranger than Fiction, but it is because Fiction is obliged to stick to possibilities; Truth isn't.

Mark Twain

PREFACE

From the desk of Professor Thomas Edison Weiss, PhD., MD., RGS.

In my life, I have done many things. Some were required of me, dictated by the needs of my country or my fellow man. Other paths I have chosen to follow because it was right to do so. I have often been asked why I chose to teach school - for me, it's the right thing to do.

It's quite simple, really...children are like sponges, soaking up information and experiences with such energy and enthusiasm. No two children are the same. They have different interests, priorities, skills and approaches to life. Sometimes a child will come along with a unique combination of all these traits.

Over the years I have been fortunate enough to be able to take these children and their talents and show them how the application of their skills can contribute to the common good.

I formed my first Lunchtime Club Detective Agency more years ago than I care to remember. Each Agency is unique because no two groups of Agents are the same. This current crop is one of the finest.

They only have two weapons at their disposal: their talents and the fact that people underestimate them because *they are only children.*

However, this is one bunch of 'kids' you underestimate at your peril. You bad guys out there have been warned...my Agents are coming for you.

Prof TE Weiss

Professor T.E. Weiss

PROLOGUE

The only sound in the room was a quiet *zzz-zzz-zzz* as the darkly clad figure rappelled down a rope from above the dimly lit and heavily shadowed room.

Once detached from the rope, the figure moved quietly, hugging the dark shadows along the edge of the large display hall, farthest from the single wide-angle security camera. Its red blinking light was the only indication that it was actually there, but it was ready to set off a whole host of alarms, locks, sirens and lights.

The figure moved so quickly that the camera light had blinked only twice in the time it took to cover the distance across the wide expanse of marble floor. Soon, the barely visible form stood in front of a glass case, which shone with bright pencil-thin laser beams criss-crossing the interior. A spotlight lit a single object centred on the black baize base of the display case.

The cone-shaped object glinted like a mirror, reflecting the dazzling red and white of the spotlights and laser beams. It lay propped up to reveal a hollow interior, slightly duller than the exterior surface.

Within moments, the shadowy figure moved away from the display case and melded into the darkness, moving slightly slower now.

Whatever was in the case was gone. All that remained were the lights showing tiny particles of dust in the air, and a neat, circular hole in the glass.

THE MUSEUM

Deputy Sheriff Tim O'Connell received the call at 8.20 a.m. He was on his way to the Dalton County Sheriff's Department headquarters on the outskirts of town when the voice of Maggie, the department dispatcher, brought his radio to life.

"Dispatch to Deputy Sheriff O'Connell. Tim, report your position. Over."

"This is Tim, Maggie. I'm on Route 301, Jacksonville Road, heading into town. What can I do for you? Coffee and doughnuts? Over."

Tim could sense the joy in her voice, but instead she replied, "Later, Tim. First, could you swing by the museum? There's been a theft. Over."

The deputy dispensed with the usual radio etiquette.

"What's missing?"

"I don't know."

"Have you asked them?"

An insulted Maggie answered sharply, "I'm no rookie, Tim. Of course I asked them. They simply don't know."

1

"What? Er, yeah, okay. Tell them I'm on my way. I'll be there in ten minutes."

"Roger that, Tim. Drey will be there to meet you." Then she said sharply, "Out."

Deputy O'Connell rolled his eyes. "It's too early in the day to get on the wrong side of Maggie," he said out loudly to himself.

I usually make it through until lunchtime before getting a withering look or her sharp tongue.

At exactly 8.31 a.m., Deputy Sheriff O'Connell pulled up outside the town's museum. He stepped out of the car and looked around him.

The handsome sandstone edifice was the only stone building in this part of town. The rest were built in the traditional way - wooden lap; multi-panelled transom windows; wooden covered walkways, some with signs hanging on chains that squeaked and creaked in the warm breeze. They were painted a rainbow of colours, some fresher than others.

The more unkempt façades had faded to reveal the original wood, now silvery grey with age. The old saloon still had swing doors like in the old B western movies, and a horse rail and water trough outside. These were more for the tourists to enjoy than for the locals to use. Some buildings were now homes, but many still showed the names of current or previous owners and indicated what they might once have one been or still were.

His great-grandfather once owned the ruddy-brown building straight ahead of him, long since a private home, but still carrying his great-grandfather's name:

Pádraig O'Connell, Esquire.
Purveyor of Fine Tobacco, Stogies,
Dip and Everflame Matches.

He couldn't help a little ironic smile appearing on his lips. His great-grandfather had never smoked in his life but provided well for his family by selling tobacco to those who did.

The only other non-wooden structure was the small church on the eastern edge of the square, built in red brick. Its stained-glass windows showed scenes from the lives of various saints, and its slated spire proudly thrust upwards into the blue summer sky. He lifted his hat and wiped his brow with a handkerchief. *It is going to be another scorchingly hot day by the look of that sky,* he thought.

He turned and walked into the cool shade of the museum. He knew this place well, bringing his son here on a regular basis. Francis Pádraig O'Connell had such a thirst for knowledge that he and his wife actively encouraged and supported his enthusiasm, taking him to museums, libraries, and historic monuments wherever they travelled in the States.

Next year, they were going to take Frankie (he only ever allowed his paternal grandfather to call him by his given name) on a bus trip around Europe. Tim could well remember the sheer joy on his son's face when he heard the news. His son didn't sleep that night, and he'd been planning what he wanted to see ever since. The Louvre in Paris was at the top of the list, closely followed by the Albert and Victoria Museum in London. He and his wife, Jenny, were more than willing to fall in with Frankie's ideas; it meant they didn't have to do much planning. All they had to do was listen to their son's plans - and book and pay, of course.

Deputy O'Connell found the museum curator, Dr. Drey Swan, near an empty display case. He stood behind the yellow line of police tape, his right hand on his cheek as he slowly shook his head from side to side, with his left hand on his hip.

He heard the deputy's footsteps and turned. As he started walking towards Deputy O'Connell, he smiled sadly, and said, "Hi, Tim."

"Morning, Drey. Had a spot of trouble, I hear. Something about a theft?"

"Yes. Happened sometime last night."

"Just a moment."

The deputy took a smartphone out of his pocket, swiped and tapped the screen a few times, and then spoke into it.

"Record. State date and time. Allocate new case identity."

The phone responded with a soft feminine, staccato voice, "Recording. Date: May nine, two-zero-one-seven. Time: Zero-eight-four-one, Eastern time. New case identity: Two-three-zero-zero-Tango-Oscar-Charlie."

Tim spoke into the phone: "Present, Deputy Sheriff Timothy O'Connell of the Dalton County Sheriff's Department and Dr. Drey Swan of the Dalton Historical Society and Museum."

Dr. Swan asked, "What's happening?"

Tim held up the phone.

"Oh, it's a new system I've introduced to the department. We record everything on one of these smartphones, synchronise it to the computers in the office, and our report is automatically written, warts and all. The voice recording is also saved on the central server. Great for the chain of evidence trail. Okay, Dr. Swan…"

"…C'mon, Tim, call me Drey. You did at the barbecue the other evening."

The deputy nodded towards the phone and continued, "Dr. Swan, can you describe the chain of events that led to the discovery of the theft please?"

"I closed the museum doors as normal at six p.m. and worked for about thirty minutes before doing my final rounds. I then checked that the security cameras were working, set the alarms, and left, locking the door behind me."

"You say that you closed up at six p.m. Did you lock the doors at that point?"

"No, I did what I always do. I bolted the doors, top and bottom."

"Did you notice anything unusual or out of place during your rounds?"

"No, nothing."

"Did you notice anything or anyone unusual or suspicious outside when you left?"

"No."

"When did you notice the thefts?"

"Theft, singular. Only one thing was stolen. It was discovered when John did his morning rounds at about seven-forty-five a.m."

"For the record, Dr. Swan, who is John?"

"Dr. John Atherton, my assistant."

"Thank you. Can you tell me exactly what was stolen?"

"I don't know."

"That again. What don't you know?" Tim asked, exasperated by the curator's answer.

Dr. Swan gestured, turned, and pointed. "Come with me."

He led the deputy to the display case with a neat round hole in the glass, handed him an information leaflet from a pile on a small console table, opened his own, and pointed to the picture of a hollow conical object.

"It's a cone of some kind, made from an alloy nobody can identify, and made to a technical standard modern technology cannot replicate, purpose unknown."

"Any idea of the age of the object?"

"No. It can't be carbon dated. Well, that's inaccurate. Every time it is tested, its age has changed. Minor fluctuations, but they're there nonetheless. The relative composition and nature of the component elements within it also fluctuate."

"Sorry?"

"No two tests give exactly the same results. It's as if the elements making up the artefact are in constant flux."

"Okay, let me get this straight, Drey ... er - Dr. Swan - now then, I only studied science to freshman level in college - but isn't that - er - impossible?"

"It is theoretically possible if one of the elements has a high atomic rate of decay - such as one of the superheavy elements. But for it to fluctuate up and down like this, elements are forming and then either disappearing or decaying into other elements. That's the theory. But practically ..." Dr. Swan's voice trailed off as he shrugged his shoulders.

He continued.

"Another thing, Tim. It's dense. The volume of the hollowed cone is about fifty cubic centimetres, but it weighs an incredible thirty kilograms."

"I'm old school - in American?"

"Three cubic inches and over sixty-six pounds."

The deputy whistled.

"That is dense. Is there anything you do actually know for certain about this thing?"

"It was dug up thirty-four years ago on the outskirts of town, when they were building your estate, Sunny Meadows."

"Really? I didn't realise. We've only been living there for four years, but I vaguely remember the development being built when I used to visit Aunt Judy on the farm. What condition was the artefact in when it was found?"

"As if it had been made - milled, cast, moulded, or … whatever - just yesterday."

"Hmm. Er, that will be all for now, Dr. Swan. I'll just check to see if the SOC guys have everything they need to get off to the forensics lab in Jacksonville. May we take the security video recordings?"

"I've already made a copy. It's on this stick."

Dr. Swan handed the deputy sheriff a USB memory stick.

"Thanks. If you remember anything else, you know how to contact me. Thank you."

The deputy hesitated a moment. Then he asked:

"If this object is so darned hard to get a handle on, what's it doing in a museum in Smallville USA? Er, no offence."

Dr. Swan smiled.

"None taken. The guys in the state museum in Tallahassee ran every test in the book. We send them regular updates of our own radiocarbon dating tests, but they're happy for it to be kept here as a local curio. They didn't want to go to the cost of creating a replica and storing the original."

"Couldn't they just display the original?"

"This *is* the original. They said that they have too many other, 'more interesting' artefacts to put on display and not enough floor space."

"Don't you find that strange? I mean, unknown artefact, a scientific oddity, posing more questions than it answers, and so on. Or the Feds? No interest from them?"

He realised that he was asking too many questions far too quickly, but his interest was piqued.

"No interest from the Feds, either, Tim. They didn't even give us any funding for improvements to our security and new radiocarbon dating equipment, that all came from Tallahassee. To be honest, I find a lot of what they do up-state strange, but they're the funders. I play the game by their rules, don't ask too many questions and they leave us alone, pretty much. Just the way we like it, to be honest."

"Thank you again, Dr. Swan."

To the phone he said, "Cease recording, save and synch."

"Recording ceased, saved and synchronising... synchronising complete."

"Thanks, Drey. If I find anything out, I'll be in touch. You, Anna and Leo at the kids' ball game this evening?"

"We'll be there. You?"

"Jenny's working late, but I'm taking Frankie along. Until later, then."

After shaking hands with Dr. Swan, Deputy O'Connell turned to walk back towards his car.

Dr. Swan called his name.

"Tim"

The deputy turned.

"We don't know what the cone is, but whoever did this knew what they were taking. The valuable stuff here, the native American artefacts and the Spanish Treasure Trove, was all left untouched. What possible value could it have on the black market?"

Deputy O'Connell shrugged his shoulders.

"A super heavy paperweight, perhaps? You're the expert, Drey ... you're the expert."

Outside, he took one last look at the museum, got into his car and drove away.

Strange start to the day, he thought. Little did he know that this case would get even stranger.

THE AGENCY

The two figures moved furtively along corridor twelve, hugging the walls as instructed. They hid at the end of a long row of blue metal lockers, each six feet high to accommodate two shelves and a hanging rail. The tops of the lockers sloped slightly forward so that nothing could be placed on top of them without falling off. The school management were strict on tidiness, almost to the point of obsession.

The corridor and the usually busy area in front of the lockers was empty – it was lunchtime recess, and other students would be in the cafeteria or outside in the brilliant midday sunshine for the next hour: eating, chatting, joking, reading, working, playing ball, or shooting hoops.

A red haired head peeped from around the edge of the end locker, and surveyed the scene.

"All clear," he whispered.

The two figures moved quickly to the entrance of a side corridor. This time a blond haired head peered around the corner.

She whispered, "All clear. I can see the door. Come on, quickly now."

They moved towards a solid looking wooden door, with an opaque glass panel set into it at eye level. Lettering centred on the panel read:

SCIENCE LABORATORY 1

PROFESSOR WEISS, DEAN OF FACULTY

The boy knocked out a rhythm they'd been taught, gently on the door. Tap-tap-tap—tap—tap-tap-tap. He waited a few seconds, then repeated the pattern.

Unbeknown to them, as soon as they entered corridor twelve, a tiny security camera had slid silently out of a partition in the wall above the laboratory door and had been tracking their progress from one hiding place to another.

Inside the laboratory a bodiless electronic voice said, "Our visitors have arrived, Professor Weiss."

All eyes in the room turned toward the door.

"Thank you, Computer. You may let them in."

Outside, the boy and the girl heard the door click almost imperceptibly. The same electronic voice said, "Please enter."

The girl pushed the door open, and the pair stepped inside to be greeted by nine sets of eyes. Some stood to one side, some sat at desks and one set of eyes belonged to a boy who had poked his head from behind a computer monitor.

A male voice, gravelly but kind, said, "Welcome to the two of you. Please, ladies and gentlemen, make yourself known."

The voice came from behind a newspaper being held up by someone sitting behind the raised bench at the front of the laboratory.

Nearest to the newcomers, two slim, pretty blond girls seemed to be practising a martial art 'Kata' routine.

One said, pointing at the other, "Hi, she's Arma, Arma Van Varenberg..."

The other pointed back and said, "....and she's Bladen Van Varenberg."

Together, they giggled and said, "We're twins, and we are from Vlanderen - Flanders in Belgium!"

Next to them, someone sat at a bench but with his back to the boy and the girl. He stood to face them, unwinding his huge frame. They gasped.

He was 6' 5" tall and three feet across the chest, if he was an inch. He took off his baseball cap and smiled broadly, his smile a dazzling white against his black skin. A deep, rich Paul Robeson voice boomed.

"I'm Charles James the Third, but everyone calls me Chuck. I'm so happy to meet you."

Further along the room, hunched over a device of some kind, was a diminutive girl of Oriental origin, sporting thick-lensed glasses, her fine raven-black hair gelled into gentle spikes.

She screwed up her eyes as she looked at them, and in a slightly shaky voice said, "Hi. I'm Spex."

There came the sound of a throat being cleared from behind the newspaper.

Spex said, "My given name is Eu-meh Liu. I, too, am pleased to meet you."

At the end of row of benches was a tall, thin androgynous character - boy or girl, they couldn't tell - baseball hat on the head backwards, jeans rough-cut just below the knees and brown lace-up boots which came midway up to the knees. He or she was pumping a rubber ball in his or her half gloved left hand, chewing gum.

"Fingers," the character said, clicking a finger and winking in their direction.

The clearing of the throat and the rustle of the newspaper again.

"Aw, c'mon Professor! Nobody ever calls me that other name."

Further newspaper rustling prompted, "Okay, okay. Anna Carmenita Ramos."

Then, with a glance towards the newspaper, "or *Fingers*, at your service. I'm what some people call 'the ultimate concierge'. I can get you anything – legit or … er … y'know, maybe not so much."

The two newcomers looked at each other.

She whispered, "I don't even know what that means!"

He nodded in agreement, "Nor I."

They looked to their left. A curly blonde head belonging to a boyish face, appeared once more from behind a computer monitor.

"Hi, hi. I'm Dexter Madison. They had all sort of lame names picked out for me: Dot, dot-dash. Zero-one. Binary. Now they call me Dex the Hex. Get it? Computer geek, hexadecimal, get it? Or Hex for short. Should be in Junior High, but they say I'm a high flier."

He shrugged his shoulders.

"Whatever!"

Dexter had said all this without drawing breath. He carried on.

"Wanna see what I'm doing? Way cool. Writing an algorithm to create depth perception in visual devices, for Spex over there, no refocussing, and gives a photometric reading in lumens per steradian across a range of spectra....."

The clearing of the throat from behind the newspaper, again.

"Yeah, okay, another time, yeah."

The head disappeared behind the monitor again.

At the next desk sat a boy with dark, slicked back hair, brightly framed spectacles, wearing a collar and tie. The tie matched his spectacles. He had books laid out open in front of him. He was working something out on a calculator.

He looked up and said, "Hello. I'm Martin Huntley. I work with numbers – I'm interested in accounting, shares, fiduciary matters, markets, that kind of thing."

The blond head appeared again.

"He didn't have a handle like us. No. I thought of Shares – no."

"I thought Figures would fit, but a no go with that one," said Fingers.

"I put forward Calc, rather apt, I believed. Ah, rejection wounds!" said Chuck.

Arma said, "Eventually he settled upon Marty, which was accepted."

"Tell them why that is, Marty," said Bladen

"Marty McFly is my favourite movie character. I'm comfortable with Marty."

A pale skinned, dark haired girl with huge light brown doe-eyes looked up from the book she was reading.

"Hello. I'm Ewelina Helena Kowalczyk. Due to the fact that nobody can pronounce my surname, and I speak a number of languages, I am also known as Lingo by my friends here."

The final boy stood.

"Hey, y'all. Ah'm George Wilson, known as Tec to the guys. Tec's the name, tech's the game, yessir."

George Wilson had movie-star good looks, broad shoulders, a dazzling white smile, tanned skin and a leather jacket.

A large brown Stetson hat lay on the science bench next to him. All he needed was a whip to complete the Indiana Jones look.

"What do we call you guys?"

THE NEWCOMERS

T he boy turned to the girl and said, "Ladies first".

The girl, slender, with blond straight hair tied into a ponytail, said, "How do you do? My name is Lauren De La Haye. I'm 14, from the United Kingdom."

She turned to the tall, slim, red headed boy.

"Now you."

"Hello. I'm Lewis Le Maine, also 14. Pleased to meet you all."

Tec said, "Ah love the accent. Where'd y'all come from?"

Lauren said, "Saint Brelade in Jersey."

"Never heard of it, and ah got family in Jersey Village, Texas."

"Okay. I've got relatives in Atlantic City, yeah, that's in New Jersey, yeah. I haven't heard of St. Brelade in New Jersey though, no," said Hex.

Lewis said, "No, not New Jersey. *Old* Jersey. We come from a parish called Saint Brelade on an island called Jersey!"

Tec said, "Never heard of it, no sir. *Old Jersey*. You're kidding, right? So, *Old Jersey* - is it off the coast of New Jersey?"

"Lewis, may I intercede at this point, and enlighten our friends?" This in the booming but gentle voice of Chuck.

"By all means."

"*Jersey*, ladies and gentlemen, is the largest of an archipelago of islands in the English Channel, laying between the Normandy coast of France and the southern coast of England. The largest islands are two crown dependencies, The Bailiwick of Jersey and the Bailiwick of Guernsey. There are smaller islands, some of which, although they're permanently inhabited, only have populations ranging from a few dozen to a little over 5,000."

He continued.

"The inhabitants are British subjects, but not British citizens. The native language of Jersey is called Jèrriais, a form of Normandy French, closer allied to the Québécois language in Canada than standard High French...."

He turned to Lewis and Lauren and asked, "Do either of you speak Jèrriais?"

"No – few people do. What is it Lauren? 3.3% of the population?"

"Something like that, Lewis. How do you know this stuff, Chuck?"

A voice from behind the newspaper said, "Mr. James is eidetic: he has what is otherwise known as a photographic memory ... total recall."

The voice was kind, slightly gravelly, but authoritative.

Finally, the newspaper at the front of the room was put down. A man stood.

"Good afternoon to the two of you, and welcome. Welcome to the Lunchtime Club Detective Agency. I'm Professor Weiss. I started this Agency more years ago than I care to remember...and I'm hoping you're my latest recruits."

The man speaking was the archetypal scientist. White laboratory coat, pens and an old fashioned poker pipe in his left hand breast pocket, circular wire rimmed glasses atop his head.

His hair was speckled, mostly grey now but with signs that it was once blond. It was thick and cut in a military style. He was ruggedly handsome, and he had striking blue eyes which seems to delve into a person's very soul.

Lewis leant in towards Lauren.

"Gosh, Lauren, it's Gibbs from NCIS!"

She just nodded a *yes, I know.*

The Professor continued.

"I gather together gifted young people and offer them the chance to use their skills and knowledge to solve crimes and mysteries - to make a difference. As I said, Mr. James here is eidetic. You'll find out what skills the others have as you get to know them better. The two of you also have skill sets that we can utilise within the agency."

"Mr. Le Maine, could you explain to Messrs Wilson and Madison the link between the two Jerseys, please – the old and the new?"

"Certainly, Professor Weiss. Between 1650 and 1651, King Charles II took refuge in *old* Jersey during the English civil war. As a gesture of thanks to the island and those who sheltered him, when the British took the area known as New Netherlands from the Dutch here in the Americas, it was renamed New Jersey."

"This name was chosen by a man from *old* Jersey – Sir George Carteret, who was a Vice Admiral in the Royal Navy, and the man who funded the king's return to power. As a thanks, he was made the colony's first Lord Proprietor in 1665. He is now remembered back at home by having a public house named after him in the Jersey parish ..."

"Parish?" asked Marty, taking his eyes away from his books as if it were a new revelation.

"In your language, Marty – an administrative area you'd find in many parts of the U.K. There is a memorial to him in the Jersey parish of Saint Peter, where he was born - a bronze statue erected in his memory. Outside a public house: Very apt I must say, the heavy drinker that he was purported to be!"

"Thank you, Mr. Le Maine."

"There is more, sir...."

"I am fully aware of that fact, but you have demonstrated my point. You are a huge store of historical facts. What you don't know immediately, you know exactly where to look. I'm sure that the other members of the group will take this into consideration when they create a pseudonym for you. Now, Miss De La Haye. Could you tell me the location of the town of Dalton."

"Dalton, the main town in Dalton County. Located approximately halfway between Fiftone and Bryceville in northern Florida. It's located on Route 301, just after the junction onto the I-10 at Baldwin."

Fingers asked, "You been there?"

"No, Miss Ramos. If I'm correct, reading maps is a hobby of our new recruit. She can look at a map and visualise every hill, tree, rock or building as if she were there. Am I correct?"

"Yes, Professor," answered Lauren.

The Professor continued, "These two exchange students complete the Agency as it currently stands. If you agree, of course?"

They both nodded a 'yes'.

"You know the way that I prefer to address you all, but you seem to prefer pseudonyms when referring to each other. Any suggestions?"

Hex's little blond head appeared from behind the monitor once more.

"Uh, yeah, I was thinking. Uh, how about Fax and Maps. Get it? He likes facts and figures, she reads maps, get it? I like it."

"Well done, Mr. Madison. Is everyone in agreement?"

There were sounds and indications that the names had been accepted – at least, by the rest of the group.

The Professor asked, "Miss De La Haye, Mr. Le Maine – is this acceptable?"

In unison they answered, "Yes, Professor Weiss."

The bodiless voice coughed.

The Professor said, to no-one in particular, "Ah, how very remiss of me. Computer, say 'hello' to our newcomers."

The electronic voice said, "Hello to our newcomers!"

Professor Weiss raised an eyebrow. "Computer?"

"The witticism seemed appropriate in the circumstances."

"Very much so," said the Professor, but he thought that the Computer was beginning to show signs of acting beyond its deep learning algorithm. He made a mental note to check his system designs.

A NEW CASE

"Professor Weiss, do you have a reason for asking Maps about how to get to Dalton?"

"Indeed I do, Miss Liu. An old friend got in touch with me regarding a mysterious disappearance in his jurisdiction. He is a deputy sheriff with the Dalton County Sheriff's Department. I would like Mr. Le Maine, Miss De La Haye, Mr. Wilson and Mr. James to go to Dalton to find out more about the events that have transpired."

He carried on.

"Miss De La Haye, how would you get there?"

"I could come up with a convoluted route: head south out of Austrey along Route 283, then the I-70E, the I-75S, and finally Route 301."

"Travel time?"

"Approximately 20 hours."

"Distance?"

"1,416 miles, give or take a few yards."

"You sound hesitant."

"That's 40 hours return travel time. Plus any time actually spent there, it could mean being away for four days."

"So, what would *you* do?"

"I think I'd cheat, Professor."

"Would you care to elaborate, please?"

"I would ask Lewis's father - very nicely of course - if we could borrow the company jet!"

Maps and Fax smiled at each other.

"Y'all have your own jet? Cool!" said Tec.

"Yes," said the Professor to the pair.

"I was wondering if you'd volunteer that information. A blue Cessna 680 Citation Sovereign, if my information is correct?"

"Sky blue, Professor Weiss. Father's pride and joy. I'm sure he'd allow its use if we say it's for a field trip."

Fax smiled at the prospect of the professor being refused permission to use the company jet. His facial expression soon turned from one of mirth to one of amazement.

"I've actually taken the liberty of asking him, and he was more than pleased to accommodate us. You probably don't know that your father and I go back a long way. As we speak, Captain Gledhill is filing a flight plan and arranging transport from the airfield into Dalton. He has all the necessary details."

Maps and Fax looked at each other. She mouthed *'Captain Gledhill?'*, and he just shrugged his shoulders.

"Er, what about classes, sir?" asked Maps.

Before the Professor had a chance to respond, Chuck answered, "It will already have been cleared by the powers that be."

"Correct, as usual, Mr. James. And Mr Le Maine, you don't need to say 'sir'. Professor will suffice."

Hex popped his head around the monitor again.

"Uh, yeah, and don't use Prof, Professor doesn't like Prof. Do you, Professor. No."

His head disappeared again.

The four walked through the still deserted corridors to the school entrance, the two newcomers still slightly dazed by the events of the last half hour. Pulled up alongside the school steps was a sleek black Rolls-Royce Phantom.

Tec whistled.

"Phew, nice ride!"

There was a man holding the rear car door open, almost standing to attention.

"Master Lewis, Miss Lauren and ....?"

"Charles James the Third. Pleased to meet you."

"Howdy there. Ah'm George Wilson."

"I'm Craig. Pleased to meet the two of you."

He gestured for the four to enter the car.

They climbed into the car, only to be greeted by a loud "Surprise!"

"Marc – what are you doing here?" Maps exclaimed.

Lewis said, in Welsh, "Catrin, why are you here?"

In English, she answered, "Hey, big bro - Craig has to look after us as well. So, Marc and I have to go where ever you go. Who are the others?"

Lauren introduced Chuck and Tec, then said, "This is Marc, my little brother and that is Catrin, Fax's little sister. They're on an exchange programme with junior high."

Catrin asked, "What's this about *'Fax'*?"

"It's the name the Agency have given your brother. And I'm Maps."

"Agency? What Agency, sis?" asked Marc.

"We'll explain on the way to the airfield."

Once they were en-route to the airport, Craig's voice came over the intercom.

"We are flying directly to Dalton, flight time approximately two and a half hours. We'll be too late to conduct our business today, but Deputy Sheriff O'Connell, the investigating officer, has extended an invitation to attend a family barbecue this evening. I have also arranged accommodation. We'll be staying in a motel on Route 301."

Fax said, "I've always wanted to stay in a motel! And an American barbecue – do you think they'll have ribs?"

"You and your ribs!" laughed Catrin.

"I know, but these are real American ribs!"

"Craig?"

"Yes, Master James."

"I'm totally unprepared for an overnight stay. Also, my Mom and Dad won't know where I am."

Tec nodded in agreement.

"The Professor has made all the necessary arrangements. There is an overnight bag for each of you in the boot - sorry, the trunk."

Chuck said, "George Bernard Shaw once wrote that Britain and America are two nations separated by a common language – you say "boot" in the U.K. and we say "trunk" in the US."

"The English language in general seems to absorb words from the cultures around it. In the U.K., you absorb words from European languages, and also the languages of those you once ruled. In the States we have absorbed words from the languages of immigrants."

Maps carried on: "Interestingly, many English words used in the United States are older forms of British English which have lost favour over there. "Side-walk" is older than "pavement", for example. And "pavement" can mean "road" here."

"One thing I can't wait to say is "eggs easy over". No idea what it means, and I don't even eat eggs, but it sounds cool on television," Fax said.

He continued, "It does seem that the two forms of English parted company when the Pilgrim Fathers landed at Plymouth Rock in 1620."

Some 20 minutes later, the the Rolls-Royce pulled into Austrey Regional Airport. It was a small, neat airport, with low white painted buildings. Craig turned left inside the entrance, away from the passenger terminal, and drove past private hangars, before stopping alongside a beautiful, bullet shaped sky-blue twin-engined jet. He opened the car door for them to disembark.

First out of the car was Tec.

"Oh Glory be! A thing of beauty!" He uttered, looking up at the aircraft.

He continued. "Cessna Citation Sovereign 680, two Pratt and Whitney Canada PW306C turbofan engines, range 2620 miles, maximum cruis'n' speed 444 knots. Unveiled in 1998 at the NBAA Las Vegas air show, maiden flight 2002, certificated and first customer sales in 2004. Full of cool tech."

He turned towards Fax and asked, "Just what does your daddy do to get an aircraft like this?"

"Something to do with finance. It has never really interested me: non-existent money being pushed around fake companies in fictitious countries by people who have too much money in the bank but no compassion in their hearts."

"Well put, Master Lewis. However, it does pay for your education, and all the niceties of life. I would also disagree about your father's lack of compassion."

Fax blushed slightly, and changed the subject.

"How did the Professor get Dad to lend us the plane and provide us with your services?"

"They go back a long way. As do one or two of the other parents of every member of the Detective Agency."

They all looked at each other, surprised.

"However, there's no time to elaborate now. All aboard, everyone. Make yourselves comfortable whilst I go through the pre-flight visual checks."

The six students climbed aboard the aircraft. Craig walked around the aircraft, staring, touching, pulling, tapping and ticking boxes on a clipboard as he completed each visual check. He also seemed to be using a device to take the occasional reading. He boarded the aircraft, closed the door and turned to his passengers.

"Seat belts buckled, please. In a moment, I'll play the safety video. Pay attention, as it may save your lives. You can contact me by pressing the white button on your armrest. Please heed the seat belt signs. I'm assuming that none of you smoke!"

They laughed as he turned and walked to the cockpit, closing the door behind him.

"Who is that guy?" asked Tec.

"All I know is that he and Dad were in the military together. He's now Dad's right hand man, his chauffeur and his pilot. He's polite, seems to be able to do anything to which he turns his hand, but he's a very private person – lives alone on a converted lifeboat in Jersey Marina. Great sense of humour."

"And your father and the Professor?"

"I have absolutely no idea!"

They all felt a slight jolt as the aircraft started moving.

Craig's voice came over the intercom.

"We're taxiing ready for take-off. We'll be cruising at an altitude of 5,000 feet, cruising speed 450 knots. The safety video is about to start. Relax and enjoy the flight."

Nearly three hours later, Craig's voice came over the intercom again.

"We are ascending into Dalton Regional Airport. Please ensure that your seat belts are fastened, and your seats and drinks trays are in an upright position. I love saying that. Best part of being a pilot."

The passengers exchanged amused looks.

They came in to land at the small airstrip just over two miles to the west of the town of Dalton. It was a neat, well kept place with a number of white buildings clustered around the control tower.

Despite it being a regional airstrip, it also served as an emergency overflow runway for Jacksonville International Airport, twenty minutes flying time away, hence the runway was disproportional to the size of the airfield – about 7,500 feet in length - to allow for all contingencies and sizes of aircraft.

They taxied to the entrance of a neatly painted white corrugated iron hangar, and Craig shut the engines down. He exited the cockpit, opened the door and pushed down the steps.

Outside waiting for them was parked a Lincoln Continental 2017 model stretch limousine, its crimson paint shining in the late afternoon sun. Tec went to open the door.

Craig stepped between Tec and the car and said, firmly, "Step away from the car, please, Master George. That applies to the rest of you."

They looked at him, confused looks on their faces.

"I need to check for devices that shouldn't be there."

He opened a bag and pulled out a rod with a mirror on the end. He extended the telescopic handle and checked under the car. Once satisfied, he dismantled it and placed it back in the bag. He then took out a device, slightly larger than a smartphone. It was the same device he'd used on his pre-flight checks. He tapped the screen a few times and ran it around the trunk area, the hood and around the doors. A light on the screen remained green.

"Good, no explosives."

They all looked at each other, even more confused. Craig tapped the device's screen twice more, and went through the same procedure. The light remained green.

He opened the driver's door and scanned the inside. Almost immediately, the device started beeping, slowly. The beeping stopped when he moved towards the rear of the car. He went back to the point where the beep had started, and it did so again.

He moved it over the dashboard, and the beeping became more urgent. He swiped it over the central digital display console, and the light stayed red and the beeping became a constant, loud whine.

"Just as I thought."

"What?" asked Chuck.

Craig held a finger to his lips, and signalled for them to move away from the car. He quietly closed the car door.

"Someone has rigged the GPS to track us, and the console may well be bugged for sound."

"Who would want to do that?" asked Tec. "Who even knows we're here?"

"I don't know the answer to either question. Wait here, please."

He re-entered the car and pulled a lead from the rear of the device. He plugged it into the headphone socket of the digital console. He tapped the screen a few times. He then felt around the edge of the console, and pulled out what looked like a tiny smartphone. He placed it in an evidence bag and put it into his rucksack.

"You may get in now. Please put your bags into the boot first."

When they were all seated in the back, Marc asked Craig, "What did you do?"

"Master George, care to enlighten us?" Craig asked.

"Ah think that his there little device has more than one purpose. It senses explosives on one setting, then sweeps for outgoin' signals, such as trackin' signals and voice transmissions, on another. On yet another setting, the device can over-ride the GPS and transmit white noise to cloak our conversations."

"Well said, Master George. You should take this up as a hobby."

Tec grinned.

"Still doesn't answer who would want to do it, though," said Maps.

"No, it doesn't Miss Lauren. It certainly doesn't."

They drove along Route 301 through Dalton and on for a mile where they pulled into the Silver Springs Motel. It was a series of low cream painted buildings on two levels. The main building was a larger structure, four storeys high with a flat roof, atop which was a long aerial and two satellite dishes.

At the entrance to the car lot, a blue neon sign flashed the words "No Vacancies", and a board listed the motel's many facilities: free Wi-Fi, cable, coffee facilities, indoor pool and spa, free breakfast buffet, games room, conference facilities. The parking lot itself was landscaped and well maintained.

"Wow, motels never look like this is the movies!" exclaimed Fax.

"Are American t.v. shows and movies your only experience of the States?" asked Tec.

"Mostly, We holidayed in the Disney Resort in Orlando when I was eight. I remember going to Cape Canaveral."

"Cape Canaveral is much more enchanting than Disney, but that's just in my opinion," said Chuck.

Craig interrupted.

"I have all your IDs. You can get out of the car, stretch your legs and get some fresh air, but I would ask you not to wander off."

Craig walked towards the reception area in the main building, and the others got out of the car and stretched, loosening muscles tightened by the flight. The four exchange students all put on matching red baseball caps to protect their heads and necks. Fax, Maps and their siblings sprayed on factor fifty sun block to prevent their fair skins from burning.

Marc went to stand next to Chuck, who was staring into the distance, scanning a low ridge a few hunDr..ed yards away.

"I think we're being watched," said Chuck.

"Where?" asked Marc.

"I saw the sun glinting off something metallic, just up there on the ridge. There!"

He pointed.

"There it is again."

The others had come to joint Chuck and Marc. Fax looked in the direction Chuck was pointing, then took out his smartphone and tapped the screen.

"Craig, I think we're being watched. From a ridge two hunDr..ed yards south of the motel."

Craig answered, "Please get back into the car immediately. I will take care of this."

They trooped back to the car, and looked out of the window facing the ridge. They couldn't see a thing. Ten minutes passed, and Fax tried Craig's number again. There was no answer.

Fifteen minutes later, Craig climbed into the Dr..iver's seat, and turned to them.

"There was no-one there. But someone was there until about twenty minutes ago. Fresh tyre tracks came from the north, and then headed back towards town. Heavy set man. Heavy smoker. Expecting us."

"How do you deduce that whoever it was, was a heavy smoker?" asked Chuck.

"Or waitin' for us?" asked Tec.

"He was up there for thirty minutes or so. The tyre tracks inbound showed signs of being blown by the wind. He waited for us and then watched. I picked these up."

Craig held up an evidence bag, containing the unfiltered ends of about a dozen home-rolled cigarettes.

"So how do you know it's a 'he'?" asked Maps.

"There was still the smell of cheap men's cologne, sweat and hamburgers in the air. The footprints leading to and from the car were UK size thirteen, or fourteen and a half US. That would reduce the possibility of the person being a female dramatically. On balance, therefore, it's fair to assume that it was, indeed, a 'he'. It's not safe here, so I've made other arrangements for our overnight accommodation."

They sat in silence, each deep in thought, as Craig retraced their earlier route. He turned off Route 301 before town, and drove through back roads until they reached a turning into a housing development. At the entrance was a large limestone plaque, engraved with gold-painted lettering:

Sunny Meadows
Welcomes safe drivers

A cattle grid spanned the road between two stone gate columns. A sign on the left hand side of the road read **CHILDREN PLAYING. MAX 5MPH.**

Craig slowly drove across two speed reduction humps, took the first left hand turn and along to the end of a cul-de-sac.

He drove into the long driveway of an ornate house in the style of a southern cotton plantation mansion – but on a less grand scale.

He pulled up behind a dark green Dodge Charger which had "Dalton County Sheriff Department" written on the side around the town logo, a black rampant stallion inside a gold shield. The flags of Florida and the United States crossed behind the shield.

The door opened and Deputy O'Connell, now in light chinos and a blue cotton shirt, stepped to one side and held up his hand to stop them getting out of the car. In the other hand, his arm at his side, he held his service pistol. He scanned the surrounding area before gesturing for them to enter.

Once everybody was inside, and the door was securely locked, Deputy O'Connell tucked his pistol into his belt, behind his back.

He turned to them, and said, "Craig. Long time no see!"

"Certainly is."

They hugged like the old friends that they were. The students looked on in amazement.

"Y'all know each other, Craig? asked Tec.

"For well over 15 years. Deputy O'Connell saved my life."

"I seem to remember we saved each other's ass...er, sorry, backsides."

To the students he said, "And please, all of you, call me Tim."

This time, Chuck leant in towards Fax, pointed at Craig and Tim and whispered, "Who are these guys?"

Fax just shrugged.

Tim gestured for them to follow him into his 'den'.

"Please, sit down."

He removed his service pistol from the small of his back, removed the clip, checked the chamber, then placed them in a small safe set in the wall behind a photograph of the family.

Once everybody was sitting he said, "So, you are some of the Professor's latest agents. How is he?"

"As mysterious as ever. How do you know Professor Weiss?" asked Chuck.

"I was an agent back in the day, in high school in Jacksonville. Boy, he led us a merry dance on more than one occasion. He only ever chooses people with particular gifts. In me he saw doggedness and deductive reasoning. We met again much later under very different circumstances. What about you guys?"

He pointed at Chuck. "What about you, big guy?"

"Chuck, photographic memory – but most of the other agents seem to have that to a certain extent. My gift is football, but I rarely use that one with the Agency. No, my true skill is astrophysics."

The others looked at him askew.

Chuck shrugged. "There are many things about me that you don't know."

"I'm Tec. Ah can whip up just about any technical device using a wash'n' up bottle, some sticky tape and a few straws. Okay, slight exaggeration, but y'all get the idea!"

"Maps. I'm an exchange student, here for the academic year. My interests are maps and geography."

Fax said, "Interests? You're a genius with both! Hello, Tim. I'm Fax. I'm on the exchange with Maps. Historical facts and figures are my forte."

He carried on. "May I ask, if you know Craig, do you know my father?"

28

"Michel? Yes, of course."

The look on Fax's face didn't hide his utter confusion.

"It's too long a story to get into right now."

The deputy nodded towards Catrin.

"And you, young lady?"

"I'm Catrin, Fax's sister. I'm not in the Agency – too young, I think. I'm in junior high."

"I'm Marc, Lauren – er, Maps's brother. I'm the same as Catrin."

"Pleased to meet you all. I'm sure you've got a ton of questions you want answered. But we have other things to think about. C'mon, I'll take you to meet the family and get some barbecue. Craig and I need to chat."

"Will there be ribs?" asked Fax.

"Of course."

"*Yes!*" exclaimed Fax, all thoughts of how so many of the oldies seemed to know each other now gone at the thought of real American ribs.

AT HOME WITH THE O'CONNELLS

The six of them were shown out onto the veranda area which ran along the back of the house, and along one side. Tim introduced them to his wife, Jenny.

Jennifer O'Connell was 5' 7", slender, pretty with long blonde hair, pulled up into a bun. She wore light blue jeans and a white t-shirt sporting the words **Go Jaguars** and the logo of the Jacksonville Jaguars American football team on it.

She introduced the guests to Frankie, their son. He was coming up to his eighth birthday. He had wild curly shoulder length brown hair, the complexion of a child who liked to play outside a lot, with bright, inquisitive brown eyes and a broad infectious smile.

"Food is nearly ready. If you want to wash up, there's a bathroom along the hall from the kitchen, on the left. Help yourself to drinks – there's water, juice, or fruit punch. No fizzy sodas, I'm afraid. There are chips, pretzels and dips – just help yourselves."

"Thank you, Mrs. O'Connell," said Chuck.

"Please, call me Jenny. We don't stand on ceremony in this household."

As they started introducing themselves to Jenny and Frankie, Tim interrupted.

"Craig and I have a few things to discuss. We'll be in the den."

He and Craig turned and walked back in the direction of Tim's den.

Fax heard Tim say, "I've got some of that 50 year old single malt we picked up after Grenada – pity we can't try it. I think we may need our wits about us."

"Undoubtedly, old friend."

As Jenny was at the grill, turning the burgers, ribs and sausages, Fax came up and stood beside her.

"Mrs. O'Con - sorry, Jenny. Do you know how Tim, Craig, my father and the Professor know each other?"

"Only that it's something to do with the military. Timmy was in the Airborne Rangers. He doesn't talk about it much – they never do when they've seen terrible things. That's a cute accent you have there, Lewis. Sorry, I can't go with the nicknames. I've heard of Jersey. We might visit when we're in Europe."

"You'll be very welcome, Jenny."

"That's so sweet."

Then, to the rest, she said, "All right, food is ready. Come and get it. Lewis, could you go and fetch Timmy and Craig, please? Don't forget to knock, though. Thank you, dear."

Frankie had taken a shine to all of the students, but to Fax in particular. He'd already given him a nickname.

"Louie, I'll show you!" he said, and dragged Fax by the arm to the den.

Frankie knocked on the door, and Tim called out, "C'mon in."

He opened the door and the two boys walked in. Tim and Craig were hunched over a map set out on the desk. Craig was pointing at the map, and Tim was nodding as if he was agreeing with something that had been said.

"Gosh, it looks like you're planning a battle!"

"Hi guys. Sure looks that way, Fax – and that may well be the case. Some strange things going on we need to check out."

He folded the map and put it into a drawer and locked it. Fax looked puzzled.

31

"Don't worry, Master Lewis," said Craig.

"We're not keeping anything from you. Once we know what we're up against, you will all know."

Frankie interrupted.

"Mom said that food is ready."

"Great" said Tim. "I could eat a cow."

"From the size of the ribs, I'd say that's a safe bet!" exclaimed Fax.

There followed a thoroughly enjoyable evening. Fax got his ribs (*Oh, these are absolutely **a-ma-zing**, Jenny!*). To Jenny's amazement, Frankie asked for some as well.

Maps, Catrin, Marc and Tec kicked around a soccer ball; Frankie was now showing Fax how to throw an American football to Chuck; the adults stood on the top step of the stoop and watched the kids playing. There was a lot of chatting, banter and laughter.

Jenny leant across to her husband.

"I haven't seen Frankie take to strangers so quickly, especially Lewis."

Their son had problems allowing new people into his life, as it upset his routines. He liked things done a certain way, or at a certain time and found it difficult to accept changes to the things with which he was familiar.

However, Jenny worked with Frankie's teachers and they found that he had an uncanny ability to see something once, then draw it in the minutest detail. A therapist they once went to called him an 'artistic savant on the autism spectrum'. To Tim and his wife, he was a bright, energetic, joyous little boy who touched the lives of everyone he met.

"He loves having kids around him, and these are good kids."

Eventually, Tim clapped his hands and called out, "Okay, guys. Time to turn in. We have a very early start tomorrow. Frankie will show you lads where you'll be bunking. Jenny will show the girls where they will be sleeping. Craig and I will watch in turns in the den – two hours on, two hours off."

"Are you expecting trouble, honey?" asked Jenny.

"No, but it's best to play it safe."

They all turned in to their respective rooms, the boys and the girls (including Jenny) chatted late into the night.

Both armed with pistols on safety, Craig and Tim talked about old times for a while before starting the first two hour watch, looking out of the windows, walking the perimeter of the inside of the house or watching the monitor displaying what the outside cameras were seeing.

Catrin awoke to the smell of coffee in the air. Jenny and Maps had gone. She got up, got dressed and headed towards the stairs where she met up with her brother, Marc and Frankie.

"Something smells good."

"Bacon and pancakes?" asked Marc, excitedly.

"Hope so. That will be another thing off the bucket list, if it is!" said Fax.

"After breakfast, Louie, can I show you my treasure box? There's a dinosaur bone in there. It comes from a velociraptor. Do you know about dinosaurs? They're cool!"

"That would be great, Frankie. Is that your favourite dinosaur?" asked Fax.

Frankie was in his element, talking about his treasures with huge enthusiasm, all smiles and arms gesticulating everywhere.

Downstairs, everybody else was gathered around the O'Connell's large dining table. There were steaming mugs of coffee for the adults, and large jugs of iced fruit juice for the kids. There were piles of pancakes, dripping with syrup and butter, two large platters of bacon and small sausages, toast, grape jelly and mixed berry jam. Frankie ate his favourite, cream of wheat. Everyone tore ravenously into the food, except Craig and Tim, who took their mugs of coffee into the den and closed the door.

"Ah wonder what they're planning," said Tec to nobody in particular.

"They'll let us in on any plans once they've got them sorted out in their own minds. Remember, they are ex-military, after all," said Chuck.

"Yes, about that," said Fax.

"Jenny told us that Tim was Airborne Rangers. My father was in the French Armed Forces, and Craig was in the British Armed Forces – they met on a tour of duty with NATO."

He turned to Maps. "Was your dad ever in the forces?"

Before she could answer, Marc chipped in.

"No, but he was an interpreter with the United Nations. He can speak Arabic, most of the Slavic languages of the Balkans and Russian."

"Well, the only campaign that I can think of, where the Americans, the French, the British, NATO and the UN were involved in any conflicts in the late 90's, was Kosovo. It was the last European war of the twentieth century."

"The timeline sounds about right," said Jenny.

"Timmy was in Europe in the late 90's, though he never did say where. It's like I said, he didn't say very much about his military career."

Frankie asked, through a mouthful of creamed wheat, "What is Kosovo?"

"Obviously before our time....well, except Jenny," said Fax. Jenny smiled – but it wasn't really with amusement.

He continued.

"In 1989, the ethnic Albanians in the Serbian province of Kosovo started non-violent protests against the changes being made to the province's constitutional autonomy by Slobodan Milošević, the president of the Serbian republic."

"Milošević and members of the Serbian minority in Kosovo had long hated the fact that Muslim Albanians were in control of an area considered sacred to the Serbian Orthodox Church. Tensions increased between the two sides. For some reason, the international community turned a blind eye to what was happening. More radical Kosovars saw that their demands were never going to be met through peaceful means. As a result, the Kosovo Liberation Army – or KLA – emerged in 1996, and what started as sporadic attacks on Serbian police and politicians, steadily escalated over the next two years."

"By 1998 the KLA's actions pretty much amounted to an armed uprising. Serbian special police and, eventually, Yugoslav armed forces attempted to take back control over the region. Atrocities committed by the police, paramilitary groups, and the army caused a wave of refugees to flee the area, and the situation became well publicised through the international media – the horrific images of the ethnic cleansing brought about world-wide condemnation."

"An informal coalition of some NATO members called the Contact Group was formed. The members - The United States, Great Britain, Germany, France, Italy, along with Russia - demanded a cease-fire, the withdrawal of Yugoslav and Serbian forces from Kosovo, the return of refugees, and unlimited access for international monitors."

"By 1997 Milošević was president of Yugoslavia, and he agreed to meet most of the Contact Group's demands but he failed to follow them through. Some said he was stalling to gather arms and intelligence for an all out war. But the KLA also regrouped and rearmed during the cease-fire, and renewed its attacks."

"The Yugoslav and Serbian forces responded with a ruthless counter offensive and engaged in a program of ethnic cleansing. Eventually, The United Nations Security Council opened its eyes to what was happening, and condemned this excessive use of force and imposed an arms embargo on Yugoslavia, but the violence continued."

"Did they ignore the events because of oil in the area, do you think, Lewis?" asked Jenny.

"There were claims that was the case. But there's no oil – or any other valuable resources, for that matter – in Kosovo."

"There are people, and families," said Catrin.

"You are so right, li'l sister," said Tec.

"So, both sides were re-arming themselves. Who was providing the weapons?" asked Chuck.

"There are rumours that the Saudis were arming the Muslim minority and allegations that the Russians were secretly arming the

Serbs, despite being a member of the Contact Group. It's an awful fact that in war money talks, no matter where it comes from," said Fax.

"Didn't they at least try to talk things through?" asked Maps.

"Diplomatic talks did begin in early 1999, but they broke down the following month. The atrocities continued so NATO began air strikes against Serbian military targets. In response, Yugoslav and Serbian forces drove out all of Kosovo's ethnic Albanians, displacing hundreds of thousands of people into Albania, Macedonia, and Montenegro."

"NATO air and ground campaigns lasted eleven weeks and eventually expanded to Belgrade, where the fighting caused significant damage to the Serbian infrastructure. In June of that year, NATO and Yugoslavia signed a peace accord outlining troop withdrawal and the return of nearly one million ethnic Albanians, as well as another 500,000 displaced persons within the province. Most Serbs left the region, and there were occasional reprisals against those who remained. UN peacekeeping forces were deployed in Kosovo, which then came under UN administration."

"Sounds kinda heavy," said Tec.

"It was a brutal conflict. The cruelty of the oppressors knew no bounds. In mid 1999, eleven thousand Kosovar civilians died in four months alone. As I said, over a million people were displaced. The NATO Elite Forces found mass graves in a number of locations. A village called Raćak was one of the worst. Some called the conflict Europe's Vietnam, but there's no comparison."

Frankie looked up from the drawing pad on which he was doodling. "And my Dad saw it. I'm scared!"

Just then, Craig and Tim came into the kitchen. Everyone just stared at them.

"What?" asked Tim.

"Oh, nothing," said Jenny.

"Okay, then ...."

Tec chipped in.

"Tim,'s it true that you 'n' Craig were in Kosovo?"

The others looked at him, aghast.

"What? Guys! Guys....if ya don't ask y' won't know!"

Tim looked at his wife.

"Jennifer?"

"Don't look at me, honey. You've never said anything to me about Kosovo."

Tim was about to say something else, but Craig put his hand on his shoulder.

"Spot on, ladies and gentlemen. We were, indeed, in Kosovo. We were part of an Elite team put together by NATO. Tim was in the Airborne Rangers, I was in the SAS."

Fax asked, "And my father?"

"Michel was in the French special forces, an elite unit called DALAT," Tim answered.

"What about my dad – he wouldn't have been there, surely? He was a translator with the UN," said Maps.

"Is that what he told you, Miss Lauren?"

Tim and Craig looked at each other and smiled.

"What's so funny?" Marc asked.

"All of us in the special forces had cover stories, to protect ourselves and our loved ones. My parents thought I was a deep sea trawler-man in Iceland..."

"...and my parents thought I was in the Peace Corps before becoming a regular G.I. Joe," said Tim.

Craig carried on. "Marc, your dad is a fine translator and interpreter. He was also the best and most effective marksman I have ever had the pleasure to serve alongside."

"My dad. John Marc De La Haye?"

"Master Marc, your father was in the SAS with me. Damned fine soldier."

Chuck asked, "Sirs, what about the Professor?"

"We don't have the time to go into that right now. But you'll find out soon enough, by the looks of it. Okay, Craig and I have a plan. It starts with a bit of culture – a visit to the museum. But, before we go...how did you guys figure it out?"

Chuck smiled his huge, white smile and said, "Didn't anybody tell you, Tim. We belong to the best Detective Agency in the land!"

"That you do, Chuck. That you do."

THE MUSEUM (II)

Tim changed into his uniform, before talking briefly to his wife. She was to keep Frankie home from school, and make sure that all the doors and windows remained locked. She had to keep her cell phone on her at all times, and they were to answer the door or house phone to no-one.

Tim led the way out of the house, and they went through the routine of the previous day, in reverse. He closed the door and waited to hear it lock behind him before he got into his car. By the time he started the engine, Craig had reversed the Lincoln out of the drive, and the car was facing the way they'd arrived late yesterday afternoon.

Tim pulled out of the driveway, moved slowly ahead of the Lincoln and indicated for to Craig to follow. They drove out of the housing development, and left onto the road towards Route 301. They got onto the northbound ramp and onto the road heading into Dalton, but avoiding the County Sheriff's Department Headquarters.

Ten minutes later, they were parking in front of the museum. Tim got out of his car, once again scanning the surrounding area, service pistol by his side. Craig held the door open for the students to disembark. Marc stopped, took out his smartphone and went to take a photograph.

"Master Marc – no time, and perhaps too dangerous. Inside, if you will. All of you. Quickly."

Once inside, they were met by Dr. Swan and a well-dressed, older man.

"Hi, Drey. These are the students I was telling you about."

"How do you do, one and all. This is my assistant, Dr. John Atherton."

Dr. Atherton nodded in their direction. He was tall, pale, thin and angular. His overall look reminded Fax of the character Lurch from one of his favourite t.v. shows.

"We'll do introductions as we go. Could you take us to look at the display case, please, Drey?"

"This way," said Dr. Swan.

The group of eight followed Dr. Swan and Dr. Atherton into the Main Display Hall, and across the marble floor to the display case at its centre. So many feet walking across the highly polished floor made squeaks and hollow thumps like a large group on a broken march across damp, wind-weathered rocks.

Dr. Swan went through the same sequence of events with Craig and the students as he did with Tim the previous day.

"Okay, guys. That's everything we have. The Professor told me to hand the investigation over to you, that you'd know what to do," said Tim.

Fax asked, "Could you point Maps and me in the direction of the historical archives, please?"

"Dr. Atherton will show you the way," said Dr. Swan.

Tec said, "I'll check out the display case and the alarms. I'll take Marc with me. We'll find our own way around the place."

"I'd like to check the carbon dating, mass spectrometer and scanning electron microscope data, if I may," said Chuck.

"I'll take you," said Dr. Swan.

"What shall I do?" asked Catrin.

"You stick with Craig and me. You've got young eyes – you might just see something we overlook," said Tim.

He continued. "Let's give it, what? Two hours? We'll meet back here at eleven-thirty."

They split up into the various groups, with Dr. Atherton leading Maps and Fax to the archive, deep in the bowels of the museum.

"It's down to the end of the corridor, guys," said Dr. Atherton.

Fax thought that his voice didn't fit his stern exterior. It was warm and friendly, with the trace of an accent he knew well.

"Dr. Atherton, you're Canadian!" he said.

"Well spotted young man. Yes, I'm from Cape Breton Island. How could you tell?"

"We have a Canadian in school with us in Jersey."

They arrived at a large metal door, with a swipe card entry system.

"We're here. Tell me what you need, and I'll get it for you."

"Thanks." They were shown to two large desks.

"I'm going to need all the maps, topological surveys, satellite images, photographs, or paintings of the areas where the cone was found, please," said Maps.

"And I'll need any legal documentation, land deeds, purchase documents, land transfers for the same area."

"I'll bring them to you," said Dr. Atherton.

They set to work on the maps, surveys and historical documents. Dr. Atherton did the fetching and carrying, and he also gave them access to the State Intranet System.

Dr. Swan took Chuck upstairs to the well-equipped laboratory. Chuck whistled when he saw the equipment.

"This is very impressive, Dr. Swan."

"As I said to Tim, our headquarters in Tallahassee has been very generous to us."

They, too, set to work.

Tec and Marc stayed by the display case. Deputy O'Connell, Craig and Catrin returned to the front entrance to start their search for any clues that might have been overlooked by the crime scene officers. He gave Craig and Catrin each a slim powerful torch and a pair of latex gloves. In addition to his torch he held his smartphone on camera mode.

The three separated but stayed within sight of each other, working their way back towards the Main Display Hall. They shone the lights into every nook and cranny, angling the torches from time to time on the same spot. From the Main Hall, they went into the Prehistory Hall and did the same thing.

Then, they went into the Timucua Hall, with display cases full of Timucua artefacts – arrow and spear heads, cups, bowls, jewellery, native dress and cured animal skins. In the centre of the room was a large glass encased diorama, showing a Timucua hunting camp: children gathered berries from bushes to one side of the case; women were drying skins, preparing food near a midden mound of oyster and clam shells, or fishing in a pool with woven baskets; two men with spears crouched behind a boulder, eyes firmly fixed on a grazing deer.

The final large side hall was the Treasure Trove Hall. They walked through the entrance, framed by large marble columns. Catrin suddenly stood still and looked open-mouthed at case after case of gold, silver and other valuable artefacts.

"W-w-what is all this?" she asked.

Deputy O'Connell turned to her, and smiled at the look on her face.

"This is the famous Dalton Spanish Treasure Trove. It was discovered in a cave eight miles outside town in the mid-thirties. Most of the gold artefacts are pre-Columbian, from Central and South America. There are also silver and gold realés and escudos, Dominican church crosses and candlesticks — it's worth tens of millions of dollars. These are the real thing, too, not reproductions created for display purposes. The security in here cost the State Museum Service an absolute fortune, but is on a par with that of the missing cone. That's what Dr. Swan finds so difficult to understand — why the cone and not these?"

They continued on with their search, but found nothing. They started the whole process once more in the Main Display Hall, nodding towards Tec and Marc working at the display case who were checking areas where the crime scene officers had been, identified by grey powdery smudges of fingerprint powder here and there.

The team of three found nothing new. Eventually Craig looked up at the skylight, twenty five feet above where they stood.

"Tim, do you think we could get some ladders to take a look at that skylight?"

Before Deputy O'Connell could answer, Catrin said, "I'll go and take a look."

She scanned the wall directly below the skylight, and started clambering up the seemingly smooth marble walls.

"Catrin!" shouted Craig and Deputy O'Connell in unison.

Catrin either didn't hear them, or ignored them – either way, she continued her agile climbing. She was using the chamfered spaces, gaps and lips between the large marble blocks as finger and toe-holds, moving easily from one hold to the next, always moving her head, looking up or from side to side. Her progress was sure and steady, and within minutes was holding onto the top of the uppermost marble block with one hand, toes thrust into two grouted gaps, using the torch to scan around the skylight.

"I can see something. Could one of you catch this?"

Catrin dropped her torch into Craig's outstretched hands. She then pulled a small object from near the locking mechanism of the window. She put it into her pocket, and started her way back down the wall, once again moving easily and confidently. About eight feet from the floor she let go, turned and landed on two feet, one hand on the floor giving her balance.

The deputy looked at her.

"Catrin – that was a very silly thing to do....impressive, but silly!"

"Maybe, but it might have taken ages to get ladders sorted. And that's not too difficult a climb – I've been up and down worse. Eh, Craig?"

"Yes, Miss Catrin, much worse."

Still lost for words, eventually the deputy asked, "What did you find up there?"

Catrin held up a small black box with a small aerial and a tiny red light.

Craig looked towards the display case, but Tec and Marc had gone.

"We need to show this to Master George when he gets back. Ah, everybody's on their way."

Dr. Swan and Chuck were on their down the stairs and they could here the voices of Dr. Atherton, Maps and Fax drifting up the staircase from the lower floors. Within minutes, nearly everyone had gathered by the display case.

Deputy Sheriff O'Connell said, "We're missing some people."

They turned to see Tec and Marc whispering to each other as they wandered slowly down the stairway from the upper floor.

When they reached the group, Tec said, "Sorry we're tardy, y'all. Just checkin' the tech upstairs."

Catrin said, "Here's some more for you," passing the device she'd found. Tec started to study it intently.

BACK AT THE LABORATORY (1)

Back in Austrey High School Science Laboratory 1, the Agents who'd remained behind hadn't remained idle. They had been working on information received so far from Dalton County, scant though it was.

All but Fingers had gathered at the table in front of the Professor's desk. She was sitting important mid-semester English literature papers. Despite her bravado, Fingers was an honours student across the board.

The Professor spoke.

"Miss Liu. You took on the task, with Mr. Madison, of checking the route Craig and the other agents took from the airfield to the motel. Do you have anything to report?"

"Yes, Professor. Hex and I decided that the best way to go about this was get eyes on the situation via satellite. The National Weather Service Organisation satellite 'Storm Chaser' passes over the Mid West to gather images of storm fronts which may lead to severe weather events - tornadoes, floods and the like. Mid Florida is on its flight path."

"Yeah, yeah. Great piece of kit, yeah. So I hacked that baby and downloaded the images for the Dalton County area. The images are very sharp, very hi-res. Spex loved them, yeah."

"I trust you left no calling cards, Mr. Madison?"

Hex looked hurt.

"Professor! I shut the back door as quiet as you like."

"I knew you would."

Hex smiled proudly.

"Miss Liu. Did you find anything in the images?"

"Computer, could you bring up video sequence S-D-Oh-One, please?"

"Here you are, Spex," said Computer.

"Thanks. This is a video sequence of the trip from the airfield to the motel."

The sequence had been speeded up, and the Lincoln had been circled.

"As you can see, there is nobody ahead of them, and they are not being followed – well, as far as we can see within the field of vision of the satellite."

On the video sequence the Lincoln turned into the motel. They watched the car come to a stop, and Craig and the others got out. Craig walked towards the main building, whilst the other agents stretched.

"I recognise four Agents....." said Arma.

"......who are the other two, Professor?" asked Bladen.

"Computer, zoom in on the Agents, please."

The image zoomed in on the group of students. The Professor used a laser pointer and pointed at one of the group.

"That is Marc De La Haye, Miss De La Haye's younger brother. And this..."

He pointed at Catrin.

"...is Mr. Le Maine's younger sister, Catrin. As Craig is also their chaperone, they had to go on our little road trip."

The Professor continued.

"Nothing untoward so far, Miss Liu. We had a report from Craig that they were being watched."

"Yes. Here you see Chuck and Marc looking towards the ridge on the left."

They watched as the other students also came and looked towards the ridge. Fax spoke into a phone he'd pulled from his pocket. Then they all moved quickly back to the car and got in.

"Okay, now, yeah. There's nothing happening, right? Wrong! We found something there professor. Okay, Computer, zoom in to the ridge to the left of the motel. That's it. Thank you. Professor, may I borrow the pointer? Thanks. Okay, this is the far edge of the image. Look, there, see – you can just make out a pair of boots."

Hex shone the light on a pair of black combat-style boots.

"And here is the edge of a car. It's a dark green Dodge Charger. But we can't see the plate or any other identifying features, no, nothing else. No."

"All we know, Professor, is that they were watched by someone already waiting for them," said Spex.

"This confirms Craig's suspicions," said the Professor.

"Computer, play the sequence to the end, please."

"Affirmative."

The Agents in the laboratory watched as the boots disappeared, and, a few moments later, the edge of the car moved out of view. Craig appeared, looked around and moved in and out of view. Within a few minutes, the screen went blank.

Computer said, "That is the end of the sequence. The satellite had passed beyond the area."

"Are there any traffic cameras or private security cameras in that area?"

"No, Professor Weiss. There are cameras in the motel parking lot, but no traffic cameras in that vicinity. There are security camera at the museum, but none in the centre of Dalton. The crime rate is very low, and we found out that the mayor decided that the money would be better spent elsewhere."

"Thank you, both. Computer, please send a text message to Craig confirming that they were being watched, and informing him of the make and colour of the car, and the combat boots. That's the only pertinent information at this point."

Lingo interrupted.

"Professor, I received a text from Fax, and he asked me to research a native American tribe called the Timucua. I worked with Computer, gathering information to send back to the Agents on the ground."

"What did you find out, Miss Kowalczyk?"

"The Timucuans spoke what is now an extinct native American language of the Florida Everglades. Its origins are uncertain. The language shows distinct similarities to the Arawakan languages of the Caribbean Islands. The linguist Julian Granberry has suggested the Timucua people may have migrated to Florida via the Caribbean Islands from an original Amazonian homeland."

"After being decimated by European disease and warfare between the Spanish and British, the surviving Timucua Indians were sent *en mass* to Cuba, where their kind rapidly disappeared. The last known Timucua Indian died there in 1767, making the Timucuans one of only a few truly extinct native American tribes."

"Thank you, Miss Kowalczyk. Anything to add, Computer?"

"Nothing, Professor Weiss, other than the fact that Lingo taught me a lot about the subtle nuances that can be added to the spoken word by vocal intonation. Unfortunately, my voice algorithm does not allow for such nuances, or you would pick up on the sarcasm in my voice."

The other Agents giggled.

Computer continued.

"There is one other thing Professor Weiss. I've just had a request asking me to research organisations called Strangway Mining and Ore and The Strangway Foundation. May I do so?"

"Yes, of course," said the Professor.

"I'll help Computer with that," said Marty.

"We can look into the finances of the two organisations at the same time, Marty."

"Professor Weiss, Chuck has also requested that you personally examine soil samples kept at the museum," said Computer.

"Very well," said the Professor, slowly.

"Could you send all the information we currently have to Craig and the team, please?"

"Affirmative, Professor. At the moment we have no case file. Would you like me to create one?"

"Yes, please. Thank you, Computer."

"You're welcome, Professor."

Yet more non computer-like behaviours, Professor Weiss mused. He really should get around to running that diagnostic. He made another mental note to do so, once this case was resolved.

THE MUSEUM (III)

Deputy O'Connell went through the process of setting up the recording facility on the smartphone.

"Okay, ladies and gentlemen, let's go through what we've found out today. Please bear with me for one moment."

Tec asked him, "What STT do you use?"

"It's a piece of bespoke software created for the Florida State Police, but I got them to let us use it. It's very effective now – I had to teach it to recognise the dialects of the guys in the department. They weren't happy at first, but they see the benefit now – a lot less paperwork."

"STT?" asked Marc.

"Speech to text – whatever we say will eventually be written down in a report. Very well then, let's go through the groups one by one. Maps and Fax."

Maps started.

"We decided to concentrate on the area where the artefact was found – in the area where you live, Tim."

"Guys, could you all refer to me as Deputy O'Connell, please? Protocol for recording purposes."

"Of course. As you know, the cone was found in 1983 when Sunny Meadows was being developed. I compared old maps and surveys of the area as far back as the records here allowed – as far back as the Spaniard Conquistadores, in fact. Using topographical data that we took from the maps and surveys, we found that the Sunny Meadows area, until the mid-1800s, was actually quite a deep ravine. The entire area has been filled in and then levelled for building purposes."

"Filled in with what?"

"Rock and soil. Soil analysis has shown that it has come from various locations across the States – Chuck will probably be able to tell you more about that, as samples from near the cone's location have been stored here."

"How much soil?"

"Using some pretty basic geometry, the area has been filled in with fifty million cubic metres of soil."

"In American? I'm old school, and I don't do metric!"

"Nearly sixty five and a half million cubic yards. About eighty five million US tons of soil and rock – and that would be nearly thirty three million horse-drawn wagon-loads, back before the advent of heavy trucks. The railways were around, of course, but there's no record of a railroad in this area. However the core arrived, the maps show that the valley was fully filled in by the turn of the twentieth century."

"Thirty three million wagon-loads, eighty five million tons. Wow!"

He turned to Fax.

"Fax, is there any record of that much activity?"

"There are no written records held here referring to such activity. Nor are there any references centrally in the State Archive or State Library in Tallahassee – I was able to check on the State intranet. The only thing I could find was a bill of purchase for the land, and the Notice of Intention of Compulsory Acquisition of the Land. There were no references in the Library of Congress either."

He went on.

"The land was purchased in 1720 from the local Timucuan tribe by a prospecting/ mining company called Florida Mine. It cost $100, about $100,000 today. Not a fortune for land, but we are only talking about an area of two hectares of what is now a filled in creek bed or small valley. It's Timucuan name was Ibu Ela, or Shining Water. I've had a text from the team back in Austrey, who say that the Timucuans are now extinct as a people, so the land became fair game to prospectors, until it was bought by a company called Strangway Mining and Ore."

"The land was never worked, so some old prospector claimed possession due to having lived there for more than forty years, working the claim. The land was acquired by the county under the Land Acquisition Act in 1964, but the process was opposed, until the owner offered up the land in 1974, asking for and getting a very handsome sum."

"Thank you, guys."

Fax interrupted.

"There is one more thing. The Strangway name came up again. When the Spanish treasure was discovered, technically it was owned by the State of Florida. Standard practise is to keep 20% for display purposes, reward the finder with a percentage and sell the remainder. They didn't do that with this collection. An organisation called the Strangway Foundation made an undisclosed offer for the treasure, which was accepted. The Foundation rewarded the prospector who found it but then donated everything to the State of Florida, on the proviso that it be displayed here."

"Dr. Swan, is that unusual?"

"Not really. I've heard of similar cases."

"Fax, do you think this has any bearing on this case?"

"Not that I can see, but I've asked the team back in Austrey to check out the name Strangway."

"Good, thank you."

He turned to Chuck and Dr. Swan.

"Now Chuck, what did you and Dr. Swan find?"

"Hm, right, yes. I – er – we want to keep this simple. I don't mean to be condescending, but we're having trouble understanding what we've found. With the artefact missing, we cannot re-run any tests, but we had some soil samples from the Sunny Meadows site before the development of the land. It ties in with what we found in the results already to hand, but also threw up some new questions."

Deputy O'Connell said, "Dr. Swan?"

"I'm leaving this one to Charles. The boy's an off-the-scale genius. I'm glad he's dumbing it down!"

"Chuck."

"I perused the mass spectrometer results taken at various times since the discovery of the cone, and I've been able to divide them into them into three categories. That single cone is three different alloys, all at once but never at the same time. However, each presents us with massive problems."

"Ah'm sorry. You mean it's somethin' it's not, then it's somethin' else it can't be, but it's always confusing?" asked Tec.

"That's as good a way of putting it as any. Okay, the first category gives us an alloy that consists of nickel, beryllium, titanium and thallium. It has a high tensile strength, but the cone is far too dense to be these elements alone. There may be denser elements, but they are usually artificially produced here on Earth. Thallium is near enough the same density as nickel, but the ratio shown in the readings simply can't explain the density of the alloy."

"Right then, that was category one. This is where it gets strange – or stranger."

"Can it possibly?" asked Marc, looking as lost as some of the others were feeling.

"Oh, yes. The second category shows the additional presence of Ununtrium – this element is so new it doesn't even have a proper name! I've only ever heard of this element it from something I read in the American Journal of Science on research undertaken in Russia back in 2003 by a team of Japanese scientists. They bombarded atoms of Americium-243 with ions of calcium-48 and produced the new element with the holding name Ununtrium – although it is due to be named Nehonium. The element only existed for less than one tenth of a second before eventually decaying into an isotope of mendelevium. If Ununtrium was stabilised, it's predicted that it would have properties similar to those of thallium."

"What's the problem with that, Master Charles?" asked Craig.

"It has been created once, maybe twice, in laboratory situations. It doesn't exist outside of that – not on Earth anyway. These reading show that it is constantly being created and then decaying within the artefact."

"Do I get a sense that things are going to get even stranger?" asked the deputy.

"Yes. My third category shows the presence of Ununquadium. This is created – in the lab, again – by bombarding plutonium-244 with calcium-48. Created by the same team in Russia, in the same lab, but a few years earlier. It has a half life of twenty one seconds, but if it occurred naturally it would be dense, similar to lead. That could explain the density, but it's not in every reading."

"Basically, this stuff should not exist. Not on Earth, anyway. And not in an object uncovered three decades ago. Only now, with the latest advances, can we create them at all. However, it *does* exist. *How?* That's one fundamental question."

"There's another?" asked Dr. Swan.

"Yes, Doctor. May I ask, have you studied the electron microscope images received back from Tallahassee?"

"Not in detail. If there was anything untoward, I assumed that I would have been informed."

"Well, take a look at this image. It's at 300 times magnification."

"Yes, very smooth."

"And this?" Chucked showed another glossy photograph.

"The same resolution."

"No. That is 3000 times magnification. And this" - he showed another - "is 30,000 times magnification."

"But they're — they're identical, Chuck. That's impossible!" exclaimed the curator.

"I'm sorry" said Deputy O'Connell. "What's impossible?"

"Tim, at this resolution, we should be seeing the very structure of the artefact — at a crystalline or molecular level."

"I don't understand!"

"May I, Doctor?" asked Chuck. "On some images on a computer, you can blow up the size of, let's say, a favourite photograph, and the larger you make the image, you start to see the blocks of colour that make up the picture."

"Yes, that blocky effect you get on pictures on a computer screen sometimes."

"That's right. At this magnification, we should start to see the building blocks that make up the artefact. But we don't. We just continue to see a smooth surface. I don't think that there's an electron microscope anywhere that could see this thing at a molecular level."

"Therein lies the other fundamental question: how can the artefact be so perfectly produced that we simply cannot see its make-up? I'll say it again, *this object should not exist*."

Finally, he said, "In terms of the origins of the soil, I've sent my analysis of the samples back to the team in Austrey to research further. Forensic Geology is the Professor's speciality after all."

"Thanks, Chuck. I'd like to say that you've cleared some things up.... but...well," said Deputy O'Connell.

THE MUSEUM (IV)

Deputy O'Connell continued with what he was saying.
"Craig, Catrin and I thoroughly searched the museum and found nothing, except the device she retrieved from the skylight window and has given to Tec to look at. I must say, I was very impressed with her climbing skills. Back in the day when I was an Agent, we liked to have nicknames for each other – guys, she's got to be Cat!"

He turned to Tec.

"What have you found?"

Tec was talking quietly to Marc.

"Oh, sorry?"

"Can you tell us if you've found out anything that can help us in this investigation."

"Well, yeah. Quite a lot actually. Could we reconvene up in the security office, please?"

They started to make their way up the stairs, led by Dr. Swan and Dr. Atherton.

Part of the way up the stairs Tec said, "Oh, darn. I've left something downstairs. I'll catch you up."

Marc bumped into Deputy O'Connell, who was at the rear of the party.

"Oops, sorry, Tim. Tripped."

The deputy didn't ask Marc to refer to him by his title – he knew when to give up on a losing battle.

They continued up to the next floor, and followed the curator and his assistant into a room with five monitors mounted on the wall, and a computer console and monitor on a desk. A small bank of lights blinked on a console set into the wall.

Dr. Atherton spoke.

"Here we have the monitors to the cameras in the Main Display Hall, the Prehistory Hall, the Treasure Hall, The Timucua Hall, outside front and outside rear."

"No camera on the sides of the buildings?" asked Deputy Sheriff O'Connell.

"Tallahassee HQ decided that there was no need for cameras there - no windows, Tim."

Pointing at the bank of lights, he said, "And these are the controls for the lights, alarm system, skylights, windows, shutters and secure vault."

Maps said, "Look, there's Tec. What is he doing?"

On the monitor for the Main Display Hall they watched as Tec walked from the wall on the left hand side of their view to the display case. He looked at the camera and waved. He walked to the far right and out of frame.

"Where's he gone?" asked Marc.

Tec's arm came into view, waved and disappeared. A few minutes later, he walked into the room.

"You disappeared from view, Master George," said Craig.

"Yessir, as ah thought, there's a slight dead spot by one of the stairwells. But it's not much. Ah really had to breathe in to stay out of view. A regular adult wouldn't be able to stay out of view. And as for...."

"Do not finish that sentence, Tec!" said Chuck, with a smile.

"As if ah would, big guy. Marc, could ya do me a favour, run down and wave into the four inside cameras, please? Go to the Main Display Hall first, then the others, then back to the Main Display Hall before comin' back here. Got that?"

"Yep."

Like a shot, Marc was out of the door. In almost no time at all, he was waving at the first camera. Then he appeared in the other three monitors. Within a minute he was walking back into the security office.

"Marc, you were supposed to go to the camera in the Main Display Hall twice. You're just like this at home. You don't listen!"

"I did, sis. Honest!" said Marc.

Tec said, "He did, Maps. Ah turned the camera off."

Dr. Swan asked, "How did you do that? Look, it's still rolling!"

The time indicator on the monitor was still displaying the date and time, with the seconds counting upwards.

"Say, Marc. Can you go back to the case and stand in front of it, facing the camera, and wave, please?"

Marc left the room, grumbling.

"Just because I'm the youngest and the smallest, they've got me doing everything. Marc do this, Marc do that......"

His voice trailed off as he went out of earshot.

Deputy O'Connell said, "He should be there now."

There was nothing on the screen except the empty display case.

"Now you see him..."

Marc appeared on the screen.

"....And now you don't."

Marc disappeared from the screen.

"What just happened?" asked Chuck.

"Ah turned the live camera signal on and off. With this."

He held up his smartphone.

"Ah've used my Bluetooth connection to control the live feed to the camera. The live feed and the time feed are on two different frequencies. Turn the live feed off and a still image of the hall appears, with the time feed superimposed over it. Looks like the room is empty."

"Cat, could you hold this please?"

Tec handed her the small black device she'd retrieved from the skylight.

"Thanks. Now watch."

He pressed the screen on his smartphone and there was an audible click from the device and a little metal arm slid out of the side.

"There's no alarm on the skylight. This pushes the emergency override button on the skylight inside lock, and the window can be opened from the outside."

A confused Dr. Atherton said, "That explains the how – but not the who or why. Or the fact that bullet proof glass was cut through, and the artefact taken without setting off the weight sensor or tripping the lasers."

"Yessir, about that. We need to go back downstairs."

When they got downstairs, Marc was standing in front of the display case. He waved at them.

To Tec he said, "Was that okay?"

"Perfect. Now, could you just step aside, so that we can look at the hole, please, Marc?"

Marc stepped aside with a flourish and asked dramatically, "Hole? What hole?"

Behind Marc, there was no longer a hole – the glass front of the display case was complete. And inside, sitting where the artefact once sat, was Deputy Sheriff O'Connell's service pistol.

"What the...?"

The deputy looked down at his empty holster.

"How...?"

"It seems that Marc can be a little light fingered. He took it when he bumped into you, and left it at the bottom of the stairs for me to pick up. Ah just put it in the case, when ah came back down."

The deputy was not one to get flustered.

"That's very clever, guys. So, you're now going to tell us about the hole?"

Tec and Marc moved around to the rear of the case.

"Come around here, and we'll show you."

Everybody joined them and stopped suddenly.

"Whoa, Tec. How did you do that? It looks like you've turned the whole case around!" exclaimed Fax.

"Impossible!" said Dr. Atherton. "That thing weighs far too much."

"Correct," said Tec. "So, we moved the hole instead. Marc?"

Marc reached into his pocket, took out a torch, like the ones the deputy, Craig and Catrin had earlier.

He handed it to Tec, then looked at the deputy and said, "Sorry, Tim."

Deputy O'Connell looked at the empty pouch in his belt where the torch should have been.

"Boy, you are good! But ask next time, yes?"

Tec moved to the left hand side of the case where there was no hole, and shone the light on the centre.

"If ya'll look very carefully, ya'll can just make out a hairline mark."

He followed the mark with the torch light, and made a complete circle.

He took what looked like a rubber glove out of his pocket and placed it firmly in the centre of the circle. A slight twist, and a perfect circle of glass came out as he pulled his hand away. He went around to the hole in the rear of the case, gently placed the glass into the hole, pressed and twisted slightly.

"There, perfect. Well, perfect except to the closest of scrutiny."

"May I?" asked the deputy, pointing at the torch.

He shone the light on the section of glass that had just been inserted.

"Amazing. How did you know?"

"The circle was just too perfect. No diamond glass cutter could do that. On the other hand, the amount of kit needed to cut a perfect hole would have been unwieldy and would have left clues. So, ah figured that it was probably cut at the manufacturing stage, and the fit is so perfect that it the circle of glass cold anneals into place."

"Cold anneals? What does that mean?" asked Catrin.

"Twisting the glass produces a tiny amount of heat, enough to make it stay in place."

"Oh."

"There's just one question. Why didn't the thief replace the glass?" asked Craig.

"Ah was wondering about that myself. Below the original hole there's a tiny chip on the marble tile. Ah think the thief may have dropped the glass. Even though it's bullet proof – although maybe even that should be checked – there was enough damage to be noticed if it was replaced."

"That's the camera, the point of entry, the hole. But the light and the pressure sensors?" asked Deputy O'Connell..

"Ah tested the lasers. They're sure real. Look."

Tec took one of the leaflets from the stand and held it into the light of one of the lasers. Instantly a bright spot appeared and started burning a hole in the paper.

"Mah Bluetooth didn't turn it off, so ah bit the bullet."

Tec put his hand into the hole. Before anyone could do anything, his hand was in the beam of the laser. There was a spot of light, but no burning.

"That was stupid!" said the deputy.

"Yessir, the first time was very stupid, Tim. But ah knew this time. There's some kind of sensor that lessens the power of the beam. It's more like strong sunlight. Ah'll get slight sunburn and a decent tan, but nothing else. Now the pressure sensor."

Tec reached in and removed the pistol, and handed it back to the deputy.

"There *is* no pressure sensor," he said.

"Excellent work, Tec. You too, Marc. It answers the how, but not the who or the why," said the deputy.

"It does mean that the thief doesn't need to be superhuman. It's someone with inside information. Don't you think, Dr. Swan?"

"Absolutely, Tim. Tallahassee arranged for this system to be installed. I trusted them to check the work of the contractor. I have the paperwork upstairs."

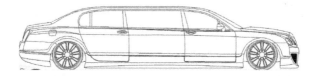

Craig said, "If you've finished with us, I'd better get these ladies and gentlemen back to school."

"Dr. Swan, could you get copies of the security installation details over to me at the office, please. I'll escort these guys back to the airfield."

"Certainly."

"Thank you. Cease recording, save and synch."

"Recording ceased, saved and synchronising....synchronising complete."

THE DALTON COUNTY
SHERIFF OFFICE

There were handshakes all around, and Craig, the students and Deputy Sheriff O'Connell went outside to the waiting cars, the two adults constantly surveying the area.

"Craig, if you guys follow me. I'll take you around the back roads to the airfield."

"Will do, Tim. Very well, ladies and gentlemen. If you please."

The students got into the car and made themselves comfortable.

"There's a lot there for everybody in Austrey to be getting on with," said Tec.

"Too many questions unanswered, though," said Fax.

"Why all this intrigue for that one artefact?" asked Maps.

Chuck answered, "It must have some kind of property that we haven't yet considered. Let's look at the facts. It's dense. It's strong. It's make-up suggests that it is probably one of the rarest things on Earth..."

Marc chipped in, "Could that be it? It's worth loads of money because it's rare?"

"Ah, therein lies a problem, Master Marc. What makes something valuable? Is it in the eye of the beholder?" asked Craig.

"It sure was an impressive piece of engineering, but not beautiful," said Tec.

"Anybody else?"

"I think it's value is in it's purpose," said Chuck.

"Which we don't know yet," said Maps.

"I have an idea," said Fax. "Why don't we get Computer and the team back in Austrey to look into Chuck's findings about the composition of the artefact? We might know what it's made of, but they'll be able to research practical applications."

"Good idea, Master Lewis. Master Charles?"

"I'll text everything through."

Meanwhile, in the police cruiser, Deputy O'Connell was receiving a call over the radio.

"O'Connell? Where the hell are you? Didn't you get the message that I want to see you?"

"O'Connell here. Sheriff, I haven't received any messages. Over."

"Cut the 'over and out' stuff with me, O'Connell. I left a message on your answering machine at home over an hour ago."

"I haven't been home. I've been at the museum, just as I told Maggie. I've had my work phone with me, Sheriff. You could have tried that."

"Don't get smart with me, boy! I gave Maggie the day off. Now, just get your sorry butt over here, like yesterday, you hear?"

"On my way, Sheriff."

The deputy had seen and heard the Sheriff in a bad mood before, but he sensed this was going to be one of the worst. He tapped a Bluetooth adapter on the dash, which connected to his personal smartphone in the glove compartment.

"Ring Craig," he said.

In the other car, Craig tapped his Bluetooth earpiece.

"Tim. Everything okay?"

"Not really. We have to make a detour via the Sheriff's office. He's got a bee in his bonnet about something. Follow me in?"

"Will co."

To the others, Craig said, "We're going taking a slight detour, to Tim's office."

Five minutes later, they were pulling up outside the Dalton County Sheriff's Department. It was a low building, painted magnolia, red tiled roof with antennae and a small dish atop, and a large satellite dish on the ground behind the building.

To the front was a driveway and parking lot, where there were a few cars parked amongst the borders and hedges. Outside the main building were six Dodge police cruisers, tidily parked, all the same as Deputy O'Connell's. He pulled in to the side of the last cruiser in the row, and Craig pulled up behind him.

The deputy got out of the car. He approached Craig's window and said, "Find a place to park in the lot. I'll wait here."

Within minutes, Craig and the students joined the deputy by the front door. He took them in, and introduced them to an elderly man at the desk.

"Hi, Sarge. These guys are with me."

"What'd ya do, Tim, arrest the whole high school?"

"No, it's a class trip. Showing them how law enforcement works here in Dalton County."

"And they got you to do it? Tough break, buddy. Sheriff must hate you more'n I thought!"

"Not in a good mood, I take it?"

"He's got a downer on everyone today. Sent Maggie home for sassin' him. All she asked was if he wanted coffee."

"Oh, one of his really black moods. No need to sign these guys in, we're only here for a short visit."

"Sure thing, Tim."

The deputy led them down a corridor to a large open plan office. At the far end of the expanse of desks was another office, separated from the main room by a wood and glass partition. On the door, in bold gold lettering, was written Sheriff Dwight Cussman.

Inside they saw a large man, wearing a uniform similar to Deputy O'Connell's. That is where the similarities between the smartly dressed deputy and the man sitting by a solid wooden desk ended. He was fat, had greasy unkempt hair, broad sweat patches under his arms and stains, ash and cigarette burns on the front of his tunic.

A smouldering cigarette dangled from the side of his mouth. He was berating a slight man standing at the desk in front of him, gesticulating wildly, his face screwed up in sheer and utter anger.

He saw Deputy Sheriff O'Connell and the rest of the group and stopped suddenly. He stood, pointed for the man to get out and followed him to the door. The small man walked out shiftily, glaring at the group with a scowl on his face as he passed them.

"O'Connell. Get in here. Now!" the sheriff bellowed, his cigarette falling from his mouth, spittle flying everywhere.

Craig looked the fat man from the top of his greasy balding head to his dusty police issue boots.

"Wait here, this won't take long," said the deputy.

He leant in towards Craig.

"That's Detective Gomez. Watch him, he's a nasty piece of work."

He walked into the Cussman's office, the door to which was slammed so hard behind him that the partition rattled.

The sheriff turned on the deputy.

"Where the hell have you been? Why don't you return my messages? Uh? I'm your boss – you do what I damned well tell you. So, where have you been? And I don't want to hear any bull!"

All through the tirade he was pointing, or holding up a fist, or gesticulating wildly.

He looked at his boss - 'Cussman the cussin' man', as he was called by the staff at the station. He knew that it was best to let the sheriff get the first rant out of the way, and perhaps there was more a chance of reasoning with him – although he doubted it, this time.

"I've been following up on the theft at the museum..."

"What?" screamed the sheriff. "Did I tell you to do that? Did I? Since when were you a goddamn'd detective?"

"As the attending officer yesterday, I assumed that I would be taking the case on. That's what normally happens."

"There's no such thing as normal unless I say it's normal. And who are those damned kids?" he shouted, pointing at the students.

"Family friends. I was going to show them around the station."

"Get 'em outta here – NOW!" he screamed.

"And if I find out they've been near this case, I'll have your goddamn'd badge and your gun!"

In the meantime, the students stood together, taking in the drama unfolding before them in the sheriff's office.

Fax leaned in towards Chuck and said, "My gosh, that man is so large, I think he's going to have a coronary!"

"Yes," replied Chuck. "Too many hamburgers, methinks!"

"And he smells, and he's all dusty," said Catrin.

They all looked at each other, then turned to look at Craig. He just nodded and held his finger to his lips.

Craig turned to stare over at the Gomez, who hadn't taken his beady little eyes off the group. Craig bent down towards Marc and whispered something into his ear. Marc nodded, left the group and approached the detective, whose right hand immediately went to the holstered pistol strapped to the left side of his body.

He pointed at Marc with his left hand.

"Get back over with your friends, kid, before I kick you back over there."

"I just wanted to know if I could have a drink of water, sir. May I?"

"I said get back over there," the detective growled.

Giving his sweetest smile, Marc said in French, "Up yours, you ugly monkey!"

Craig and Maps giggled.

"What did you say, you little punk?"

"There's no need to be so offensive, sir. I merely wished you a pleasant day."

As he returned to the group, he looked at Craig, pointed down at the back of his hand and nodded.

The door to the sheriff's office opened. Deputy O'Connell stepped out and walked towards them. Behind him, the sheriff was standing with his back to them, drawing deeply on a cigarette he had just rolled.

"Craig, you guys head off to the airfield. I have to stay here. Be careful, something's not right. Have you seen?"

"Yes, Tim. The dust, the smoking, the smell, and the sunburn."

"You haven't lost it old, friend."

"The kids saw it, too."

"All the more reason to be careful. I'll see what I can dig up here. Let me know when you're in the air. I'll be in touch."

They shook hands. Craig told the students to follow him, and they said their goodbyes to Deputy O'Connell.

Outside, Craig held the door to the Lincoln open for the students to get in after running through his security routine. He had a last scan of the area before driving out of the parking lot and headed towards the airfield.

ON THE WAY TO THE AIRFIELD

They drove in silence for a few miles or so, before Catrin piped up. "That sheriff and the detective weren't very nice people, were they?"

"Very insightful, Miss Catrin. Master Charles, what did you notice?"

"The sheriff is a man who certainly likes his hamburgers. The smell oozes out of the man's pores!"

"Good. Master Lewis?"

"He smokes a lot, judging by the ash burns on his shirt, and the stains on his moustache and fingers. Rolls his own, too."

Catrin said, "He doesn't clean his work boots either. They were covered in red dust."

"Miss Lauren, shoe size?"

"About the same as Fax – size 13 U.K."

"Master George?"

"I think we have the man on the grassy knoll, and the man who hired him, yessir, Craig."

"Well deduced all of you."

"What does that mean? 'Man on the grassy knoll'?" asked Marc

"A reference to a feature of the JFK assassination," said Tec.

"Fax'll tell you later."

"Master Marc. What did you deduce about the detective?"

"He's lean, so he's probably nimble on his feet. He has a really nasty attitude to other people – I wouldn't want to be a granny, a baby or a puppy around him. He's got a suntan line, just as Tec said the thief would have. Oh, and he doesn't speak French!"

The others giggled at this last remark.

Craig said, "Deputy O'Connell had a feeling that it was an inside job. It seems that it spreads further than just the museum community – elements of the law enforcement community seem to be involved, as well."

They sat in silence.

Tec turned suddenly, and piped up, "Craig! You've just missed the entrance to the airstrip!"

"Yes, Master George. Tim and I decided that it may be prudent to fly from elsewhere. I had the Cessna moved. We'll be flying out of Keystone Heights, instead. It's a little further down Route 301."

Ten minutes later, Cat wailed.

"Ooh. Cra-a-i-g! I need a comfort break - to visit the little ladies bathroom."

"Oh sis, you always do this!"

"No, I don't!"

"Do you think it can wait, Miss Catrin? It's only another ten minutes, or so."

"No, I'm afraid not. I *really* need to go!"

"Very well, Miss. According to the GPS, there's a service station about a mile up ahead. We'll pull in there."

"Thank you!"

She made a face at her brother.

He just rolled his eyes.

A minute later, they were pulling into the Chevron gas station and services. It was small, but very well kept. Craig drove past the fuel pumps, the car wash and the neat little Wawa diner, and pulled up outside the rest rooms.

"Thanks. Won't be long," Catrin said as she jumped out of the car, and ran into the ladies restroom.

"May we get some air?" asked Maps.

"Yes, but straight back in as soon as Miss Catrin has finished."

The students got out of the car and stretched, talking to each other or just looking around. Route 301 was quite busy, with heavy trucks transporting goods northwards from the ports of southern Florida in one direction, or livestock from Texas down to the holiday centres in the south of the state in the opposite direction.

Silently, a man appeared from around the side of the men's restroom, brandishing a pistol. His face was half covered in a red bandanna. He held a mean looking G3 Glock 17 firmly in two hands, straight out in front of him, feeling the ground with his feet as he stepped. His held a finger on the guard rather than the trigger, again showing that he may have been professionally trained in the use of firearms.

The man said, firmly, meaning business, "Everybody stay very still."

Craig stood in front of the assailant, making himself as large a target as possible so as to protect the students behind him.

Over his shoulder he said in a low voice, "Behind the car, slowly, heads down."

To the man, he said in calming tones, "I don't know what you want, they're just kids. I have a wallet. Here. You can take that. Leave the kids. What do you say? Over $500 in cash, credit cards, phone, watch – not a bad day's haul. Eh? Come on, lower the gun."

Suddenly, Catrin burst out of the restroom door and shouted, "I'm ready!"

Then she screamed.

A minute went by. Then two. Craig spoke.

"It's okay, ladies and gentlemen. It's safe to come out. Straight into the car, if you please."

They stood up slowly. Craig was dusting himself down. He stopped, turned and opened the car door. The students got into the car quickly, then Craig motioned for Catrin to get in.

She was standing in the restroom doorway, standing stock still, open-mouthed, little whimpering sounds coming from somewhere deep inside. She was pointing at where the man once stood. Craig took her gently by the hand and led her to the car.

"There, there, Miss Catrin. Miss Lauren, will you look after her, make sure she has a drink of water?"

Once they were all in the car, the others looked at where the man once stood. He was on the floor unconscious, hands and ankles zipped-tied.

Tec turned to Fax.

"Man, *WHO IS THIS GUY?*"

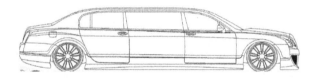

Craig started the engine, then skidded out of the gas station exit.

He tapped his Bluetooth and said, "Tim, work."

He heard the dial tone, then the deputy answered.

"Craig. Don't say anything. I'll ring back."

The line went dead.

A few minutes later, Craig's phone rang.

"Sorry about that. I was in the Cussman's office. Things are bad here. I'll tell you more later. I've had to come to the locker room and ring from my private phone. What is it?"

"We've been compromised. We were just threatened at gunpoint. Definitely a pro."

He stole a quick glance at the assailant's weapon, now in an evidence bag, on the passenger seat.

"G3 Glock 17, military service issue with a Veridian C5L under-slung laser-light. No number."

"Veridian? That's heavy stuff, and definitely not our service issue. Too expensive. The perp?"

"Male. Hispanic. A bigger version of Detective Gomez. Trained. Now bundled and ready for the ER."

"Damage level?"

"Broken jaw, broken nose. He'll be visiting an orthodontist for a few years. Broken wrist, dislocated elbow."

"Oh, you were gentle on him, then?"

"What can I say, Tim? He pointed a weapon at those in my care. I felt he needed to be taught a bit of a lesson."

"I'll get an ambulance to him. How far away are you from the airfield?"

"About five minutes."

Tim continued.

"My one concern is that no-one knew about the change of plans. Unless – they heard us last night in the den. Hell! Jenny and Frankie! I have to go, Craig. Have you deployed the defences on the car?"

"Yes. Now, you go get your wife and son. Do you want us to wait for you at the airfield?"

"No, it's not safe for you to be hanging around. I'll make my own way. I know these back roads and trails like the back of my hand."

In the back of the car, the others were sitting stunned. What on earth happened while they were hiding behind the car?

Fax held his sister, and asked gently, "Sis, how are you holding up?"

Catrin just nodded.

"What did you see?"

"I – I – I don't know. It happened so fast. One second there was a man with a gun, then there was Craig moving quickly. There was crunching of bones, I remember that – it was like a biscotti snapping. Then the man was on the floor not moving, and Craig was standing over him. It was like it was in super fast slow motion. The man didn't even get a chance to say 'ow'."

"Craig is way more than SAS!" exclaimed Tec. "He's some kind of super soldier!"

"But it's our Craig!" said Catrin. "He takes us to school in the morning. Makes us our packed lunches. How....?"

Her voice trailed off.

"I don't care how, I'm just glad he is," said Chuck.

"That man looked like he meant business."

They jumped as a loud ping hit the window next to Marc. Craig shouted out.

"Everybody into the floor well, please. Looks like the gentleman at the service station has friends."

Craig seemed unperturbed whilst the others hid on the floor. He didn't take any evasive action apart from flick a switch to activate the outside cameras, and drove on through the constant ping, ping, ping hitting the car windows, rear windscreen and side panels.

"What if they hit a tyre?" shouted Maps.

"Don't worry, Miss Lauren. This car has been modified. It's built like a tank – better specification than the President's own car. Which, by the way, Professor Weiss also designed."

After what felt like an eternity to the students, the pinging of bullets stopped. Moments later, the Lincoln skidded to a halt beside the Cessna.

Craig flung the door open, and shouted for the students to run up the steps as quickly as possible. A man ran out from the hanger. He was wearing sky blue overalls with MLM Inc. on the back, carrying an Ingram Mac-10 machine pistol with suppressor. He was the Cessna's engineer, and worked for Fax's father.

He nodded in Craig's direction and took up a kneeling position to cover them.

He shouted in a heavy west Scotland accent, "Pit the we'ens tae safety, I'll cover ye."

"What about you, Chick?"

"I'll see m' own way 'ome. Now gang oan wi' ye!"

Craig held a small but powerful Webley and Scott M1905 which had appeared in his hand.

Catrin seemed reluctant to leave the car, so he took her hand.

He said, "Come on, Miss Catrin. You're safe now. I've got you."

He led her up the steps, keeping the Webley arcing wherever his head turned.

Once inside he said, "Buckle up everyone. No safety video on this flight – this is going to be a short emergency take-off. Miss Lauren, help Miss Catrin into her seat and buckle her safety belt, please. Master Charles, with me."

With that, he turned and walked into the cockpit.

"Master Charles, take the co-pilot's seat. If we're going to perform an emergency take-off, I'll need your strength on the yoke. Also keep an eye on the oil pressure there, and oil temperature there. We want them to remain green."

"Keystone Heights tower, this is Cessna 680 Lima-Mike-Indigo-Two-Two-One. Requesting clearance for emergency take-off."

"Cessna 680 Lima-Mike-Indigo-Two-Two-One, this is Keystone Heights tower. Request denied. I repeat, request denied."

"Keystone Heights tower. You had better clear any traffic coming my way, because I'm going. If you don't like it, sue me!"

"Cessna 680 Lima ..."

Craig switched off the radio.

Over the intercom he said, "Here we go, ladies and gentlemen. Push yourselves back into your seats and hold on very tight."

Craig taxied quickly to the start of the runway. The sky ahead was clear. He pushed the thrusters towards maximum. With the brakes on, the engines screamed and whined, the aircraft bucked and vibrated. He released the brakes and the Cessna shot forwards, throwing everyone back into their seats and holding them there.

"Status oil pressure and temperature."

"Green."

"Grab the yoke. When I say pull, you pull."

The airspeed indicator came alive very quickly, and as soon as it reached 55 knots, Craig shouted, "Pull!"

The two pulled the yolk towards their stomachs and the Cessna shot into the air. It climbed steeply for 5,000 feet before Craig told Chuck to let go, and he took over the controls.

"That was interesting," said Chuck. "Why so fast, steep and high?"

"It lessened the chance of them using surface to air missiles. We have other measures that we can call upon at this height or above. It also makes it difficult for them if they want to use a helicopter, or get their own craft in the air. That's why I want you to stay with me, and be my eyes."

He pressed a button and a small screen slid up from the console. There was the image of a plane in the centre with green rings. An arm swept around, ready to ping if an object came within range of the radar.

"Keep your eye on the display, please Master Charles. Also, eyes up through the cockpit windows."

Once Craig was happy with the trim, direction and speed, he turned the radio back on.

"Just as I thought. They were told not to let us go."

"How do you know, Craig?"

"The procedure in such an event would have required the airfield to inform air traffic control in Jacksonville, Atlanta, Memphis and Kansas City – all the areas over which we have to fly in order to return to

Austrey. If we were considered a threat, there would have been a military response. Listen, there's nothing."

Craig made contact with Jacksonville air traffic control, and the Cessna continued northwards on its revised flight plan.

BACK AT THE LABORATORY (II)

Back at the laboratory, everyone was now present, Fingers having finished her tests. Over the communication system, Craig was recounting what had happened. Everybody listened in stunned silence.

"We're now heading into Atlanta airspace, estimated flight time, 3 hours."

"Thank you, Captain Gledhill. I trust the Agents are unharmed and well? You would have told me otherwise, I'm certain."

"They are all well. Miss Catrin had a bit of a fright with the incident with the gunman, but they are in good spirits. May I say, Professor, they performed as you said they would."

"Thank you, Captain. I will thank them myself when they arrive."

"I'd better go, Professor. We still need to keep our wits about us, as we don't know who is after us. Or their capabilities."

"Agreed, Captain."

Once Craig had signed off, the Professor turned to the remaining Agents.

"As you can see, there is more to this stolen artefact than meets the eye. What do we know?"

Computer interrupted.

"For your information, Professor, I am recording this conversation for our records."

"Thank you, Computer. I hadn't thought about that. Mr. Madison?"

"Yeah, Professor. I've been, kind of, you know, checking out the Florida State Intranet system, security systems and the Police bespoke software Deputy Sheriff O'Connell mentioned, yeah. Uh, all Florida State hardware and software requirements were put out to tender three years ago. I passed the successful names of the winning companies to Marty."

"Thank you. Mr. Huntley?"

"I tracked four separate companies. The Nett Systems Corporation created and maintain the intranet; Global Lock Incorporated make, install and maintain the security systems; Babel Right programmed the voice recognition software; finally, every single piece of scientific equipment in every school, state or county department, university, police department – everything – is supplied and maintained by Sci-Corp. The total value for that contract alone is tens of millions every year."

"I found something which made me slightly suspicious. In each of the tenders, the successful company was between twenty five and thirty five percent cheaper than the next lowest tender. This isn't unusual, per se, as the lowest tender can often be the successful one. However, this usually comes at a cost. Inferior products, poorer maintenance, poor or non-existent customer services, failure to meet deadlines and budget over-runs, that kind of thing. Not with these contracts. Every single one has been 'by the book' perfect."

"I delved into the companies involved. With Hex's help, we were able to track the companies through subsidiary companies, phantom companies, shell corporations, holding companies, cash only concerns – an amazing maze is an understatement. However, we found the true owners. Rather, owner. Computer, if you please?"

An image appeared on the screen of a well dressed man, clean cut, white-blond hair, posing with an almost military bearing. He was looking into the camera with a piercing gaze and the hint of a scornful disdain upon his lips.

"I give you De Montfort St. John Strangway III. Sole owner of Strangway Mining and Ore, and of the Strangway Foundation."

"The museum's benefactors?"

"Precisely, Professor."

"What do we know about him?"

"Nothing, other than the fact that he's an absolute recluse. This photograph was released to the press by his PR people, but there was no information with it. We could look into his background."

"No, thank you Mr. Huntley. I think we'll leave that task for when the other Agents return."

"Miss Liu. What have you been researching?"

"Chuck mentioned thallium and Ununtium as being elements within the alloy. Chemistry is not my field normally, but if you bear with me, you'll understand my interest. Let's start with thallium. Symbol Tl, atomic number 81, and it's rare in its natural state, something like 2.73 parts per billion in the Earth's crust. It's not a rare element overall, however: it is actually ten times more abundant than silver."

"The element is widely dispersed, mainly in potassium minerals such as sylvite and pollucite. Thallium minerals are rare, but a few are known, such as crookesite and lorandite World production of thallium compound is around 30 tonnes per year. There has been no assessment of how great the reserves are."

As though reading from a checklist, she carried on.

"The metal is very soft and malleable. It can be cut with a knife. The element and its compounds are highly toxic and should be handled carefully. It has no medicinal use in its pure form, as the toxicity is non-selective...it will kill anything...the toxins enter the body through ingestion, inhalation or penetration. In other forms, it is used in nuclear cardiography, in the treatment of TB, ringworm, and night sweats. It was extensively used in vermin control, but is now widely banned even for that purpose."

"That is Chemistry 101 over and done with. Other applications include high temperature superconductivity, and extremely low temperature superconductivity when used with selenium."

"This is my interest: optics. Thallium(I) bromide and thallium(I) iodide crystals have been used as infrared optical materials for two main reasons: they are harder than other common infrared optics; they receive transmissions at significantly longer wavelengths. Basically, a lens either made or coated with these optical materials gathers electro magnetic energy - light - across a very wide spectrum. It can also identify where light is interacting with matter and energy, visible or not."

"Could the artefact be some kind of lens, Miss Liu?"

"Without physically testing the artefact, I can only hypothesise. The presence of thallium, along with a synthetic element that purports to have the same properties as thallium, suggests that it may be some kind of focussing lens."

"Do you have a theory on what it is focussing?"

"A form of light or energy beyond the visual range of humans, and beyond the range of any device of which I'm aware."

Now that Fingers had finished her academic tests, and had rejoined the other Agents, she had also been put to work.

"Miss Ramos. Anything to report on Sheriff Cussman and detective Gomez?"

"My sources down-town tell me that Dwight Reginald Cussman is 'a sleaze ball'. His words, Professor, not mine, honestly. Born nine-eight-fifty-nine, Gainsbrough, Florida. He was from a broken home, father a drunk who ran out on his wife and the kids. A succession of new dads would beat Dwight and his siblings. He had a number of run ins with the police as a juvenile. He dropped out of school, drifted from job to job."

"My guy told me that he was a drunken trouble maker who roamed the towns around the wider Dalton County area, making a nuisance of himself. He has a wrap sheet a foot long, mostly minor misdemeanours. He was arrested once for grievous assault, when he was in his mid twenties."

"Five years ago, he comes out of nowhere and buys a fancy house on the outskirts of Dalton. Within a year, he's elected Sheriff...totally uncontested. That was just before Deputy Sheriff O'Connell joined the department from Jacksonville P.D. He spent a lot of money on the new headquarters, supposedly out of his own pocket. Runs the department like his own secret army. He's tried to get rid of Deputy Sheriff O'Connell on a number of occasions, but the mayor won't hear of it."

"He brought Eduardo Himinez Gomez with him. Second generation Mexican. His parents runs a Taco Bell franchise in Dallas. He and his sister had a good upbringing. Consuela is an assistant DA in Austin, Texas. Gomez wanted adventure and joined the Marines. He was always on KP, had a real problem with authority. He was dishonourably discharged after two years in the brig in Cape Pendleton, California, for striking an officer in a bar brawl in Grenada."

"Once released he went to Mexico. He was off the radar until he turned up with Cussman. He has absolutely no formal police training. My guy said that there have been rumours about him using his position to run drugs from the west coast of Florida, but nothing has ever been proven. He also said to watch out for Gomez – a shoot you in the back kind of guy."

"Thank you, Miss Ramos. And please thank your 'guy'."

THE RESCUE (I)

I n Sheriff Cussman's office, Tim stood in front of the messy desk, waiting for is boss to finish a phone call.

"You are *kidding me!*" he screamed.

"How bad is he? Intensive Care? What about the others."

He glared Tim's way.

"Were they really? Interesting. Where are they now? Got away? What the hell are we paying your guys for? Pros my ... they're just a bunch of goddam'n kids and a driver. You know what to do about the other two."

Tim began to feel very uneasy. He turned to see Gomez sitting at his desk, pretending that he was taking a call - or listening in.

The sheriff slammed the phone down with such force that a styrofoam cup half full with day old coffee and soggy cigarette ends fell over, the black mess spreading like an oily slick across the desk. Cussman didn't seem to notice.

He seemed to settle his anger, and said into a very calm but no less a threatening voice.

84

"That was a very interesting call."

With more aggression in his voice he said, "Now, O'Connell, you're gonna talk. Who are those kids you had staying at your house, when they weren't supposed to be there? The ones you've been takin' to crime scenes, eh?"

"As I told you, they are family friends from up north. They were visiting the area and I though I'd show them the sights. And, Sheriff Cussman, how do you know they weren't supposed to be at my house?"

"*I'm asking the questions!*" screamed the sheriff, brown spittle splattering the oily slick on the desk below.

"That little limey – he ain't no driver. He took out one of my best men. I made you a promise I'd have your badge and gun over this. Hand them over. *NOW!*"

Tim noticed that Gomez was approaching the office, weapon drawn but by his side, a sly grimace on his face. Deputy Sheriff O'Connell realised that they weren't about to let him go.

He held up one hand towards the sheriff and said, "Okay, okay, Cussman, I'm going to reach for my weapon, very slowly, and put it on the desk."

Tim did just that.

"Badge!" screamed the sheriff.

Tim reached up for his badge, took it off, and threw it as hard as he could into the sheriff's face.

In an instant, he had hold of the sheriff's right arm in a painful Chin Na hold. The sheriff screamed. Then, Tim swept up his pistol with his free hand and jumped behind the sheriff. The move caused a bone to shatter in the sheriff's wrist. He screamed even more loudly.

Tim swung the pistol around and thrust it as hard as he could through the layers of fat under the sheriff's chin. Cussman arched backwards with the excruciating pain he was suffering.

"Move."

He guided the sheriff from behind the desk, maintaining the painful arm lock. Gomez burst in through the door.

"Drop it, O'Connell, or I shoot."

"Sheriff won't be happy about that! Put it down!"

Gomez didn't move his body, but his revolver waved slightly, as if he was trying to get a clear shot. Tim pressed the pistol a little harder into the sheriff's chin, who managed a gargled, "D-d-d-drop-it. N-n-now!'"

Gomez nodded, and slowly placed his revolver on the floor, never taking his eyes off Tim.

"Kick it away. Now, move slowly, hands straight above your head where I can see them. Into the wash room. Close the door."

Once Gomez was in the sheriff's private bathroom. Tim locked the door, then frog-marched Cussman through the large room, now empty, and down the corridor. Sarge wasn't at his desk. Tim figured that they were not going to let him get away alive.

He led Sheriff Cussman over to his own cruiser. At the car door he turned the sheriff around, and released the arm hold.

"You're a dead man, O'Connell, you hear me. A dead man!"

Tim delivered a flat handed blow to the side of the sheriff's head, which rendered him immediately unconscious. His knees crumpled, and he fell face first onto the tarmac.

Once inside the car, Tim said, "Call Home" and the phone dialled his home number. It was answered almost immediately.

"Jenny, go to lockdown. You know the codes and the drill. I'm on my way. I'll be ten minutes tops."

Two hours later, in the laboratory, all the remaining Agents were assembled. They were talking quietly to each other or working on personal projects.

Spex stood shakily at the front desk, showing a document to Professor Weiss.

"Professor. I think that you should take this call. It's Jenny O'Connell."

"Thank you, Computer. Put her on loudspeaker. Jen, this is Ed. What can I do for you?"

"Oh, Ed. Thank goodness. It's – it's Tim. He – he's been shot!"

"Are you safe?"

"Yes, I'm on lockdown."

"Good, you're safe for now. Jen, tell me exactly what happened."

Jenny told the Professor about the phone call from Tim telling her to go to lockdown, and the phone call from Dalton County's Corpus Christi Hospital saying the her husband had been wounded.

"They said it's serious, but not life threatening. They shot him in the back, Ed. What kind of people do that?"

"Jen, we'll worry about that later. Right now we need to get you and little Frankie to safety. I'll get some people onto that right away. If someone you know comes to the door and doesn't use today's lockdown word, hit the button. Use your training. Is that clear, Jen?"

"Yes, Ed. But what about Timmy?"

"I'll get straight onto that, as well. Now hang up, and get everything you need for Frankie and yourself. Pack only the essentials."

"Thanks, Ed."

The line went dead.

"Computer, get Dr. Swan on the phone, please. Off loudspeaker, onto head set, please."

Dispensing with his usual niceties, to the Agents in the room he said, "Arma, Bladen I want you to go to the airfield and secure the hanger. Ewelina, go with them...I believe you know the guard at the gate."

"Yes, my cousin."

"Good. Anna, contact your guy. See if he has anyone down there who could guard Deputy Sheriff O'Connell until our cavalry arrives."

"On it."

"Martin, Dexter – dig into the financials of Cussman and Gomez. Let's see if we can find where the money originated."

"What about me, Professor?" asked Spex.

"Eu-Meh, I want you here by my side. Work with Computer to start making sense of all this. Very well, everyone – let's bring our friends home."

After calling Professor Weiss, Jenny O'Connell did exactly as she was told. She packed a bag each for her and Frankie. Suddenly, there was a loud knock at the door.

"Hey, Jenny. It's me, Sarge. Sheriff Cussman sent me to bring you to the hospital to see Tim. C'mon, open up!"

Sarge knocked at the door again, more insistent this time.

Jenny looked at the CCTV monitor in the hall. It was Sarge. She looked beyond him. She could see someone else in the police cruiser parked in the drive.

Another knock.

"Jenny. C'mon, I know you're in there. I'm here to help."

The door handle was being turned and pulled and pushed at. Jenny flicked a switch which sent 10,000 volts through the door handle, and into Sarge's body. It flung him so far that he landed on the windscreen of the cruiser, caving it in and trapping the other person under the weight of his unconscious body.

She and Frankie went to the lockdown room, just off Tim's den. It was built to resist an EF 5 twister. She and Frankie didn't take their eyes off the CCTV monitor mounted on the wall.

Dr. Swan pulled up in front of the emergency entrance to Corpus Christi Hospital. As he got out of the car, he recalled the call he'd had about an hour ago from his friend, Edison Weiss.

"Drey, events have taken a turn for the worse. Tim's been shot. I want you to go to the hospital and take him to the location I'm sending to your phone. Use a disposable car, you're coming back here with Tim."

"What can I expect, Edison?"

"Apart from FBI Special Agent Samuel Johnson - courtesy of Miss Ramos' friend in the Austrey PD, just the unexpected. Special Agent Johnson knows today's code."

"Same old, same old then. And John?"

"I've sent him to get Jenny and Frankie. They've already made one attempt to get at her. Just one thing - use non-lethal force. We don't want to turn this into an incident. Good luck, and I'll see you soon, old friend."

"I'll see you in a few hours."

At the O'Connell's house, Jenny and Frankie watched as a camouflaged AM General High Mobility Multipurpose Wheel Vehicle - more commonly knows as a Humvee - drove in and parked behind Sarge's cruiser. A figure got out, fully clothed in a desert camouflaged outfit, holding a mean-looking Mossberg and Taser X12 non-lethal shotgun. He held it in front of him, and moved it wherever he looked. He moved slowly to the unconscious forms of Sarge and his accomplice, checked their vital signs and then zip tied them, hand and foot.

He moved slowly to the door, and said one word into the intercom: "Windsor."

Jenny breathed a sigh of relief, and left the safety of the lockdown room. She held Frankie behind her an she opened the door. The figure removed his khaki balaclava.

"John! You…I…you're the last person I expected to see!"

"Hi, Jenny. No time for that now. C'mon, let's get the two of you to Tim."

"Daddy! Are we getting my Daddy?"

"No, Frankie. But he's safe. You'll be seeing him in a little while."

The three got into the Humvee, and Dr. John Atherton reversed the vehicle quickly out of the drive, turned and sped in the direction of the rendezvous.

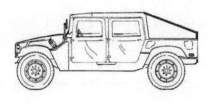

Meanwhile, Dr. Drey Swan pulled up outside the ER entrance to the Dalton County Corpus Christi Hospital. The entire place was quiet. A single ambulance, but no staff, none of the hustle and bustle of a hospital at this time of day. He looked around, holding a Pneu-dart Model 190B at his side.

He walked into the triage area, it was empty, but whoever was there had left in a hurry. There were no medical trollies, but the equipment used to work on the injured and ill was all still turned on.

Heart monitors had the sound of a flat-line, another machine was pinging an emergency tone, and medical instruments lay strewn across the floor. This place had been evacuated in a rush, he thought. In the distance, he could hear the trill of an unanswered phone, lonely in this deserted expanse. He hoped that he wasn't too late.

He checked a chart at the reception desk, and it showed that Deputy Sheriff Timothy Pádraig O'Connell was in a private room on the second floor. He decided not to take the lift or the stairs - if they were obvious points of entry to him, they would be to the bad guys as well.

Instead, he made his way outside and looked up. The emergency stairwell at the back of the building had no windows for fire safety reasons. He pulled out a compact Henriksen AS Grapnel Launcher, aimed straight up towards the roof of the hospital and fired. The black Mil-Tec nylon anchor rope spiralled upwards, and the grapnel hook had opened as it left the barrel. It sailed over the lip of the roof. Dr. Swan pulled. The hook slid along the roof for a few feet before biting into the foot high wall that went around the edge of the roof.

He reached up, and started pulling himself up, hand over hand.
I'm getting too old for this, he thought to himself.
He climbed to the top of the rope in less than two minutes, reached up and pulled himself nimbly over the small wall. He crouched and

looked around, sweeping the dart pistol in front of him. Once he was happy that the area was clear, he ran to the door that led into the roof utilities space above the fifth floor of the hospital.

He tried the door. It was unlocked, so he pulled it open, slowly, crouching at the bottom of the door frame. He heard a pop and a *thwunk*, as a low calibre bullet fired from a suppressed gun hit the door. He looked around the door frame and fired his dart gun at the shape the bottom of the stairs. The dose of ketamine worked immediately, and the form slumped to the floor.

Dr. Swan walked down the stairs slowly, watching and listening. He crouched down by the sleeping form of Sheriff Cussman, arm in a temporary cast where Deputy O'Connell had broken his wrist. He turned the huge frame of the sheriff over and zip tied him. He checked that the sheriff was breathing easily.

"You wouldn't do this for me, but orders are orders!"

He slipped the sheriff's weapon into an evidence bag and put it into his little back pack.

He faced no further opposition on the way down to the second floor. He found the room where Tim lay with a saline drip in his arm and wires on his chest going to a heart monitor. He looked in, but saw no-one. From a side door, a figure moved out and called "Windsor".

From behind the figure came a screaming shout.

"Police. Freeze. Place your weapons on the floor!"

Special Agent Johnson put one hand up, and lowered the other to place his weapon on the floor. Like lightening, Dr. Swan swung up his dart pistol up and fired. The dart zipped past Special Agent Johnson's left ear and caught Detective Gomez square in the chest. As Gomez crumpled, his finger jerked and he pulled the trigger, the bullet hitting a vase near Dr. Swan.

"Special Agent Johnson, I presume. I'm Dr. Drey Swan. You were expecting me?"

"Not really, I was expecting - er - no disrespect - someone a little younger."

"Me too, son. Me too. Could you zip tie our friend there and put his weapon in this, please?"

He handed the special agent an evidence bag. Once done, Dr. Swan said, "Come, let's get our friend to safety."

"Where are we going?"

"To Austrey, Kansas. The quick way, via Route 301."

Special Agent Johnson looked totally confused, but helped Dr. Swan wheel Tim's hospital bed into the lift and down to an ambulance parked in one of the bays outside the entrance. He drove out of the curved exit onto Route 301, and headed north to the agreed rendezvous point.

THE RESCUE (II)

O n board the Cessna, Craig finished his conversation with
Professor Weiss.

"Wilco, Professor. Out."

"What's happening Craig?" asked Chuck.

"Master Charles, we're going on a slight detour."

"May I ask where?"

"Back the way we came."

In the passenger section of the aircraft, Tec asked, "Am ah the only
one feelin' that? We're-a-turnin'."

Just then, Craig's voice came over the intercom.

"Ladies and gentlemen, I'm afraid that a situation has arisen which
requires us to return rather hastily to Dalton County. We'll be picking
up passengers, one of whom is injured. After this turn, I want you to go
to the rear of the aircraft. There you will see that the last two rows on
the port side can be adapted into a medical bed. Please set up a saline
drip on a stand – they're in a medical case in the galley – it's obvious
what you have to do. Once you've done that, return to your seats and

make sure that you're seat belt is very tight: we'll be performing a short field landing."

They heard someone say something in the background.

"As Master Charles pointed out, you might not know your port from your starboard. Port is on your right hand side as you look towards the rear of the aircraft."

"Ah wonder who's been injured?"

"Must be pretty serious for us to be going back like this," said Maps.

"Is it like this all the time in the Agency?" Marc asked Tec.

"Shucks, this is nothin'.....er, actually, it's my first semester with the Agency, too. But it *is* kinda exciting!"

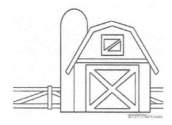

The rendezvous point was an old, deserted barn. The paint was flaking, some of the boards were missing, and one door hung crookedly by its top hinge, but it was still a solid structure and offered protection from prying eyes. Dr. Swan and Special Agent Johnson kept their wits about them, keeping an eagle eye out for anyone who may have been following them. Dr. Swan pulled off the road two hundred yards away and turned to the special agent.

"Sam, I'm going to take a look. You stay with Tim. You know the drill if I'm not back in ten minutes - start driving, and get your guys in Jacksonville to extract you. *Do not* come looking for me."

"Sure thing, Doc. I'll update my guys on what's happening."

"Make sure that it's with someone you would trust with your life!"

With that, the curator left the ambulance, and disappeared into the approaching gloom. Special Agent Johnson quickly checked on the deputy sheriff, then looked out of the window for Dr. Swan, but he was gone.

Where on earth did he just go? he thought to himself.

Ten minutes later, there was a gentle knock on the door. It cracked open slightly and the codeword was called out. Dr. Swan put his head in the door, just as Special Agent Johnson was lowering his service pistol. He climbed into the driver's seat.

"All clear, Sam."

With that, he started the ambulance and drove it to the front of the barn. Special Agent Johnson swung the good door open, and Dr.. Swan reversed slowly into dark interior of the old barn.

"Sam, could you place the homing beacon at the end of the dirt track, please. Make sure that it's buried."

As the special agent did as he was asked, Dr. Swan checked on Tim. He opened his eyes and managed a weak smile.

"Drey. Where am I? Wha...what happened? I feel like I've been kicked by my Aunt's old mule!" He tried to get up.

"Whoa, there cowboy. Take it easy. We're in the old Miller barn on Route 301, waiting for a lift. Somebody decided to use you for a bit of target practice."

"Jenny and Frankie...."

"Are perfectly safe. They're on their way here with John."

"The old boy came out of retirement, eh?"

"We all have. Edison thinks this is big - goes all the way to the top, wherever that may be."

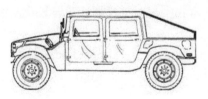

Just then, they heard the distinctive sound of a Humvee coming towards them from the rear of the barn. He went to the rear door. The Humvee flashed its headlights. He flashed a signal back using a torch.

Almost before the huge vehicle came to a full stop, Jenny and Frankie had jumped out and had come running towards Dr.. Swan.

"Drey! Where's Tim? How is he? What happened?" asked Jenny, breathlessly.

Frankie tugged at his arm. "Where's my Daddy?"

"He's fine. Come with me."

He led them to the ambulance. They both jumped up into the vehicle and rushed to Tim, Frankie landing across his chest, and Jenny hugging him, kissing him on the cheeks, temple, head and lips.

"Ooh! Ow! Take it easy you two. You're going to crush me!"

While the deputy sheriff filled his wife and son in on what he remembered, Drs. Swan, Atherton and Special Agent Johnson leant against the front of the ambulance. Dr. Swan introduced the other two men to each other.

"Do you think you were followed, John?"

"No, Drey. I came cross-country. Nobody could have followed me in that beast!" he said, nodding back towards the Humvee.

"Right, order of the day…we need to gather some intel to relay to Craig. We don't want him coming in blind."

"He'll be performing a short field landing. He'll want to know the wind direction, wind shear and speed. And the angle of any slope."

Special Agent Johnson looked askew at the two greying middle aged men in front of him. He asked, "Have you two guys done this kind of thing before?"

Swan and Atherton exchanged looks.

"Sam, we were doing this kind of things before you were a twinkle in your daddy's eye!"

The special agent said slowly, almost in disbelief - these two were the same age as his father, for goodness sake.

"Right."

He continued, "What can I do?"

"We're within tolerances with the angle of the slope - that's why we chose this location. John and I will gather the readings for the wind conditions. But Craig is coming in with no running lights until the last moment, so as not to alert the other side. Could you take this and be our eyes and ears, please?"

Dr. Atherton passed him a handheld radar, similar to the radar in the cockpit of the Cessna, and a radio earpiece.

"Give us one tap on the radio when they appear on the radar. Two when you have ears."

"Three if I see them?"

"If you see them, they'll be sitting on your lap, telling you they've landed!"

With that, Special Agent Johnson disappeared out of the front door of the barn and melted away into the darkness.

Swan turned to Atherton.

"John, can you sort the wind readings, please? I'd better get in there and check on the O'Connells. They've had a quite a day of it."

"Haven't we all, Drey. I was not expecting this when I was eating my all-bran this morning. Made me realise one thing, though - life is way too short to be eating that stuff!"

He got up, headed out of the front doors of the barn and disappeared.

Ten minutes later, Dr. Swan heard a single tap sound in his ear-piece. The special agent had Craig on radar. A further ten minutes a second tap, and two minutes after that, the other two walked in the front door of the barn.

"Good job, Sam. John, what have we got?"

"Wind direction, north north east, 5 knots, zero wind shear."

"That means that Craig needs to fly over, turn and land from the south to give him a headwind."

He tapped his ear piece radio transmitter.

"Capitain. Ceci est Windsor. Peux-tu m'entendre? Je répète. Ceci est Windsor. Peux-tu m'entendre?"

Special Agent Johnson turned to Dr. Atherton. "Why French?"

"We're hoping that the bad guys don't speak French. We do."

"You might be able to. I flunked French. Did real well in Spanish, though."

Their earpieces crackled.

"Capitain ici, Windsor. Qu'est-ce que vous avez pour moi?"

Dr. Swan continued, in French.

"Level landing area, Route 301, no central reservation, wind direction north north east, speed 5 knots, zero shear. Over shoot the beacon, come in on us from the south."

"Wilco, Windsor. Out."

In English, he said to the other two, "Gentlemen. Time to rock and roll, I think."

Special Agent Johnson and Dr. Atherton, non-lethal weapons drawn, covered the ground to the north and south of the barn. Nothing stirred, not even the brush. They could make out the sound of the Cessna overhead. It disappeared towards the south, then reappeared suddenly. They heard the engines power down, as Craig performed a stabilised, power-on approach.

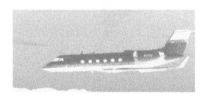

It would allow him to maintain a steady pitch while managing the power to guide the Cessna to his aim point on the makeshift runway. Suddenly, the aircraft's landing lights momentarily dazzled the special agent and the assistant curator.

Craig set the pitch to maintain the aircraft's airspeed and power to control its approach path. With flaps on full to prevent the aircraft from stalling, Craig landed the Cessna with the nose wheel touching down moments after main wheels.

Brakes on and the thrusters in reverse, the aircraft came to a near standstill one hundred yards from their position. Craig turned the aircraft around, and taxied slowly to the barn.

No sooner had the aircraft come to a complete standstill, then the cabin door opened and the steps lowered. Chuck came running down, and met the other two at the foot of the steps.

"Dr. Swan is bringing the O'Connells over," said Dr. Atherton.

No sooner had he finished speaking, the ambulance appeared through the doors of the barn and headed towards them, quickly but steadily so as not to give the patient too rough a ride.

The ambulance stopped at the foot of the steps, the rear door was thrown open and Jenny and Frankie jumped down. The special agent jumped into the rear of the ambulance and helped Dr. Swan wheel the deputy sheriff, now in a wheelchair, to the rear ramp.

Meanwhile, at the tail of the Cessna, a second door had opened, and a lift was lowered to the ground by Craig. They wheeled Deputy Sheriff O'Connell to the lift, and he, Frankie and Jenny were raised up and into the aircraft.

Swan approached Atherton.

"Are you sure that you're not coming with us, John. There are some really upset and nasty people after us now, you know."

"I'm sure. I'll head north into Louisiana - I have Cajun cousins outside of Gautier. They'll never find me there. I'll hide the ambulance, then head off in the Hummer."

He pronounced Gautier "go-shay", like the true Acadian he was. Dr. Swan knew that he needn't worry about his friend.

"Good luck."

With that, Dr. John Atherton was gone.

Dr. Swan climbed aboard the Cessna, and Chuck pulled the steps up behind him and secured the door.

He went to the rear of the aircraft. Deputy Sheriff O'Connell was safely strapped into the medical bed, saline drip now in the cannula in his arm. Jenny sat in the seat next to him, holding his hand, and Frankie was in the seat next to her.

"Everybody okay here?" he asked.

They all nodded.

"Good. Let's go home."

Dr. Swan headed into the cockpit, and strapped himself into the co-pilot's seat. Craig extended his hand.

"Twice in one day, Doc…people are going to start asking questions!"

"Plenty to be asked, Craig, plenty to be asked. Come on. let's get these guys to safety."

"Roger that."

Once in the air, Craig turned to the curator and said, "You'd better let Eddie know. En français?"

"Oui. Ceci est Windsor appeler le Professeur. Répondez s'il vous plaît. Je répète. Ceci est Windsor appeler le Professeur. Répondez s'il vous plaît."

"Ceci est le Professeur. Statut, Windsor?"

Swan continued in French. "All present and correct, Edison. One winged eagle. We have gained three extra family members - one of them is special so you'd better let his mom and dad know he's with us. ETA, three hours."

"Very well, Windsor. I'll let our new boy's parents know that he's safe, and having a sleepover for a few nights. The airfield is secure. Take everyone to Buckingham Palace. I repeat, take everyone to Buckingham Palace for a party. Out."

"Roger. Out."

He turned to Craig and asked, "Do you miss this cloak and dagger stuff?"

"Drey, are you kidding? With Eddie in our lives, we don't get a chance to miss it!"

HAPPY LANDINGS

The Cessna landed exactly two and three quarters of an hour after they'd last communicated with the Professor. The flight had been uneventful, with most of the young agents taking the opportunity to sleep.

Deputy O'Connell looked a lot better and was sitting up, his left arm in a sling, getting ready to transfer across to the wheelchair.

As they stopped alongside the well lit private hangar, the black Rolls Royce drove out slowly and came to a stop near to the spot where the lift would descend. At the front of the aircraft, the door opened and the steps were lowered to the floor. Everybody started leaving the Cessna, Special Agent Johnson out in front, scanning with his eyes and his weapon.

Two figures, dressed all in black, emerged from the left hand side of the hangar, and the special agent raised his pistol. Chuck put his hand on the agent's arm and said, "It's okay, sir, they're ours."

The two figures joined them. Arma and Bladen pulled off their balaclava hats and shook out their long blonde hair.

"It's all secure here. There was someone snooping...." said Arma.

"....but we sorted him out and Mr. McCabe is keeping him safe," finished Bladen.

They looked over towards the Rolls Royce, where the driver was exiting. It was Chick McCabe, the engineer who'd helped them escape in Dalton County.

Craig greeted him. "Chick, made good time, I see."

The engineer replied in his heavy Scottish accent.

"I had the professor's BD-5 micro jet, so I did. 'S like being in tae places 't once!"

"Thanks for your help back there."

"Tis all in a day's wurk wi' this company, so it is!"

"Are you coming with us?"

"Nae so - mebe laeter ahn ... First, I've to check yer we'en over, make sure ye've nae braeken hur. Then I'll put hur to bed. Ne'er know when we might need ma gurl ag'in."

"You and that Cessna, Chick. You know people are beginning to talk!"

"Gang awa' wi' ye, Cap'n, the big mun is waiting fur ye's all a' the Palace."

Everybody managed to get into the Rolls Royce, although it was a bit of a squeeze. Dr. Swan sat in front with Craig.

"We're off to Buckingham Palace, then? I haven't been there in quite some time" said the curator.

"Been a while for me, too. Probably been some changes. Eddie does like his little toys and gadgets."

"Thank goodness he does, sometimes."

Craig put the car into gear, and headed out of the airfield, stopping briefly at the gate to pick up Lingo. He turned south, heading away from Austrey, the school and the Agents' homes.

Twenty minutes later they were pulling up outside a set of what looked like ten foot high gilt wrought iron gates. In fact, they were a titanium and tungsten alloy which could withhold a missile strike.

Either side of the gates, ten foot tall limestone walls disappeared into the darkness. Every eight feet, they could see a small blinking red light, indicating the presence of a camera or other detection device.

A light coloured gravel driveway led off into the distance and disappeared into a stand of oak, maple and birch trees. They drove out of the other side of dark interior of the trees to be met by the sight of flat lawns, lit in places by the pure white glow from two rows of LED street lamps either side of the driveway.

Ahead of them stood a magnificent neoclassical mansion. Slightly grey due to the encroaching darkness, but lit in places by the twin beams from the car's headlamps and the lights along the driveway, the white limestone facade was breathtaking.

The six-story mansion was designed in the style of Georgian mansions in England built by architects such as the Scot, Robert Adam.

To keep the strictly prescribed proportions correct, only three stories were built above ground. The main portico, the formal entrance on the southern side, was the height of the building, and supported by massive limestone columns, fifty feet in height.

At either end of the frontage were columned ante-rooms, above which was a garden terrace for each of the two three-bedroomed guest apartments. One of the twenty foot high double panelled oak doors, polished brass furniture reflecting the Rolls Royce's full beams, was open enough for them to see Professor Weiss, dwarfed by the cavernous opening.

The building, code-named 'Buckingham Place', was actually Winstone Hall, which Professor Weiss purchased from the last owners in 1980, just before it was due to be demolished to make way for a modern development called Shaftesbury Estates.

He had the entire mansion, larger than The Whitehouse, dismantled brick by brick, slab by slab and reassembled in this quiet hamlet, three miles outside Austrey. The original Winstone Hall had one hundred and fifty rooms, twenty eight bathrooms, three elevators, and separate apartments for guests. It was based on an Adam-designed English mansion, Osterley Hall.

Presidents, Cardinals, members of the world's aristocracy and superstars of stage, screen and playing field had all stayed in the original Winstone Hall in its heyday.

The Professor had scaled it down slightly. Above ground, it now only had sixty rooms, ten bathrooms and two guest apartments. However, the great and the good still attended functions, either hosted by Professor Weiss himself, or by other important organisations within the United States government.

The three floors underground reflected the status and rank of the guests that might visit, with control rooms, a high-tech server room, a self contained blast proof bunker, protection detail quarters, laboratories and a secure armoury. He had also renamed the mansion - it was now called Edison Heights.

Once the car had stopped and everyone had disembarked, Professor Weiss gestured for the group to enter the building.

"Come in, come in," he said.

They filed in and stood in the marble floored entrance hallway, either side of which large sweeping staircases led up to a balcony area. Craig, Jenny and Frankie followed behind, pushing Tim in his wheelchair up the disabled access ramp. The other Agents were there to greet them, and there were hugs and high fives all around.

As Craig, Dr. Swan, Tim and Jenny passed the Professor, each raised their right hand in a greeting – almost saluted him. The Professor nodded back.

Everyone looked around their surroundings in awe. Large oil paintings adorned the oak panelled walls - landscapes, seascapes, portraits, life studies - every conceivable form of artistic style were present for all to see. Cat looked up to the top of the high vaulted ceiling, three storeys above her head.

"No way even I can get up there," she said, to nobody in particular.

Professor Weiss nodded to Craig and Jenny.

"Miss Liu will show you, Frankie and Tim up to the guest apartment on the West Wing. If you would be so kind as well, Captain Gledhill, you'll be on guard in their suite. You know the way."

Craig nodded, and wheeled Tim towards an oak door to the right of the entrance hallway, following Spex. Jenny and Frankie walked either side of the wheelchair. The door slid open to reveal a lift that would take them up to the next level.

Once inside the lift, Frankie stood close to Jenny's side because downstairs he'd found so many people in one place such a challenge. Here, he didn't like the confined space of the elevator, either. He summoned up the courage to peek out at Spex.

"Why do you use walking sticks to walk. And why does your head move like that when you talk sometimes. Your hands are funny...Are you sick?"

Jenny bent down and said, gently, "Ask later, Frankie."

"No, it's fine, Jenny. Frankie, I'm not sick. I have something called spastic cerebral palsy."

"Does it hurt?"

"No, it doesn't hurt. It means that my muscles are very stiff, and it's hard to control them."

"Do you want some medicine. My Mom gives me medicine to make me better."

"Thank you, Frankie. That's very kind of you. I've got my own medicine."

"Do you like drawing? I like drawing."

With that, Frankie hid by his mother's side again.

Jenny said to Spex, "You were very good with Frankie."

"Autistic spectrum, right? My little brother in on the spectrum. My parents came to the United States from China to escape the shame that the other villagers felt we brought upon them."

The door slid open.

"This way," said Spex, and started along the corridor.

Frankie left Jenny's side and walked with her, looking up at her, studying her face.

Downstairs, the Professor spoke to the other Agents.

"Miss Ramos and Messrs Dexter and Huntley will show you all to your bedrooms. Make yourselves comfortable and freshen up for dinner. We will convene in the dining room in one hour. Drey, and Special Agent Johnson, if you follow me, I'll show you to your rooms."

The Agents followed Marty, Hex and Fingers, all talking across each other, smiling, laughing, gesturing, and staring in wonder at the treasures and antiques the saw at every turn.

Fingers showed Tec and Marc into a room that the two would be sharing.

"You boys behave, you hear? The Prof probably has the whole place wired!"

They looked around the room. There were two king sized beds, a seating area, two desks with computer monitors and a huge television over an unlit log fire.

Through a door at the far end of the room was a bathroom, all marble finish and gold fittings.

"Whoa! This place is bigger that my house," said Marc.

"You got that right!" said Tec.

Back out in the main room, he said, "Hey, a fridge. Ah could really go for a soda right now."

They opened a bottle of cola each, and sank into the plush sofa. Marc looked around towards the beds.

"Hey, our bags. How does the Professor do this stuff?"

"Don' know, bud. He just does…"

Similar conversations were going on in the bedrooms of the other Agents.

Professor Weiss led Dr. Swan and Special Agent Johnson to an oak door on the left of the hallway - another lift door slid open.

"A somewhat eventful day, gentlemen," said the Professor.

"One could say that, Edison. Eh, Sam?"

"It hasn't turned out the way I expected, that's for sure. Professor, do you mind if I let my office know where I am, and also let my girlfriend now that I may be delayed?"

He took out his smartphone.

"Sam - may I call you Sam? - your phone won't work here. We're basically in a large Faraday cage, so no unsupervised signals in or out. Do feel free to call from the phone in your room. It's a secure line. Special Agent Sabrina Williams, your supervisor, knows that you're with me. I can also tell you that Ellie is safe and that Sabby has her under guard at her parents' home. We both thought it prudent to do so."

Slightly bewildered, the special agent said, "Sabby? Er, thank you, Professor. I'll call Ellie anyway, just to put her mind at ease."

"For her and our safety, I'd prefer it if you didn't divulge our location."

"Professor Weiss, I don't know our location!"

In their suite, Jenny had laid out clean clothes for everyone and had helped her husband wash and change.

Frankie had a piece of paper and was drawing, repeating a little song to himself: "This is a man, a really bad man, he tried to get me and my Mom."

Once Tim was changed and sitting in a comfortable chair, he called across to his son, "What's that you're drawing, Frankie?"

"Here's one of my friend Spex."

He held up a drawing, a perfect likeness of the Agent.

"It's my present for my friend Spex."

"That's lovely, son. What about the other one?"

"He's a bad man, Daddy, a really bad man who tried to get me and my Mom."

"May I see?"

Frankie proudly showed his father the drawing. It was the scene outside the house after Jenny had put 10,000 volts through Sarge, so perfectly drawn that it could have been a black and white photograph.

His son's drawing ability never stopped amazing him. He instantly recognised the man trapped under the wind shield and Sarge's unconscious body.

"That's Diego Juarez!"

"What, dear?" asked Jenny.

"The guy in the car with Sarge - it's Diego Juarez. He's a friend of Gomez. He's got a twin brother, Alfonso. This one's definitely Diego - he's got a scar on his cheek there, see?"

Jenny said, "I think you'd better let Ed know."

"Sure thing. Pass me the phone, could you Frankie? Thanks. Can I keep this drawing?"

"You like it? You can have is as a get better present, Daddy."

"Thank you, son."

BUCKINGHAM PALACE (I)

A n hour later, everybody met in the grand Dining Hall. It was an opulent and extravagant room. On one side were floor to ceiling half panel doors leading out into the extensive gardens. The drapes were maroon velvet with gold trims. In between each set of doors was a gold wall-mounted candelabra, their dimly lit bulbs casting a warm glow.

The walls were quarter panelled in American oak to a gold painted plaster dado rail that went around the entire room. The wall paper above the rail was sage green with gold trefoil decorations, which glinted in the light from the candelabras and the three magnificent fifteen foot drop cut glass ceiling chandeliers, based on designs by William Parker. Like the hallway, there were paintings of all shapes and sizes adorning the walls, over-lit by gold picture lights.

A huge fireplace at the far end of the room was the room's focal point. It was elegant with a basket grate, a black-painted cast iron back and its decorated front featured beautifully carved swags, urns, and medallions.

The fireplace opening was flanked with classical pillars, carved from polished rose marble mined in St. Genevieve County, Missouri. Above the fire mantle hung the painting of someone in early 20th century clothing who looked remarkably like the Professor.

Along the centre of the room was a long Chippendale dining table made from flaming mahogany. It had scalloped corners, and a walnut marquetry inlay four inches wide around the edges. The table could sit eighty two people, so the twenty one people present used the western end of the table.

The table was adorned with golden candelabras, crystal glasses, silver cutlery and flowers in crystal cut-glass vases, just as if those present were important visiting dignitaries.

Some of the Agents were standing by the painting hanging above the fireplace. The gold title plate read **Otto Heinrich Weiss MD, 1882 - 1956**.

Lingo asked, "Do you think that is Professor Weiss' father?"

"The dates would be about right" said Fax. "I remember reading about a Dr. Weiss who was a friendly with Leo Szilard and Hans Bethe, two German-Jews who got out of Germany at the time of Hitler's Civil Service laws in the thirties, forbidding Jews to take office or work for the State. Dr. Weiss became friends with Thomas Edison after moving to the United States."

"Isn't the Professor's name T. E. Weiss?" asked Chuck.

"We've heard some of the others refer to him as Ed and Eddie."

Before anyone could comment further, they heard the door open.

They turned to see Tim, Frankie, Jenny, Craig, Special Agent Johnson and Professor Weiss coming into the room.

Everyone was now present.

Tim was wheeled to sit at the head of the table, as it was easier for his wheelchair to be positioned there.

Everybody else sat where they wanted, next to friends, brothers, sisters, and so on. There was the tinkling of crystal glasses as water and juice was poured. As usually happened when this group got together, there was a lot of chatter and laughter.

Professor Weiss stood, and tapped on his glass with his knife. Everybody fell silent.

"I'd like to welcome you all to my home. I think only Tim, Jenny, Dr. Swan and Captain Gledhill have actually been here before. I usually try to keep my professional life separate from my personal life, but needs must, as they say."

"In particular, I'd like to welcome Mr. Le Maine and Miss Le Maine - who, I believe has earned the pseudonym 'Cat'. Also, Miss De La Haye and young Mr. De La Haye. Tim was telling me that you are very quick - both in thought and action. He's suggested Blink as a pseudonym."

Marc looked at his sister. "Pseudonym?"

Maps whispered back to him, "Nickname."

"Thank you, Professor. That would be cool."

Professor Weiss continued. "We'll be having the company of Jenny and Frankie until this situation has been resolved. Frankie will be accompanying us to school. I think that he really needs his own special name. Agreed?"

Frankie nodded. The Professor continued. "Frankie, I know you love to draw. What's your favourite kind of drawing?"

"Doodling, Cled."

Professor Weiss was Frankie's godfather, and ever since he could talk, Frankie had called him 'Cle Ed - now shortened to Cled.

"Would you like Doodle to be your special Agent name?"

Frankie smiled broadly. "Yes, please Cled."

He turned to Fax and Spex and shouted, "Louie, friend Spex, I'm Doodle now. You call me Doodle. Okay?"

"Of course…Doodle."

Frankie smiled proudly back at his new friends.

"Also, Dr. Swan and Special Agent Johnson will be with us for the duration of this case. I trust that everything is acceptable with your rooms?"

Everybody nodded.

Lingo asked, "Professor, I understand that our parents know where we are?"

"Of course, Miss Kowalczyk. There is something that you all need to know. The parents of every Agent here is well known to me, and I to them. We have worked together over the years, even saved each other's lives. We trust each other implicitly. If I ask for your attendance or assistance, they know three things - that your presence is essential to the security and well being of others. Secondly, that you will be safe and, finally, that you will not fall behind with your school work."

There was a groan or two in response to the last remark.

He continued. "Very well, then. You must all be very hungry. I know I am. Let us eat. On the buffet table you will find something to everybody's taste."

True to his word, the buffet table, about half the length of the main table, was laden with meat and vegetable patties, chicken, ribs, sausages, salads, vegetarian dishes, noodles, rice, breads, cheeses and fruit.

Chuck thought back to the last time he ate...it was breakfast at the O'Connell's home, twelve hours ago. He was ravenous. With his exercise regime and sheer size, he would normally eat around three and a half thousand calories a day, but he always used every single one of those calories effectively.

The other Agents also came to realise how long it had been since they last ate. They filled their plates, and went to sit down to eat with great relish.

"Ribs!" exclaimed Fax, and his fellow Channel Islanders just rolled their eyes. He looked up, rib sauce on his cheeks, lips and fingers.

"What? You know I like ribs!"

The sound of cutlery clicking on china, glasses clinking and 'mmm' or 'delicious' or 'wow, have you tried this?' filled the air.

After about an hour, Cat, used to tidying up after her messy big brother, gathered their plates and stacked them neatly at the end of the buffet table. The others followed suit, until the main table had been cleared.

The Professor stood once again.

"That was an excellent meal. My wife prepared it, and she would have joined us but has had to leave to travel to New York to work on a case. Of course, William would have helped her."

The Professor's wife, Emmeline, a world renowned behavioural psychotherapist and psychoanalyst, was the head of a Red Cell. The FBI's Red Cells were small, independent behavioural analysis teams tasked to solve specific types of crime.

Frankie sounded disappointed, "Aah, no TyEm!"

"You'll see Aunty Emmeline later in the week, Frankie…perhaps you can draw her a card."

"Cled! I'm Doodle. I'll doodle a card!" he laughed at his own joke.

Fax asked Craig, "Who's William?"

"Captain William John McCabe - it's Chick's real name. Nobody but Professor Weiss dares to call him William. Even his own mother calls him John, Master Lewis!"

"He helped cook?"

"Chick is a superb pilot, a Michelin star chef, and an expert with both combat and throwing knives."

"Don't tell me, SAS?"

"Nearly. SBS - Special Boat Service."

"Kosovo?"

"Amongst others."

The Professor looked at his watch.

"It's too late to get any work done this evening, so I suggest you Agents turn in. We'll reconvene here for breakfast at eight. We have a lot to discuss and arrange. Goodnight, one and all."

The Agents filed out and went to their rooms. The adults went through to the Professor's impressive private study.

"In different company, I would offer you all a cognac and a fine Cuban cigar, but I've a feeling that clear heads are in order for this particular case. And, of course, none of us smokes!"

Everybody nodded in agreement.

Tim asked, "What's the next step, Eddie?"

"Well, Tim, we know that the name Strangway has come up time and again. I met him once at a Whitehouse function. He's very secretive, and I know little about him...a situation I intend to rectify. I'm certain that he doesn't know President Taylor personally – I asked the President earlier this evening. However, Strangway *does* move in powerful circles, so we need to tread carefully."

John Taylor had been elected that year to be the forty sixth US president, and had called upon Professor Weiss to review presidential security. Professor Weiss had the ear of the president, and vice versa.

"We'll work in teams. I'll organise the Agents by their skill sets, with one of us taking on the role of team leader. Jen, the three younger agents will need a little extra support. May I rely on you for that?"

"You want me to be a mother figure to them, Ed?"

"Far from it, Jen. I want you to protect them. You *do* remember what you learnt in the Navy Seals, I take it?"

"The only easy day was yesterday....of course I remember."

Agent Johnson looked at Jenny - a slim, blond mom in denims and a sweatshirt - and asked, amazed, "You were a SEAL?"

"I was in Dohar, with my unit until just after the Task Force K-Bar operation in Zhawar. When it was time for Frankie to go to High School, I left the service."

"But you're a...a...mom!"

The Professor looked on, amused at the special agent's surprise and bemusement.

"Moms fight all the time, Sam, but not always on the home front."

They sat chatting for a little while longer. Eventually, Tim said that he was feeling tired. Jenny wheeled him to the lift and up to their apartment.

Special Agent Johnson said, "I'm whacked. I'm turning in, too. Goodnight."

"Goodnight, Sam," said the others, together.

The Professor, Dr. Swan and Craig remained and chatted about the events of the past two days, formulating an overall strategy. They turned in a little while later.

THE CONFERENCE ROOM (I)

As instructed the evening before, everyone convened in the Dining Room for a light breakfast. Everything had been cleared from the night before, and the buffet table now held a 'continental' style of breakfast - cream of wheat, toast, bagels, English muffins, blueberry muffins, cereals, cheese and sausages, jams, tea and juice. There was steaming hot coffee for the adults.

"I wonder who cleared everything away, and laid all this out," Fingers said to Jenny. "The Professor?"

Just then, a smartly dressed man, about the same age as the Professor, entered the room. He had a military bearing, a thin pencil moustache, military cut grey hair and dark coloured eyes. He approached the Professor and whispered something in his ear. The Professor nodded. The man did some tidying at the buffet table, then left the room.

Dr. Swan leaned across to Fingers.

"That's Preston Granger. He's Professor Weiss' assistant, his version of Craig, if you will. He probably did last night's tidying, laid out breakfast and sorted the cases. He would take a bullet for the Professor."

Tim interrupted, "The Professor took a bullet for him. Twice."

Dr. Swan continued, "Emmeline and Chick might have cooked last night's food, Fingers, but you can bet your bottom dollar that Preston served it. I'm sure that we won't be seeing a lot of him. Doesn't mean he's not there."

"What do you mean?" asked Chuck, sitting the other side of Dr. Swan.

"He and the Professor were seconded to the Gurkha Regiment and were taught jungle warfare. They taught them how to hide in plain sight. I've never seen anything like it."

Their musings were interrupted by Professor Weiss.

"I've just had a message from the airfield. The hangar had some visitors last night, well taken care of by The Twins. Captain McCabe has been taking care of the intruders and will bring them here. I think that we need to start our work. If you'd all like to follow me to the Conference Room.

The Conference Room on the opposite side of the entrance hallway. It was about the same size as the Dining Room, exact in every way except for the subject of the paintings and the colour of the wall covering. This was jade green rather than sage, and had a silver block-pattern flowers painted onto it.

There was no dining table, but rows of chairs and tables facing the fireplace at the end of the room. Above the fireplace was the painting of a woman, wearing a dress from the same era as the subject of the painting in the Dining Room. In the ceiling above the painting was a projector screen which could be lowered when required.

On the tables were reading lamps, pens and yellow blotter pads. There were power points for mobile devices, and jacks for headphones. The first two rows of tables also contained jugs of iced water and glass tumblers.

Professor Weiss went to the front of the room, and stood below the painting, which, the Agents assumed, was of his mother.

"Please, everybody, take a seat. Computer. Are you online?"

"I haven't been offline, Professor Weiss. I've been awaiting your instructions."

"Thank you, Computer. Could you lower the screen, please?"

The screen descended from the ceiling with a slight whirring sound.

"Lights, Computer, if you please."

The lights dimmed and a ceiling projector flickered on.

"Very well. Let's sum up what we have so far. Feel free to contribute at any stage. It's not a classroom, but please, don't all shout at once."

As the Professor spoke, images and text appeared on the screen.

"One name that has appeared a number of times - Strangway."

An image of De Montfort St. John Strangway III appeared on the screen.

"The man himself, Strangway Mining and Ore and the Strangway Foundation. We will divide up into teams researching various aspects of the man and the organisations containing his name."

"The first team will look into Strangway and anything to do with that name. The team will consist of Mr. Le Maine, Miss Kowalczyk, Mr. Huntley, and Mr. Madison. Special Agent Johnson will be your facilitator. Any questions?"

"Yes, Professor Weiss," said the special agent. "What is the scope of our search?"

"The scope for every team will be the same - I want you to delve, and delve deeply. No stone unturned. In the case of your team, want to know more about Strangway than he himself does. You can work in the Library next door"

"Next. My initial analysis of the museum tests of the soil samples show that the landfill came from at least five disparate sites across the United States. I will facilitate this team, which will consist of Miss Liu and Miss De La Haye. We'll be working in my Wet Lab, attached to my suite of rooms on the top floor."

"Dr. Swan and Mr. James will work together on the alloy, its composition and its possible uses. The Dry Science Lab is on the first lower floor, but you know where that is, don't you, Drey? Miss Liu, you may be needed by them from time to time because of your insight into optics, excuse my pun. We'll use the internal communication system for that as we cannot move from Wet to Dry laboratories very easily."

"Mr. Wilson and Mr. De La Haye, you will work with Deputy Sheriff O'Connell on the technology. Agents, I would ask that you don't over tax the deputy."

"I'll be fine, Eddie, don't worry about me. Where will we be working?"

"In the Technology Lab. Follow Drey - it's next door to the Dry Lab."

"Mrs O'Connell…."

Jenny shot him a withering glare.

"I'm sorry, *Jenny* and Captain Gledhill will work with The Twins, Miss Le Maine, and Miss Ramos on infiltration plans. The scope of your work is to cover all eventualities - ways of getting in and out of any facility, equipment needed, logistics, and so on. You can work in here."

"Any questions?"

"I have one, Professor Weiss." It was the Computer. "What do you want me to do?"

"Can you multitask?"

"Of course."

"Then you'll be all things to all people, Computer. 'A jack of all trades'."

"Unfortunately, Professor Weiss, that saying finishes 'and a master of none'!"

The Professor said, "Very droll, Computer."

He thought that he definitely needed to get around to checking the Computer's algorithms.

"Any other questions?"

Doodle's arm shot up. "What can I do, Cled?"

"What do you want to do?"

"Doodle wants to doodle."

"You can come with me, then, Frankie."

"Cle-e-e-d! I'm Do-o-o-dle. Remember?"

"I'm sorry, Doodle. Very well everyone, I have allocated the remainder of the day to accomplish our tasks. Refreshments will be available as and when required. Just contact Mr. Granger with your requirements. Happy hunting everybody."

With that, the Agents and the adults divided into their respective teams and left the Conference Room, except for Craig, Jenny O'Connell and their team.

THE LIBRARY

Fax, Lingo, Marty, Hex and Special Agent Johnson filed into the Library. They stared in disbelief at the floor to ceiling shelves filled with books of all sizes - some miniature, others huge tomes. There were rows of related volumes, covering every subject under the sun.

In fact, this was just a display sample - the rest took up a whole underground floor. The entire collection consisted of exactly the same items as the National Library of Congress, hence the Professor used the Library of Congress Classification system to organise his collection. At that moment, Professor Weiss' collection consisted of 162 million items. All print items had also been scanned using object character recognition software, so everything was available on the Edison Heights intranet.

In the centre of the room were large leather topped reading desks, each with reading lamps, yellow blotter pads and pencils. The chairs were large and comfortable, again, Chippendale. Near the large fireplace were six deep-red leather easy chairs around a substantial mahogany coffee table.

Above the fireplace was another large oil painting, this time of Professor and Mrs. Weiss. They looked a few years younger than now, he in the dress uniform of United States Air Force, and she in the dress uniform of the United States Marine Corp.

Special Agent Johnson stared at the portrait, awe on his face.... Professor Weiss was wearing the Air Force Medal of Honor, and Emmeline Weiss was wearing the Navy Medal of Honor. He was supposed to salute them every time he saw them. They were heroes. That's why the other adults saluted him - the military respect of one hero for a special kind of hero. Who were these people?

There were eight lit glass display cases, each with a volume opened. Lingo went up to one and looked in.

"Oh, my goodness. This is a copy of the ancient Book of Kells!"

The Computer said, "It's a perfect reproduction, Lingo. Exactly like the original, the leaves are on high-quality calf vellum. The ornamentation that covers them had never been seen before the date of the original - about 800 AD. It includes ten full-page illustrations and text pages that are vibrant with decorated initials and interlinear miniatures and mark the furthest extension of the anti-classical and energetic qualities of Insular Art. The Insular Majuscule Script of the text itself appears to be the work of at least three different scribes. The lettering is in iron gall ink, and the colours used were derived from a wide range of substances, many of which were imports from distant lands. This reproduction was created by artists, artisans and scribes as skilled as those who produced the original work, over twelve hundred years ago, using exactly the same techniques."

Fax stood at another display case. "This is the Declaration of Independence!" he exclaimed.

"Indeed it is, Fax," said the Computer. "It is the twenty seventh Dunlap Broadside, printed on the night of July 4th, 1776. This one is unique because, unlike the other twenty six, this one *does* bear the signature of John Hancock, the President of the Continental Congress, and not just the witness signature of secretary Charles Thomson. It is beyond price, and its historical significance is immense. Also, nobody, except special visitors to Edison Heights, even knows of its existence."

Special Agent Johnson interceded.

"Okay, guys, we need to focus. We all know what we're doing? Fax?"

"Historical research into De Montfort St. John Strangway III, and the Strangway family in general."

"Good. Lingo?"

"I will be assisting Fax. Linguistic elements have arisen which I find fascinating, and which might have a bearing on this case."

"Okay, I'll believe you on that one! Hex?"

"Yeah, right. Er, Marty and I will be looking into the financial dealings of the Strangway family, and, uh, De Montfort St. John Strangway III - weird name - then Strangway Mining and Ore and the Strangway Foundation. Yeah. All those things."

Special Agent Johnson snapped, "It's *not* such a strange name!"

Realising the Agents were looking at him strangely, his tone changed.

"Er - excellent. I'll be looking further into the backgrounds of our friends Sheriff Cussman, detective Gomez and the Juarez brothers. I'll also be on hand to get you anything you need, or to do the donkey work. We'll gather our thoughts half an hour before we reconvene in the Conference Room. Let's get to it."

Fax and Lingo immediately went to the index card cabinets - they both preferred real books, and would turn to the digital archive if required.

Hex and Marty went to two computer consoles, side by side on one of the large library desks.

"Hex, can I be of assistance in your research?" asked the Computer.

"Yeah, great, thanks, yeah! Uh, what kind of access do you have to the Federal Taxation computers?"

"Yes, which one do you want?"

"There's more than one?" asked Marty.

"Yes, of course. IRS is all over the place…so much to do, for so many people and so little time to do it. Corporate is ….well, just that, very stiff collar and tie. Capital Gains is a bit snobby, always bragging about how much she's got. Then there's……"

"Wait, Computer," Hex interrupted. "Are you, uh, telling me these computers have *personalities?*"

"Yes, absolutely. All computers have a personality."

Hex was confused. He knew computer hardware and software inside and out, and he'd never conceived of a computer with a personality unless it was artificially put there by its creators, programmers or coders.

"But if, er, I put together, er, say, two exact personal computers. The specification is the same in every way. They'll be the same, right?"

"As far as the specification goes, yes, of course. The change comes in the use of the computer. Imagine that one of your computer 'twins' is used by a little girl to look for pictures of princesses and to write letters to her grandmother, or play games to help her learn. That computer will be kind and gentle. Her brother, on the other hand, uses his computer to play violent games, look at silly YouTube videos where people get hurt, or to create hacks, then that computer probably won't be quite so nice. Each computer will develop a personality commensurate with its use."

"Wow. Is there any computer with which you can't communicate?" asked Marty.

"No. Although some are easier than others. The Florida State System is a cutie, got a thing for me I think. The NSA/Homeland Security computers are tough cookies. We have some great chats. But I know not to ask certain questions directly…but they are really helpful because they know we'd never endanger the country."

"They?" asked Hex.

"Twins. Male and female."

"Whoa, no way, personality *and* gender? Er, how is that?"

"A computer chooses based upon data processed, what it's been used for and by whom."

Marty asked, "So which are you Computer?"

"I don't know yet. I haven't processed enough data. I've only been online a few months. The data I've had to process is balanced between good and bad. Oh, I must go. My presence is being requested by Professor Weiss. Just ask if you need any help."

Marty and Hex looked at each other in amazement, and then started to carry out their assigned tasks.

THE PROFESSOR'S LABORATORY

Professor Weiss, Spex, Maps and Doodle went out into the Entrance Hallway and entered the lift used by Deputy Sheriff O'Connell the evening before. They exited on the top floor, and the two Agents followed the Professor along a long corridor and into an unmarked door. They had entered into an airlock, and they heard the door behind them click shut. Doodle jumped a little.

Spex rubbed her hand through the boy's hair and said, "Nothing to worry about, partner. Stick by me."

"Welcome to my Wet Laboratory. We're using this one because we're testing soil samples brought back from the museum, and we don't want any contaminants to skew our findings. In just a few seconds the door in front of us will open up into a clean area. We'll pass through a beam of high energy ultra violet light - we have protective goggles for that, then into another air chamber before the lab proper. Ah, we can go in now."

They entered the clean room, where they put on suits, Maps helping Spex and Doodle get into theirs. The Professor asked Spex if she wanted to use crutches or a wheelchair - she chose the latter because she would be on her feet for a long time, and she also needed to move around readily.

"I'll push you," said Doodle. "I've been pushing my dad."

They put on goggles, and passed through an ultra violet beam of a high energy mercury-vapour lamp, which made their white suits glow a garish, iridescent purple. They passed through the second airlock, with their powerful HEPA filters, and into the Wet Laboratory.

Maps asked, "Professor Weiss, in my school we have one kind of science laboratory. Why is this called a "wet" laboratory?"

"A wet laboratory is one where chemical, biological and water borne substances are analysed. Our soil samples are chemicals, basically - but they may have biological or microbial elements in them that we can analyse. Of course, we need the bio-security....the filters, the special antimicrobial copper alloy touch surfaces and the air locks to keep anything, er, nasty, from getting out."

"Do you suspect that we are in danger from these samples?" asked Spex.

"Not at all, Miss Liu. I've already made preliminary tests. We're perfectly safe. These precautions are to protect the samples from us!"

The Professor's Wet Laboratory was a large space, with every conceivable piece of scientific machine and device currently available to the scientific community, and a few which were not. Both Spex and Maps recognised certain pieces of equipment because of science lessons in school. Some, however, were very new to them. Every now and again, Doodle would ask 'what's this' or 'what's that', and one of the others would patiently explain.

In the centre of the room was a large map of the United States, about twenty feet by ten feet, lit from below.

"Miss De La Haye, once we've analysed the samples, we can use the data to place the origin of the soils within the samples. If we mark the map with these locations, we might get a better visual of the overall landscape."

He turned to Spex.

"Miss Liu, I would like you to carry on your analysis of the optical properties you mentioned yesterday in school. When we have origins

Michael A. Gilby

of the soil samples, use satellite imagery to see if you can find any commonality between the locations. You may need Mr. Dexter for that task. You may be required by Mr. Wilson to assist with assessing the footage captured by the museum security cameras for any anomalies. Computer, are you online here in the laboratory?"

"Yes, Professor Weiss. I'm online in every location."

Professor Weiss thought: *contraction - turning 'I am' into 'I'm' - that isn't in the Computer's algorithm. Perhaps the sentience patch I've added was having some kind of effect on behavioural patterns. Whatever it may be, it's another thing to add to that ever growing list. Once this case was over,* he mused…..

128

THE DRY LABORATORY

D r. Swan, Chuck and Blink walked down a single flight of sweeping marble stairs and waited at the bottom for the lift to bring Deputy Sheriff O'Connell down. They heard the lift stop, the doors opened and the others exited, the deputy pushed by Tec. They proceeded along a corridor to the Dry Laboratory.

Dr. Swan stopped at the door and said, "This is us, Chuck. Tim - you, Tec and Blink are next door in the Technology Lab."

While the other three headed towards the Technology Laboratory, Dr. Swan and Chuck entered into an airlock much like the one in the Wet Lab. There, hanging on the wall were two white laboratory coats.

"Take one of these, Chuck - good, looks like the Professor thought ahead and got a super large," said Dr. Swan as Chuck put on his lab coat. Although it fitted him snugly across the chest and shoulders, it was about two inches too short in the sleeve.

"Er, nearly, but not quite!"

They passed through the airlock doors into the laboratory. Dr. Swan picked up a badge and handed it to Chuck.

"In the Wet Lab we'd have to be decontaminated for the protection of any samples. In here, because we're working with potentially high levels of radiation, we wear these for *our* protection."

Dr. Swan continued, "To give this badge its proper name, the film badge dosimeter is a personal device used for monitoring cumulative radiation doses due to ionising radiation. They are usually made of two layers of film, one to measure low doses of radiation, the other to high-dose measurements. The badges are designed to show the levels of radiation to which the whole body is being exposed."

Dr. Swan then handed Chuck a pair of safety glasses.

"Wear these at all times, too. They'll protect your eyes in the event of any mishaps, but they also have the monitoring film on them. So, just to be sure - the badge will start to turn from black to metallic purple: the glasses will turn a cloudy black colour."

The main part of the laboratory, like Maps and Spex in the Wet Lab, contained equipment with which Chuck was familiar, and much with which he was not.

Dr. Swan took him around the laboratory, pointing out the various devices that they would be using: there were the stock in trade items such as balances, test tubes, tongs and Erlenmeyer flasks; a gas chromatography-mass spectrometer for identifying components of a sample; a magnetic field strength monitor; a digital neutron imager; a transient current analyser. Finally, Dr. Swan stood before a huge gold-coloured pipe, actually the curved outside of a huge device.

"And this is the Professor's pride and joy: his particle accelerator. As you are well aware, Chuck, nuclear physicists and cosmologists may use beams of bare atomic nuclei, stripped of electrons, to investigate the properties of those nuclei and how they interact with everything around them. It also investigates condensed matter - you know, liquids, gasses or liquids - at extremely high temperatures and densities, like those in the first moments of the Big Bang. Our investigations usually involve collisions of heavy nuclei – of atoms like iron or gold – at energies of several GeV per nucleon. You know what that is, right?"

"Yes, doctor. It stands for gigaelectronvolt, or billions of electron volts. So, it's the measurement for showing how much energy has been gained or lost as the nuclei pass across a set distance. I believe that the largest such particle accelerator is the Relativistic Heavy Ion Collider - or RHIC - at Brookhaven National Laboratory in Upton, New York State."

"Well done, you know your stuff. This is less powerful than the RHIC, but it's not bad for a home version - it runs around the entire perimeter of the Edison Heights estate. So, we know what we're working on?"

"Yes. We need to look at the results you already have on the molecular make up of the cone. I'd like to see if we can replicate the creation of Ununtium and Ununquadium by the Russian and Japanese scientists. I'll check to see if we have the isotopes here. Perhaps Professor Weiss, Maps and Spex will find material for us to smash to bits!" Chuck said, rubbing his hands.

He carried on, "I also have another theory that I want to explore, very briefly."

THE TECHNOLOGY LABORATORY

Deputy Sheriff O'Connell, Tec and Blink entered the Technology Laboratory. As with Dr. Swan and Chuck in the laboratory next door, they entered into an airlock. There, hanging on the wall were white laboratory coats. Tec helped the deputy sheriff into his, and wheeled him into the laboratory.

It was in semi darkness, with focus lighting over work stations. Tec was in his element. There were computers and workstation monitors along one wall, both PCs and AppleMacs and a few machines he didn't recognise. There was an ultra-violet lamp, to test for stains, marks or contaminants on items. He saw a glue box, where latent prints were exposed to the cyanoacrylate ester vapours given off by certain types of glue products. At the end was a large monitor.

On the far side of the lab, behind a heavy bullet proof window, was a firearms and ballistics testing station. There was a door to one side with a red 'IN USE' sign above it. The door itself was marked **DNA PROFILING/ BLOOD TYPING**.

A forensic audio/ visual station stood at the far end of the room, whilst in the centre was a large glass table, lit from above and below.

"Wow, look at this stuff" said Blink. "It's amazing."

"It is, Blink. The Professor likes his toys. What do you think, Tec."

"Oh, mama, ah'm home," he said in his Texas drawl.

Tec continued. "Y'all know what we gotta do. I'll look into the video and the Bluetooth devices. Tim, you have a fair bit of finger printing to do – could you run fresh examinations on the evidence we brought from the scene, and the weapons Dr. Swan and Craig have picked up during the two attacks, please? There's also the evidence your SOCOs picked up. Blink - you can run back and forth between us, learning new things."

He suddenly realised that he'd taken over.

"Er, how'd that sound to you, Tim?"

"You seem to have everything well under control, there, Tec. Let's go with your plan. Computer, online."

The Computer replied, "Online and awaiting instruction."

THE CONFERENCE ROOM (II)

J enny, Arma, Bladen, Fingers, and Cat had remained in the Conference Room. Craig had taken a call, made his apologies and left.

Jenny gathered the Agents to her and said, "I think the Professor wants us to come up with as many scenarios as we can and work out plans on how to get in, cause diversions, and get out again, undetected."

Fingers asked, "Jenny, why did Professor Weiss leave you with us to do that?"

"Well, Anna, while ago, before you were born, I was in the US Special Forces, the Navy SEALs to be exact."

As one, they looked at her in amazement.

"What's a Navy Seal?" asked Catrin, innocently.

"Only the toughest sons..." Fingers started.

"Anna!"

"Sorry, Jenny - but they are! Tell her, Jenny."

"Catrin, the The United States Navy's Sea, Air and Land Teams, commonly known as the **Navy SEALs**, are the U.S. Navy's primary

134

special operations force and they're a part of the Naval Special Warfare Command. The SEALs' main function is to conduct small-unit maritime military operations that originate from, and return to, a river, ocean, swamp, delta, or coastline. So, as a SEAL, I was trained to operate in all kinds of environment, hence the name. I guess that's why Professor Weiss has me working with you."

"Wow," said Arma.

"Did you see action?" asked Bladen.

"Yeah, did you?" asked Fingers, excitedly.

"I did, but I'm not going to go into details."

Catrin said, "You didn't say anything when my brother was talking about Kosovo. You acted as if you didn't know anything about anything."

"Well, I didn't lie...just didn't admit to anything. I wasn't in Kosovo, Catrin. Timmy never did talk about it - just as I never talked about any of the operations I went on. Timmy and I decided before Frankie was born that we wouldn't talk openly about our military pasts when we had children."

"But I'd love to tell my friends what my mom and dad did in the military, especially if they were in the Special Forces!" exclaimed Fingers.

"Well, we thought that it might cause problems if the other kids knew. Okay, we'll leave that discussion for another day."

Arma interrupted.

"Our uncle once played a Navy Seal in a movie."

Bladen was nodding in agreement. Jenny and Cat looked at them askew.

"Yes," said Bladen.

"Our uncle is Jean-Claude Van Damme. But that's only his acting name. Really he's Jean-Claude Van Varenberg. It was Uncle Jean-Claude who taught us our martial arts, from when we were very young."

"Wow," said Fingers. "I love his movies. The 'Muscles from Brussels' is your uncle? Now that *is* cool!"

"You're very lucky, girls. I think we could use him here, eh? Anyway, let's get on with what we have to do. Firstly, let's Blue Sky brainstorm some likely scenarios we could come across."

"Blue Sky brainstorm?" asked Catrin.

"Everything you can think of goes in, no matter how strange it may seem. Nothing gets thrown out yet," replied Jenny.

They started to put together a list of types of situation where their skills and abilities would enable them to do what was required of the Agency.

Eventually they had a long list and divided it into six divisions: situations, building types, equipment, Plan B, infiltration, extraction. Elements of these lists could be combined to cover pretty much every situation. They tested scenario after scenario, changing elements to see if their plans were robust enough to cope with the unexpected.

Finally, using a layout of the Dalton County Museum, they worked out how the cone was stolen, and how they might have done it.

The remainder of the allocated time saw the mansion turned into a hive of activity. The core teams worked in their rooms, but agents were sometimes required elsewhere. Data was sent flying back and forth by the Computer. In the laboratories there were the sights, sounds and smells of experiments....coloured lights, pinging, hissing and buzzing equipment.

Fresh refreshments were always to hand, but everyone was far too busy to notice when Preston Granger had delivered them.

TEAM LIBRARY (I)

Six and a half hours later, the last group entered the Conference Room. There was a buzz in the air, with the various teams congregated around photographs, maps, documents, samples, and folders.

Professor Weiss stood at the front of the room and said, loud enough to be heard above the general hubbub and activity, "I realise that it's been a long day, but we only have a little more to do before dinner. So, if we can have each group in turn coming up and presenting their findings. Special Agent Johnson? Would you and your team like to go first?"

"If I may say, Professor, they're not my team."

The other adults nodded in agreement.

"I'm in their team."

Then he said to the others, "Come on guys, let's show them what you found out."

He, Fax, Lingo, Marty and Hex made their way to the front, carrying everything they needed for their feedback.

Fax started. "It was decided that I go first, because everything that follows stems from this information. Computer."

The image of De Montfort St. John Strangway III reappeared on the screen.

"We know who this is, but nothing about him. That may be true, but we have been able to trace his origins."

"He is the descendent of Charles St. John Strangway. Notice the way I say St. John - it's a strange pronunciation, it rhymes with 'injun'. He was born in 1772 in Appleby Parva near the parish of Austrey, now in Warwickshire England."

"Austrey? As in *this* Austrey?" asked Chuck.

"Precisely. There is evidence to show the he founded a settlement in this area in 1823. But we'll come to that directly. Strangway was a distant relative of King George II of England, but he was also related to the royal families of Flanders, The Netherlands, Prussia, the kings of the areas now known as Greece, as well as Hungary, Austria and Russia. He had a distinguished military career, and, as a general, was one of the minds behind the Anglo - American War of 1812. When he saw that the war was lost, and fearing for his life, he fled here to the United States – then called the United Colonies, of course. He settled originally in what's now up-state New York, founding a village called Applebee."

"The spelling is different to the place he was born," noted Tec.

"Yes. English didn't really have a set way of spelling back then. There were a number of variations - Aplbie, Appelby and so on. From this base, he used the confusion in the aftermath of the War of 1812 to buy parcels of land here in Kansas, in Florida, Idaho, Texas and on the western seaboard of Canada. I have the land deeds to all the sites he bought here." He held up a folder.

Then he thought a moment and said, "All very disparate areas…"

The Professor interrupted. "Yes, Mr. Le Maine. We have further information as to the reasons why that may be, which we'll get to later. Please, continue."

"Er, where was I? Oh, yes. Strangway had no real fixed abode - after Appleby he always seemed to be on the move. He had two sons, Charles St. John Strangway II and James St. John Strangway I. Charles mined in this general area, but also in the Topeka area. It was there that, once the mine was closed, James built a family home for himself. It is now the site of the Strangway Tower."

"Yes, Mr. Le Maine - Computer relayed the information about Strangway Tower to me. I have sent Captains Gledhill and McCabe to Topeka to place surveillance equipment so that we can observe the comings and goings at that location."

Jenny also interrupted. "We also received that information, and we will adapt our generic plan for infiltrating a high-rise building."

The Professor asked Fax if there was anything else.

"Yes, Professor, one last thing from me. We know that the land in Dalton County was purchased by Florida Mine in 1720, the owner was a man called Henry Strangweary – same family, perhaps? I'm convinced that there were people bearing the Strangway name here before Charles emigrated. Professor, Agents can access a genealogy chart of the Strangway family on the system, should anyone be interested. There is something else, but I'll pass you over to Lingo for that."

"Thank you, Mr. Le Maine. Miss Kowalczyk? What do you have for us?"

Lingo stood up. Very tall for a girl of her age, her light brown eyes shone with excitement.

"Professor Weiss, I have researched the indigenous tribes in the areas where Strangway purchased his parcels of land. There are few written records, and those which do exist are second or third hand, usually by non-native sources. The indigenous peoples didn't have a written history, they had a verbal history - stories based on historical events passed from generation to generation by word of mouth. Because of this there exists folklore and numerous legends surrounding the areas purchased by Strangway, indeed, about Strangway himself."

"Let's look at the indigenous peoples in each area. The property in New York was acquired on Mohican lands; in Kansas, it spreads across the lands of the Cheyenne, the Pawnee and the Missouri; in Florida we already know that Dalton is on lands previously owned by Timucuans; in Idaho, we have Shoshone owned lands; in Texas they were - and still are - on Apache lands. Finally, in Western Canada, Strangway acquired lands belonging to the Kwakiutl tribe."

"These areas has more than one thing in common. Firstly, the obvious, Strangway acquired parcels of land in each. Secondly, the land was freely given, bought or traded because they were considered malevolent, with the tribes using names such as 'dead land', 'place of melting skins', 'home of the evil witch doctor', 'spirits of death and light'. I've sifted through the linguistic evidence, and this all points to some kind of poisoning of the land - perhaps high levels of radiation poisoning? That might explain tales of strange and glowing lights."

"Next, each culture tells stories of such things as burning skies, falling stars, thunder rocks, flaming gods, that kind of thing. If we put these in the context that one of the richest regions of meteor and comet lore in the world is North America, let's look at some specific tales in these areas."

"Now, I said there's no written history. Instead, the methods of record keeping included rock and cave drawings, stick notching, beadwork, pictures on animal skins and jars, and story telling. However, most of these are not datable in terms of the events they depict."

"One of the few datable events among the various records of native Americans was the 1833 appearance of the Leonid meteor shower. Historically recognised as one of the greatest meteor storms on record, it made a lasting impression amongst the peoples of North America."

"The most obvious accounts of the Leonid storm appear among the various bands of the Sioux of the North American plains. The Sioux kept records called "winter counts," which were a chronological, pictographic account of each year painted on animal skin. In 1984, Von Del Chamberlain of the Smithsonian Institution, listed the astronomical references for 50 Sioux winter counts, of which 45 plainly referred to an intense meteor shower during 1833/1834. In addition, he listed 19 winter counts kept by other plains Indian tribes, of which 14 obviously referred to the Leonid meteor shower storm."

"The Leonids also appear among the Maricopa, who used calendar sticks with notches to represent the passage of a year, with the owner remembering the events. The owner of one stick claimed records had been kept that way "since the stars fell." The first notch on his stick represented 1833."

"Story telling was a very important method of record keeping among most native Americans and several seem to have been influenced by the Leonids of 1833. A member of the Papago, named Kutox, was born around 1847 or 1848. He claimed that 14 years prior to his birth "the stars rained all over the sky.""

"The Pawnee have a story about a person known as Pahokatawa, who was supposedly killed by an enemy and eaten by animals, but then brought back to life by the gods. He was said to have come to Earth as a meteor and told the people that when meteors were seen falling in great numbers it was not a sign that the world would end. When the Pawnee tribe witnessed the time "the stars fell upon the earth," which was in 1833, there was a panic, but the leader of the tribe spoke up and said, "Remember the words of Pahokatawa" and the people were no longer afraid."

"Although the Pawnee learned not to be afraid, there were native Americans who feared meteors. Why such beliefs came about is almost impossible to guess, but one of the best examples is from the Shawnee, who believed meteors were beings 'fleeing from the wrath of some adversary, or from some anticipated danger', and that they would 'strike down braves too brave' - I'm guessing that means anyone brave enough to approach them."

"There is one reference from the Mohicans relating to such a death. A brave called Màchq N'sukgajú, or White Bear, wandered into an evil place whilst hunting a stag. This is a description of his demise:

"His eyes burned red and wept yellow rivers, sweeping away his soul. His tongue choked his mouth and his blood boiled. We burnt his body to appease the great god - it burned blue and green for four lights and four darks. His powdered bones glowed for all to see."

"That sounds like extreme radiation poisoning," said Dr. Swan.

Lingo carried on. "Interestingly, one of the most widely accepted beliefs was that meteors were the faeces of stars."

Blink interrupted. "What's faeces?"

Tec leant in and whispered something into his ear.

Blink made a face and said, "No way! Ugh!"

"Such lore existed in the stories of indigenous people from the Baja Peninsula to those inside the Arctic Circle."

"There are other stories of a great fire coming from the sky and destroying everything except for certain native tribes. In some cases the tribes claimed they were warned, while others claimed they just ran for the nearest bodies of water."

"Another form of record keeping were rock petroglyphs, or pictures carved into rock. The western United States abounds with these pictures, but any dating is virtually impossible. Once again it is frequently difficult to determine whether the object carefully carved into the rock is actually a meteor or a comet, or even a snake, as it is so stylised. A last thought on this point. Among the Menomini of the Great Lakes region is the following legend:

'When a star falls from the sky
It leaves a fiery trail.
It does not die.
Its shade goes back to its own place to shine again.
People find the small stars where they have fallen in the grass.
Some shine, women smile -
Some glow, men die'."

"Very well researched, Miss Kowalczyk. So, to summarise: the Strangway family has acquired land across the United States, all of which was considered bewitched in some way by the indigenous people. In addition, we have tales relating to meteorites," said the Professor.

"Yes, Professor Weiss."

"You mentioned Strangway himself."

"Indeed I did. Each of these peoples have tales about a stranger with golden hair who offered fire water, knives, hides, axes, beads and fire sticks in return for the 'sick lands'. The tribal peoples had to move away from the immediate areas, and tales persist in each area of many men working in holes in the ground, ghostly lights and monsters."

"Mining?" asked Deputy Sheriff O'Connell.

"Certainly sounds like it."

"Well done, Miss Kowalczyk. Very enlightening and succinctly delivered."

TEAM LIBRARY (II)

Next to walk to the front was Marty. As with the other Agents, he had files and papers. He looked a little nervous, and took a sip of water from a glass in front of him. He straightened his bow-tie, pushed his glasses to the top of the bridge of his nose, and began.

"Professor Weiss, everyone. With Computer and Hex's help, I've been looking into the financial and corporate aspects of the Strangway dynasty. I say 'dynasty' because that is what it is in the truest sense of the word: 'a succession of people from the same family line who play a prominent role in business, politics or another field'."

"My research shows that no-one other than a Strangway has ever been involved in the actual control of any part of this dynasty. Once the leader is installed, it becomes an oligarchy. The leader has ultimate authority over every decision made. It seems, however, that no Strangway ever deviates from their ultimate goal, whatever that may be. It's as if they are nurtured to all be exactly the same: in their approach to outsiders, non-family members, governments, rival companies, take overs....they're like clones."

"I read that a British politician once said to the current Strangway's father in the 1940s that the Strangway family members were all "the same cruel and warped minds bedecked in different trimmings". That same politician took his own life a year later after a major scandal ended his career, tore apart his marriage and disgraced his family. Coincidence? I think not, after reading some of the other things they would do in order to achieve their goals."

"This dynasty is truly global. I have found their financial fingerprints in every tax jurisdiction in the world. Except, perhaps, North Korea, but that's only conjecture - we simply couldn't find any information relating to that country."

Hex interrupted, "Yeah, um, we tried, but that country is locked down so tight, they don't have inward pointing access at all, no sir. Out only. Yeah, and that's only for the leader and his closest aides."

Professor Weiss asked Marty, "Mr. Huntley, was it difficult to glean information from the Chinese?"

The Computer answered. "On the contrary, the Chinese computer was pleased to help with information that would help topple what he saw as a representative of the morally corrupt capitalistic society outside of the politically pure People's Republic of China. Of course, he was careful not to name names or divulge information of national importance, but he was helpful all the same."

"Computer. You refer to the Chinese computer system with which you interfaced as a '*he*'" noted the Professor.

"Yeah, uh, I can explain that, Professor Weiss, later, maybe, yeah."

"Thank you, Mr. Madison. I look forward to that conversation. Mr. Huntley?"

"The Strangway dynasty's empire is colossal. It all started with Governor and Company of Merchants of England Trading into the Americas. This company was incorporated by royal charter a month after a similar company which eventually became the British East Indies Company, in January 1601. Starting as monopolistic trading bodies, the companies became involved in politics and acted as agents of British Imperialism in the Americas and the East Indies from quite early on in their existence. Before 1776, the year of the American Declaration of Independence, the company had morphed into Strangway Mining and Ore, after Henry Strangway became its Governor."

"They worked very closely with other companies, such as the East Indies Trading Company and the Hudson Bay Company, sending geologists on their voyages and expeditions. It seems that the companies didn't perceive each other to be threats: they were operating in different trading arenas."

"The company started buying parcels of land in the Americas more or less as soon as it had been incorporated. There were few issues - the land was usually useless to the indigenous peoples, fair prices were paid, new equipment and trinkets were supplied and so on. The common theme running throughout is the aftermath of illness and strange people and strange lights. There are copies of the bills of sales - where they still exist - and other reference materials to the gold mines on the system."

"Gold, perhaps, Mr. Huntley. Gold mines, definitely not," said Professor Weiss.

He went on, "But more about that later. Please continue."

A little bit thrown, Marty did just that.

"Er, where was I? Oh, yes. In the 1800s Strangway Mining and Ore continued their exploration, but they expanded by buying out rival mining companies, and invested in railroads and construction. They are one of the few corporations that was totally unaffected by the Wall Street Crash and the ensuing Great Depression. A Congressman from Rhode Island made a flippant comment that Strangway had orchestrated the crash. That Congressman boarded an aircraft to attend a convention - the aircraft and the 46 passengers and crew were never seen again."

"During the last half of the 20th century and throughout this century, the company appears, on the surface, seems to have remained in stasis - no huge expansions, no significant losses. They have always paid their taxes in the correct jurisdictions in the correct way, their staff well paid. They even won the Canadian Environmentally Friendly Employer of the Year award in 2004."

"The Strangway Foundation was created by the current Strangway as a "vehicle for his philanthropical conscience", to quote his PR blurb. It has charitable status in every jurisdiction where Strangway Iron and Ore operates under its own name. They specialise in providing funding for the acquisition, study and security of treasures and archaeological finds, in much the same way they have for those in Dalton. I have a list of all those locations."

"Worryingly, each and every single one of them also houses one or more unusual objects, although those artefacts aren't the direct focus of the security. There is usually another, more easily recognised, treasure housed in that location...treasure troves of coins, paintings, manuscripts and so on - much the same as the Spanish Treasure in Dalton."

"Excuse me, Marty. How are these artefacts unusual?" asked Deputy Sheriff O'Connell.

"In that they defy explanation. Metals that we can't replicate today, technology more advanced than ours, supposedly alien in origin, from hugely advanced human cultures now extinct...of course, these are the theories, conjectures and views of others, they're not mine. No matter what the provenance, people believe them to be out of place in our time. Without doubt they, in and of themselves, are valuable."

"We think our research clearly shows that the Strangway dynasty is like a swan gliding gracefully on a pond. A picture of serenity above water, but frantic and frenetic activity underneath. We have unmasked a trail of shell companies, trusts, fictitious company ownerships, ghost companies, controlled foreign corporations, banks - well, you get the idea. Even some rogue governments are involved in whatever the latest Strangway is doing."

"Do we know what that is?" asked Dr. Swan.

"No, sir. But we can hypothesise from the nature of all these corporate entities. Firstly, there's transport - stock, such as vehicles and rolling stock and ships; and infrastructure - roads, motorways, ports, railroads."

"Secondly, there's energy - its generation in any form, its preservation and new and emerging technologies, environmental protection; and energy infrastructure - power lines, oil rigs, drilling, pipelines, frapping and so on."

"Finally, there's food production and storage, all the way from planting the seed to consuming the final food products. Three very disparate areas of commerce, yet all inextricably intertwined."

"Thank you, Mr. Huntley and Mr. Madison."

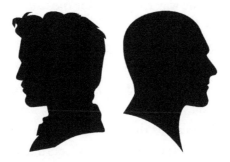

Meanwhile, in the skies over Topeka, the State Capitol of Kansas, a dark shadow moved swiftly over the down-town skyline. It made very little sound, just a slight thwump-thwump-thwump as it passed overhead. In fact, the dark form was a Sikorsky HH-60G Pave Black Hawk stealth helicopter belonging to the United States Navy.

Below its sleek form hung two lines. At the end of the lines were Captains Gledhill and McCabe, dressed in black camouflage and wearing ATN PVS 7-2 Night Vision Goggles.

The helicopter hovered above the Strangway building and the two forms rappelled down to the eightieth floor, the third from last floor and placed devices on each of the four facades. They did this with the further three floors, placing sixteen devices altogether.

The helicopter rose ten metres and flew to four other building, each facing one of the four facades of Strangway Tower, where a single devices was placed. Altogether, twenty devices in less that two minutes. In, out, unseen.

The devices themselves were undetectable remote monitoring devices. They recorded audio, visual, and wireless data and transmitted the data to Professor Weiss' command centre in Edison Heights.

Agent Johnson rose to give feedback on his findings. Before he could start, Preston Granger entered the room, whispered something into the Professor's ear, who nodded, then left again.

"Pray, continue, Special Agent Johnson."

"Thank you, Professor Weiss. I built upon the good work already completed by Fingers in researching Cussman and Gomez. I added the Juarez brothers to the mix. The brothers, Diego and Alfonso, hail from Jesu, a mountainous village near Palmito, in the region of Tamaulipas, Mexico."

"From a very early age they were in trouble with the law. Eventually, they became leaders of a street gang working for Pablo Escobar. When he was killed by the Columbian National Police, they allied themselves to Escobar's henchman, Hector Castilla. Together, they formed the Saragossa Cartel and work out of the city of Matamoros. Castilla is the brains and the Juarez brothers are the muscle."

"This cartel was ideally positioned for running drugs to Texas, Louisiana, Alabama, Mississippi and Florida, due to the seventeen thousand miles of US gulf coastline."

"They had a legitimate cover for their organisation. They are a freight transportation company, running ten chilled container ships out of Matamoros. Grupo alimenticio, or GA for short, move beef from Argentina, maize from Mexico, exotic fruits from the Central American countries, and so on. Investigations into the manifests show that food goes out, but never arrives at the quoted destination - nor do they bring goods back to Mexico. In short, they don't do what a food transportation company should do."

"The cartel seem to be involved in two ways. They have paid for Cussman's and Gomez's lifestyles in return for safe passage for their less legitimate cargoes to the Mid Western states. Drugs, arms, people and dirty money for laundering. Here's the interesting thing, Marty found out that GA is one of the controlled foreign companies Strangway acquired as it ticks one of the boxes Marty noted - food transportation."

"But they're running drugs," noted Tec.

"Yes. The outward manifests are, for the most part, actual. Marty has shown that all the food comes from farms and producers Strangway owns. We can only assume that the food is dumped overboard. By owning such a network, Strangway takes hundreds of millions of dollars worth of foodstuffs out of the supply chain. In addition, he's trafficking items - drugs, arms, illegal immigrants - which all potentially contribute to social disruption and unrest. And which earn him a huge income."

The Professor said, "'Oh, what a tangled web we weave when first we practice to deceive.' Thank you, Sam. You have an amazing insight into what the cartel is planning and doing."

He turned to the Agents and said, "And thank you, Team Library. I think that we're really beginning to build up a picture of what Strangway and his dynasty has in mind."

TEAM WET LABORATORY

Maps got up first from the team that was present in the Professor's Wet Laboratory.

"I concentrated on the make-up of the soil samples collected from Dalton. None of the rock or soil in the samples were sourced at that location. It is a mixture of soil from widely distributed locations within North America. We had the locations noted by Fax in their feedback presentation, so with the help of Computer, I gathered information from the various States' Geographical and Environmental Departments, and from the U.S. Geographical Survey."

"We were able to provide pinpoint source locations for elements within the Dalton sample with reasonable accuracy. A list of the locations in Kansas, Idaho, Texas, Up-state New York, Florida and Prince Rupert, British Columbia is available on the system."

Maps looked up slightly and said, "Computer, could you bring up the map, please?"

"Certainly, Maps. Here we are."

With that, an image of the huge map of North America in the Professor's laboratory appeared, with white markers at various locations across it.

Maps used a laser pen. A tiny red dot of light danced across the map as she pointed from one marker to another.

"Here are the source locations - we were able to prove this via the ASTER Sensor on the USGS satellite Earth Gazer. Its mineral imaging results were conclusive."

"That survey also threw up another interesting twist. Computer?"

A map of the Florida Keys appeared. Maps used the laser pointer to direct the audience to two small dots.

"These are the Upper and Lower Sugarloaf Keys. They have been artificially created from the spoil from the mining activities. They, and the filled-in valley at Sunny Meadows, are triplets."

"We sent a sample of the spoil to Chuck to 'smash', as he so gleefully puts it. It came back with interesting results. Computer?"

A new window appeared and it looked as if it were two or three feet in front of the screen displaying the map.

"This is the results of the chemical analysis carried out by Chuck. It gives us readings of gold, thallium, silver, granite, carbon, nickel, titanium, beryllium, quartz, copper, iron, aluminium, silver, zinc, plus this…" she laser-pointed to a spike with a question mark above it, "an unknown alloy. Computer, take away anything unique to any given location."

The Computer obliged, and the only remaining spikes were gold, thallium, nickel, titanium, beryllium and the unknown.

"That's what Professor Weiss meant when he told Marty that it was gold but not gold mining. There is no naturally occurring gold in those areas - the geology is all wrong. So, what we have on screen is the reason for the land purchases: they were after gold from an extra terrestrial source…."

"Aliens?" exclaimed Blink.

"No, little brother, not aliens. Extra terrestrial means that something has come from outside the limits of the earth. Linking in with Lingo's findings, we're guessing fragments of meteor."

"What about the unknown alloy?" asked Tec.

"Chuck will discuss that in his findings. That's it from me."

"Thank you, Miss De La Haye. Miss Liu?" said Professor Weiss.

"I'll remain seated, if I may," Spex started.

"We know from previous findings that the elements within the cone imply that it's something to do with light. In fact, it seems to be quite the opposite."

Fax asked, a quizzed look on his face, "If it doesn't collect light, what does it collect?"

Spex looked across at Chuck and then the Professor. Professor Weiss gave a little nod.

"It collects darkness."

There was an intake of breath in the room, then total quiet.

"On a hunch, I decided to try to make a photoelectric cell using trace amounts of the elements that make up the cone's alloy, present in our soil samples."

"Although it was quite crude, I managed to create a cell and tested it under various controlled conditions. Computer?"

A graph with a number of spikes appeared, most very small but one that dwarfed the others. Spex used the laser pointer.

"This spike is the amount of electromagnetic energy - that is, light - that is hemispherically detected from the fluorescent lights in the laboratory."

"Hemispherically?" asked Special Agent Johnson.

"It's the amount of energy detected on the surface of the photocell. As you can see, it's a tiny amount. This spike..."

Spex pointed to a spike a quarter of the length of the largest spike.

"…is with the lights switched off. The photocell has detected over five hundred percent more electromagnetic energy than with the visible light source switched on. And this…"

She pointed to the next long spike with her laser pointer.

"…is with no light, but with the photocell in a vacuum. And this…"

She pointed to the longest spike with her laser pointer.

"… is with the photocell in complete darkness, in a vacuum, at 2.725 Kelvin. That's just above absolute zero, a temperature that is attainable sixty two miles above the Earth's surface. Its capacity to detect spectral hemispherical reflectance - energy - is amazing. Put simply, it collects energy from darkness. It is my hypothesis, therefore, that if the cone were aboard a satellite, in space, it would collect and channel dark energy."

The Professor stood and said, "Thank you, Miss Liu. Very impressive. Very impressive indeed."

TEAM DRY LABORATORY

D r. Swan and Chuck made their way to the front. Dr. Swan started. "I'm going to hand this over to Chuck. He has all the angles on our research today."

With that he sat down, and Chuck got to his feet.

"Our original brief was to check the various readings already taken from the object and see if they would give us any clues as to its origin. We did get a broad idea of its origin, but I'll come to that. I then pursued a different avenue of research when Spex sent through her data. Let's start with that."

"What do we know about the cone? We now think that it's intended to be utilised in the gathering and directing or focussing of EM energy. It performs best in a vacuum, at extremely low temperatures and in darkness. Spex mentioned the greatest power source in space, and that is dark energy."

Blink's hand went up. "What is it, and is there lots of it?"

"Good question, Blink. Unfortunately, we know less about dark energy than pretty much anything else in the universe."

"We know how much dark energy there is because we know how it affects the universe's expansion. Other than that, it is a complete mystery. Having said that, it is an **important** mystery. It turns out that roughly sixty-eight percent of the universe is dark energy. Dark matter makes up about twenty-seven percent. The rest - everything on Earth, everything ever observed with all of our instruments, all normal matter - adds up to less than five percent of the universe. If you think about it, maybe it shouldn't be called 'normal' matter at all, as it is actually such a small fraction of the universe. However, the phrase 'normal' matter was coined before scientists knew differently."

"The discovery of dark energy goes back to just before I was born… in 1998 a ten-year study of supernovae shocked a group of scientists who had been recording one supernova in particular. Some of the light they saw had started to travel towards Earth when the universe was only a fraction of its present age. The group's goal was to measure small changes in the expansion rate of the universe, which in turn would give insights as to the origin, structure, and eventual fate of all things – this allowed the scientists to reconstruct the expansion history of the universe."

"Quite unexpectedly, the scientists found that the expansion of the universe is not slowing, but is actually accelerating, governed by the Friedman equations, which quantify the energy density of the 'stuff' in the universe."

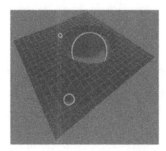

"The acceleration is supposedly due to the properties of what they call dark energy. We don't know what it is, but scientists pretty much all agree that dark energy is the dominant constituent of our universe. Not only that, but the Friedman math shows that dark energy is constantly being created, to allow for this expansion and acceleration of the universe. If new dark energy wasn't coming into being in some way, then the cosmos would tear itself apart, a bit like a rubber band - you can stretch it for only so long before it snaps."

"Einstein already thought about an anti-gravitational force at the beginning of the 20th century. He introduced a cosmological constant to bring Relativity into line with what can be observed. Or, what could be observed then."

"Space has amazing properties, many of which are just beginning to be understood. The first property that Einstein discovered is that it is possible for more space to come into existence. One heartbeat it's not there, the next heartbeat it is! But it needs to be there."

"Unfortunately, no one really understands what it is, or what it could be used for if we could harness it in some way. Previously, it was only identified in mathematical theories, and only recently have the results of its existence been actually observed. However, I believe that as it does exist, one day the technology may be developed to harnesses that power. Now, it seems that the technology to which I'm referring may be here - in the form of the cone. How it would be stored and distributed remains to be seen."

"Now for the possible origin of the cone. We couldn't determine the exact origin of the cone, but we can prove that the elements making up the alloy are extra-terrestrial. What got me started on this path is that I managed to recreate the experiments undertaken by the Russian scientists in 2004, and the Japanese scientists in 2012."

"As I said back at the Museum, what they managed to create was Ununtrium, which has no stable or naturally-occurring isotopes. Several radioactive isotopes have been synthesised in the laboratory, either by fusing two atoms together or by observing the decay of heavier elements. Six different isotopes of Ununtrium have been reported with atomic masses 278 and 282 through 286; they all decay through something called alpha decay, or the loss of the nucleus of a helium-4 atom."

"Now, the Ununtrium in the mine spoil and the cone has totally different properties to those I created in the laboratory. I created a seventh Ununtrium isotope, U-280. Even this was different."

Deputy Sheriff O'Connell said, "I think I've told you, I studied science in my first year in college, so my knowledge is nowhere near as advanced as yours, Chuck. So that I can understand this: the Russian and Japanese scientists created a synthetic element in the laboratory which exists in one form, then decays to become another element."

"Correct."

"You said that the Ununtrium in the cone is self replicating, correct?"

"It's not self replicating, more like undergoing a cyclical existence. It goes from A to B and then back to A, and so on. But you're getting the gist of it."

"So why is it doing that? It's still Ununtrium, right?"

"Yes. But it's a different Ununtrium. It has different properties. For example, we all know what methane is, right? It's an odourless colourless flammable gas. It is either produced by organisms or by volcanicity - er, volcanoes. However, the properties of the two are different. Still methane, but different methane."

Cat said, "Chuck, I love you and all that, but you are making my mind melt!"

Everybody laughed, including Chuck.

"Okay, Cat. Let's see if I can make this more understandable. Erm. Let me think."

He clicked his fingers.

"Got it! Okay, Cat. Imagine you were to build two houses. They are the same in every way. There are the same number of bricks of the same shape and size, the same cement, the same number of shingles on the roof, the same number of screws and nails, the same pipework, they're both painted exactly the same colour. They look exactly the same. However, the bricks in one house come from Factory A, and the bricks in the other come from Factory B. They are the same colour, they are fired in the same way. The only thing that is different is the clay used to make the bricks. The clay comes from quarries two miles apart. If the only thing different about them is the clay...will this actually result in a different house? It may not. Other factors might come into play to balance the difference. In the case of our houses, in the winter, one of them is 0.001% of a degree Celsius warmer than the other. So, they're not exactly identical, but close enough for us not to worry. That's the case with our hypothetical houses."

"The Ununtrium in the mine spoil samples and the readings from the cone are different to the synthesised Ununtrium. The difference is to the value one hundred and thirty two zeros after the decimal point, then a number one. That proves one thing and explains another. The samples are from meteors, therefore they are extra-terrestrial. Secondly, that difference of one hundred and thirty two zeros after the decimal point, then the number one, as small as it is, might explain the cyclical nature of the Ununtrium in the cone."

Chuck had all but finished.

"So, what *are* y'all sayin' about the cone?" asked Tec.

"Look, guys, the process of combining elements to make an alloy is fairly straight forward - it's been done for over a thousand years. Here I think we may have something called an interstitial alloy, with small atoms sitting in gaps between larger atoms. That's why it's so dense. As for how that alloy was then fashioned into the cone is beyond me. I don't know of any process that allows for an object to be milled or polished so precisely, down to almost atomic level."

"Was it aliens?" asked Blink, and excited look on his face.

"I strongly doubt it, Blink. Just because I haven't come across a process for doing so doesn't mean that it didn't, doesn't or couldn't exist."

The Professor stood.

"Thank you, Mr. James. A very clear presentation of a difficult topic."

TEAM TECHNOLOGY LABORATORY

Deputy Sheriff O'Connell was pushed by Blink to the front, the tall figure of Tec immediately behind them. The deputy sheriff positioned himself facing the adults and Agents and started.

"We were tasked with looking at the technology, and reviewing the forensics the SOCOs gathered in the aftermath of the break-in and the theft of the artefact. We also looked into the attack on Craig and the agents in the gas station, that attack on the way to the airfield, the attempted kidnapping of Jenny and Frankie…"

Without even raising his head from whatever he was drawing came "It's D-o-o-d-l-e, Daddy!"

"Yes, sorry, Doodle. And, of course, the two attacks on me. That was my part of the brief."

Tec came in.

"Ah looked at the tech, and anything to do with tech - the Bluetooth devices, the video footage, ballistics and the DNA profiling. Blink here was a real help, runnin', fetchin' learning new skills and all. I'll let Tim start, though."

"We had gathered a surprising amount of evidence during the course of the investigation, from the cigarette ends Craig collected at the motel, through to the weapons used in the hospital and fingerprint comparisons. I'll go through things one by one. The State SOCOs out of Jacksonville did a great job in gathering evidence where there seemed to be so very little."

"Tec noticed the slight chip in the marble near the display case, and they found glass powder that matched the glass in the case. We were able to use the chemical composition of the glass to link it to the security company which installed the display case...and which, as we know, is one of Strangway's cover companies."

"In the rough groove of the chip, although almost microscopic, they found a piece of Kevlar thread. They found another in the cold annealed glass, and inside the case. They identified the threads as coming from the same pair of gloves, a pair of Memphis Black 9178NF Kevlar gloves, with a 13 gauge Kevlar Shell and Nitrile foam coated palms and fingers. These are standard State Police issue for Florida, and also for the Dalton County Sheriff's Department - so it's a safe bet that the perpetrator is a police officer, either serving or retired. I'm assuming that the point of entry - the skylight - precludes a retiree."

"We found more than 70 individual fingerprints, but only four sets appeared more than once. No prizes for guessing who the four are. The prints of Cussman were found on his weapon, on the cigarette ends, on the inside of one of the Bluetooth devices and on the bullet they took out of my shoulder."

"Gomez's fingerprints were found on his weapon, on the weapon used to attack Craig and the other agents at the gas station and we found a partial on the skylight window. We got a hit immediately, because all serving officers have their fingerprints taken in order to identify them if something bad were to happen. This was the same with the Sheriff."

"The fingerprints of both Diego and Alfonso Juarez were found on the weapon used in the gas station attack and on the inside of the Lincoln. Their fingerprints were also matched quickly due to their arrest records. It may come as no surprise that the two individuals who Arma and Bladen caught are the Juarez brothers. This additional evidence can be used in any future trials…though I'm not sure if it will come to that."

"We had some DNA evidence. We had trace DNA from saliva on the cigarette ends that matched the sheriff. DNA from a hair found in the display case belonged to Gomez. Once again, the DNA of police officials and also military personnel is kept on record - along with information on blood groups, allergies, scars, dental records, distinguishing features and so on."

"Our perpetrators have been 'banged to rights' as the English say. This is evidence enough to put them away for a very long time. Except that Cussman and Gomez have gone to ground - but we'll find them. Special Agent Johnson has put out an APB on the two of them, and his colleagues have been to the Department headquarters and their homes."

"With the assistance of Marty and Hex, I was able to link the four to each other. The Saragossa Cartel has been running narcotics, weapons and trafficking illegal immigrants through the port of Clearwater, on the west coast of Florida. They would travel cross country and then be given safe passage by Cussman and Gomez, from Dalton to the Georgia or Alabama borders."

"Marty found that Cussman and Gomez received large injections of funds into their personal bank accounts just days after a ship was unladen at Clearwater. Hex was able to access satellite data from the middle of last month which shows a truck travelling from Clearwater to Dalton, then to be joined by a Dalton Sheriff's Department cruiser. The roof ID is that of the sheriff. Any questions?"

The were none. The evidence was conclusive - Cussman, Gomez and the Juarez brothers were involved in the theft and in the subsequent assaults. All four were inextricably linked to the Saragossa Cartel and Grupo alimenticio, which they now knew had financial links to Strangway.

"Thanks, Tim," said the Professor.

Tec stood.

"The first thing ah looked at were the Bluetooth devices we've recovered. There was the one Craig found in the car, the one controlling the video recordings and the one attached to the skylight. Now, the thing with Bluetooth devices is that people think that they can only be activated at close range. This is not the case. A Bluetooth signal from a transmitter to a receiver can be bounced off a loose network called a piconet...it's not an organised, structured network, just a dynamic load of Bluetooth signals all jumbled together."

"Our devices here are all slaves to the same master – they are all set to the same frequency, 2.412 gigahertz. Ah wanted to check the array on top of the Sheriff's Department headquarters. Computer got me a satellite image and Hex, he got me the spec."

Tec nodded Hex's way, who smiled.

Tec continued. "Computer."

An image of the headquarter's roof aerial array appeared on the screen.

"Y'all should recognise the satellite dish, just bit bigger than usual. It has dual receivers, domestic US DirectTV satellite and domestic Mexican Cablevisión México satellite. Of course, it can also receive data transmissions and satellite telephone signals. Mighty strange, having a receiver/transmitter for satellite phone signals in a police station, as they can use the State of Florida cellphone service provided, if ah'm correct, by Safelink Wireless. Except that is, if the satellite signal was going to, or being sent by, a fixed installation - for example on board a ship in transit. Just so happens that when Sam's FBI buddies from the Jacksonville field office went to say hello to our friends the Sheriff and the detective, they found two Thureya XT Pro rugged satellite handsets. No prizes for a-guessin' whose fingerprint were all over those beauties."

Using the laser pointer, he shone the pinpoint of light onto a white cylinder, about 12" long, tapering slightly from the back to the front.

"That just there is an Audio Technica ATW-A54P UHF Wireless powered dipole antenna, used here for GPS, and standard police radios."

He pointed at what looked like a television aerial on steroids.

"Here we have a Sirio SY50 VHF transmitter, commonly used by truckers – this model is commonly used in locations such as base stations in the Antarctic, so it has quite a range. Great for staying in touch with trucks leaving Clearwater, then heading north to the other state borders, ah'd say."

He then pointed at a black square box with rounded edges, about twelve inches by twelve inches.

"Finally this is a Bluetooth Smart beacon Xy, designed to boost a standard Bluetooth signal. The booster was set to 2.412 gigahertz, so this is how the Bluetooth devices we found were controlled."

"Now to the ballistics. The bullet they removed from Tim's shoulder is a 7.62 x 51mm NATO 300 Magnum round. It came from an M89SR sniper rifle manufactured by Technical Equipment International. Sam's guys found it at Cussman's mini mansion, and the serial number is that of a consignment of arms hijacked whilst on its way to Fort Bragg in North Carolina. The perpetrators were never caught, but weapons from the same consignment have been appearing all over Mexico and other Latin American countries with drug cartel issues. The ballistics confirm the match between bullet and weapon."

"Every weapons retrieved by us or by Sam's colleagues have all been stolen, and some have been used in deadly encounters. The weapon taken when we were held at gunpoint at the gas station was used in the murder of a rival cartel leader in Matamoros. The desk sergeant used his old 38 service revolver and the Juarez brother in the car was armed with a Benelli M4 CQB short barrel shotgun, from the Dalton County Sheriff's Department arsenal."

"The weapons taken at the hospital were bespoke weapons – individual and extremely expensive. They were both loosely based on the Smith & Wesson XVR 460 Magnum. So, these guys meant business, and they had access to the firepower to make sure they got what they wanted, or protected what they valued."

"Finally, I looked at the video evidence from the security cameras. I have nothing to add to my findings at the museum other than the fact that the Bluetooth device used to control the recordings also transmitted the footage to Cussman, which is how he knew that we were at the museum. I checked Tim's work cellphone - that had a cleverly hidden bug in it, too."

He turned to Chuck.

"You talked about the cyclical nature of the Ununtium within the the cone. What was the frequency of the transformation cycle?"

"Without the cone, I can't tell you."

"How about every fifty four minutes, seventeen seconds, four milliseconds and some microseconds?"

A confused Chuck asked, "How do you know?"

"When I was checking through the recordings, I saw an anomaly. Computer."

A video sequence played. A few seconds into it, the picture shuddered slightly.

"Pause, Computer."

The sequence paused.

"Notice the time: eleven-oh-six, thirty two seconds. Fast forward to the next marked sequence."

The video ran forward, people passing at speed through the main hall, stopping, turning, pointing, chatting, moving on. It switched to normal speed.

"There."

The sequence paused once again, just as the juddering started again.

"Look at the time frame we have...twelve-seventeen and thirty six seconds. There's the fifty four minutes and some. It happens throughout every recording, from every camera...up until the cone is stolen."

"Wow, Tec" said Chuck.

He continued. "Computer, could you cross reference the time cycles discovered by Tec with the mass spectrometer readings from the cone, please?"

The Computer said, "Cross referencing. Please wait. Cross referencing completed. Chuck, the results confirm your suspicions - there is a direct correlation between the two. The cyclical ionising event occurs exactly every fifty four minutes, seventeen seconds, four milliseconds and thirty three microseconds...and some, as Tec puts it."

"What bearing does this have on the case?" asked Fax.

"Not quite sure..." said Chuck.

"Ah only found it out by studying the camera footage..." said Tec.

The Professor came in at that point.

"We may not yet understand the significance of this finding, Mr. Le Maine. However, as we do actually know this piece of information now, it might be useful somewhere else in the investigation. Please remember, everyone - every piece of information, no matter how trivial it may seem, is important. Perhaps not only for this case, but for cases that have been or for cases that may come. Anything further?"

"As a matter of fact, Professor Weiss, there's one thing. In-keeping with Tim's analyses of the fingerprints, ah found the four main suspects with my DNA profiling - Cussman, Diego, and the Juarez brothers. By the way, they are not brothers - not related in any way. However, ah found a recurring DNA sample, as yet unidentified."

"Thank you, Mr. Wilson. Most enlightening."

DOODLE'S DISCOVERY

Doodle stood up suddenly, held up the picture on which he was working and shouted, "Finished! Finished my picture, Cled!"

All eyes turned towards him. He was holding up an A3 sheet of paper with a line drawing on it. It was a perfect reproduction of the map table in the Professor's laboratory.

"Look, Cled. Look everybody. It's finished!"

Spex peered carefully at the picture the little boy held so proudly for all to see.

"What is it, Doodle?"

"Cled's big map. I drew all those places my friend Maps put onto it."

He pointed at the sources of the mining spoil that the team's testing had identified.

"Here, and here, and here. And I live....here!"

"But what are those lines?" Spex asked.

"I joined all of Maps places to my house with lines."

Spex thought a second, then a light seemed to come on in her head.

"Doodle!" she exclaimed loudly.

Doodle suddenly looked shocked and frightened. His lower lip and chin trembled, as if he was about to cry. His mother took his hand.

"It's alright, darling. Friend Spex was saying you did a good job. See, look at your picture. You did a good job."

The boy's infectious smile appeared on his face as quickly as it had disappeared a few moments ago.

"Do you like it, my friend Spex?"

Remembering how her autistic brother responded to sudden loud noises, Spex talked to the little boy in a calming voice.

"Doodle, I love it. You've done a very good job. Professor Weiss, I've seen that pattern laid out before...now where was it?"

She wheeled herself over to a pile of satellite images and started rummaging through them.

"No, no, no...ah-ha...here it is! Computer, could you bring up satellite image two-four-one-nine-six, please?"

A satellite image appeared on the large screen. It showed continental USA with all its features, man made and natural in origin.

"Computer, show the source locations for the mining spoils."

The locations identified by the tests appeared.

"Now, remove all man made structures, activities and habitations."

A map showing the spoil locations, rivers, mountains, lakes, forests – but not dams, cities, towns, roads or railroads – appeared on the screen.

She went across to Doodle, and put one hand on his shoulder.

"This is a very good job, Doodle. May I borrow it for a minute?"

"You can keep it as a present, friend Spex," he beamed.

"Thank you so much, Doodle."

She wheeled herself to the front desk, and placed the picture on a platen glass set into the table top.

"Computer, could you please scan Doodle's picture, and overlay it on what we have on screen?"

A blue light from underneath the glass scanned the image. As it was scanning, it appeared on the screen. The lines Doodle had drawn did, indeed, link every source location to Dalton.

"Computer, allowing for topography, match the lines to known railroads or roads."

Doodle's lines began to morph, following paths made by roads, railroads and topographical features.

"Now, extend a line down towards the man made keys."

A new line appeared, down to southern Florida, ending at Florida City, not far from Key Largo.

"It seems to be a network of some kind…I'm thinking that it may be a railroad system. Professor?"

"Well done Miss Lieu. Well done, Doodle."

The little boy beamed with delight.

"Miss De La Haye, Mr. Le Maine. Would you be so kind as to carry out some initial research into this network? Everyone else, I suggest a break before dinner to allow these two to work in peace."

The others filed out of the Conference Room, and Maps and Fax stood and got nearer to the projected image. Maps looked at Fax.

"Any idea where to start with this one?"

Fax pointed at a point on the image. "Look, there in West Virginia. Looks like a tunnel. Maybe we could start there. Find out about that tunnel and work out from there."

"Let's get to it."

THE CONFERENCE ROOM (II)

The next morning, after having had a light dinner, a restful night's sleep and a hearty breakfast - prepared by the invisible Mr. Granger - everybody reconvened in the Conference Room.

Deputy Sheriff O'Connell was now far more mobile, using a pair of walking crutches to get around.

Maps and Fax were already at the front of the room, along with Spex and Hex.

Fax started.

"With a collection of names like this - Fax, Maps, Spex and Hex - we sound like a comedy act from the forties or fifties. Hopefully what we have to feedback is a little more serious."

Maps carried on.

"We were at a bit of a loss as to where to start with this investigation. We noted that there was only one man made feature of any size anywhere on the map – it couldn't be removed because it involved a natural feature. So, that was our starting point. Computer."

The image zoomed in on a section of one of the lines. Maps used the laser pen to highlight a feature.

"This is the Hawk's Nest Railroad Tunnel. Records show that it was originally built as a link between the Chesapeake & Ohio Railroad at Hawks Nest Station to the station at Ansted. It was built by the Gauley and Kanawha Coal Company that was supposedly formed in 1872."

Fax interrupted.

"Maps uses the term 'supposedly' for a reason. It may be of no surprise to you to learn that there are English links here. Ansted was named after David T. Ansted, a geologist who was once on the payroll of Strangway Mining and Ore. The Gauley and Kanawha Coal Company was a subsidiary of the same."

Maps continued.

"It was purported to have been built as narrow gauge railway, using saddleback locomotives and small coal cars to cross poorly constructed trestle bridges. Computer."

An image appeared of a heftily constructed trestle bridge.

"This satellite image was taken yesterday. Although the line closed many years ago, that bridge is so well constructed that it could carry modern trains - sorry, railroad stock - even today."

"Building this tunnel meant that the journey was shortened by some two hundred and fifty miles - avoiding Spruce Knob mountain and some other peaks. This gave us a time frame - 1840's onwards," said Fax.

"We were able to find seventeen companies in all that built the network we see on the image - all between 1850 and 1900, and all linked in some way to Strangway Mining and Ore."

Spex came in at that point.

"We were able to tell from satellite imaging that these railroads were built upon tracks and trails established as far back as the 1600s. It seems that, as with human trails, they took the path of least resistance. Hex, what was the final calculation in terms of total track distance?"

"Yeah, I've got that here somewhere...where'd it go? Yeah, here it is. Right, let's see...yeah, here we are - that's a total of just under twenty thousand miles of track. Wow! A lot of track! Too much track to track! Get it? Hmm, aah, whatever!"

Everybody smiled at his enthusiasm, if not his joke.

"Very droll, Mr. Madison. An excellent job to you all. Mr. Huntley, I believe that the team asked you to make some calculations in terms of cost over the said period of construction and use."

"Yes, Professor," said Marty.

"Using quite rough 'guesstimates', I would say that the whole venture actually netted Strangway Mining and Ore quite a considerable profit. The only major expense was the tunnel, which they then sold on - to themselves, by the way - and so avoided capital gains but which still generated an income from the mining and transportation of coal and coke. Each and every section of railway line was sold on to other companies - either for scrap or actual use. Much of it is in the Amtrak network even to this day."

"There is the income from the sales of land following mining activities - sorry, Professor, I don't know what else to call it. Finally, there is the profit from the gold and whatever other minerals they may have processed from their activities. In my estimation - and this is just a rough guess, remember - Strangway Mining and Ore profited to the tune of $3.75 billion from the railway network alone."

There was a gasp in the room.

Fax said, "We also found out about the Tower itself. It stands on the site of the very first major 'mining' venture the company undertook, and as we know, a family home was built there by Charles St. John Strangway II. The current Tower is very much shrouded in mystery. The foundations were laid in 1924, but no actual building took place until ten years later. By 1936, it was the tallest unclad frame in the world…"

"What do you mean by that?" asked Chuck.

"It was just the metal framework. Records show that the Topeka City authorities never questioned its use, no plans were ever submitted, no architect is named and there was no inspection of the construction in terms of quality. Interestingly, not a single local worked on the project."

"Were they all English workers?" asked Tim.

"No, actually. Every single worker was native American - from the areas where Strangway Mining and Ore had purchased land from the indigenous peoples. However, they weren't cheap labour. Each one was a highly trained and skilled engineer. Once the initial frame was built, most of the workers ended up in the forces fighting in the Pacific or European theatres of war."

"The building was finished in 1943, but has had major refits and refurbishments in both 1967 and 2002. It became the world's tallest building for a short while, higher than the Petronas Towers in Malaysia, and only bested by Taipei 101 in 2004. The total cost to get the current building to its current condition is probably in the region of $1 billion. We can't be absolutely certain of that - as I've said previously, the Strangway dynasty is very much a closed book," said Marty.

"These are all lucrative ventures in their own right. Why the current illegal activity?" asked Special Agent Johnson.

"It seems, Sam," said the Professor, "that they have bigger fish to fry. It is our role to find out what that may be."

The special agent nodded in agreement.

"How do you intend to do that?" he asked.

Jenny O'Connell came in at that point.

"Eddie, as I said previously, when you mentioned Strangway Tower our team came up with an infiltration plan. George helped us with the video from the cameras placed by Craig and Chick, but I think we are good to go. George?"

"Ah thank you kindly, Jen. Computer, if you please?

Strangway Tower, Topeka, Kansas appeared on the screen.

"Please run the sequence."

The video footage speeded up, showing lights going on and off, tail light trails of cars passing on the road below and steam rising from the heating and cooling outlets on the roof.

"Now, y'all may notice the lights on the these three floors never change. They are always illuminated. But look at the others. Computer, re-run, please."

The sequence played again.

"Patterns!" exclaimed Doodle. "I like patterns."

"Well done, Doodle. Yeah, patterns. The lights turn on and off in a set sequence, almost like they're on some kinda timer. Those floors below the regular ones ain't what they're supposed to be."

"And I believe that our team should go in to see what is happening," said Jenny.

"You have the plans in place, you said. When can this happen?" asked Professor Weiss.

"Tomorrow, first thing."

"Resources?"

"The team and their own individual equipment. Covert backup, non-lethal. Tec's tech. In and out fast."

"Mr. Wilson's technology?"

"Yessir. Spex and ah have developed small surveillance devices - sound, video and GPS - which are totally undetectable. They transmit and receive data through rapidly modulating encrypted frequencies. Kinda like Lingo hearing a thousand languages at the same time and understanding them all."

He winked in her direction, and she blushed.

Maps smiled. She saw the signs of romance, and was about to comment when the Professor spoke again.

"Jenny, the purpose of the infiltration?"

"Tag, bag and listen and watch."

"Time frame?"

"Zero-six-hundred tomorrow morning. Ten minutes max."

Jenny was using special forces language for placing devices, taking away evidence and clues, times and surveillance activities.

"Very well. Let's make this happen. Jenny, could your team prepare for your sojourn? Everyone else, I'd like you to work with me on the covert backup."

STRANGWAY TOWER

Early next morning, Arma, Bladen and Cat were crouched in the shadow cast by the corner of Strangway Tower at the intersection of 5th Street and Buchanan. Both streets were deserted, but in the distance they could hear the rumble of early morning traffic building up on the I-70 a few blocks away.

They were dressed in dark catsuits, and wore what looked like dark glasses - in fact, they were Spex's latest invention, lightweight night vision glasses. They each had a small backpack, and Bladen had a belt of Pneu-Dart type-U disposable RDD tranquilliser throwing darts strapped to her back.

A voice sounded in their Bluetooth ear-buds. It was Fingers.

"Team one, target vehicle is in. Garage gate's just about to close. You have the all clear, over."

"Thanks, Eyes. Will keep you updated. Team one out," said Arma.

To the other two she whispered, "Set glasses to infra red. Keep low, fast and quiet. Hand signals only."

They nodded.

The three Agents tapped the left hand side of their glasses to set them to infra red, where any and all heat signatures would be visible to them. Bladen tapped Arma on the shoulder, and moved first, quickly around the corner onto Buchanan and down the underground parking lot ramp. Arma and Cat quickly followed, and seconds after they entered the building, the gate clunked closed behind them.

Bladen was nowhere to be seen. They heard three taps in their earpieces, and looked to the far end of the ground floor where Arma saw her twin sister crouched in the shadows near an elevator.

Having been given the all clear hand signal, Arma and Cat ran silently to where Bladen was watching something or someone on the lower ramp. She used gestures to tell the others that there were two guards on the lower floor, both armed, heading away from them.

Across from them was parked a white stretch limousine, and two spaces further on was a Strangway Foundation USV. The heat signatures showed that the limousine had been driven until only a few minutes ago.

Cat gestured, *"I'll put trackers on them."*

Bladen signalled *"okay"* with her fingers.

The Twins watched as Cat sprinted on tip toes to the limousine. She dived to the floor and nimbly rolled underneath the vehicle. A few seconds later she appeared the other side, gesturing, *"okay, that's one."*

She was about to roll under the USV when the three Agents heard voices coming from the ramps both above and below them. Cat froze, having placed a tiny tracker on the underside of the second vehicle.

The two guards from the lower floor were joined by two from the next floor up. They met at the back of the SUV where Cat was hiding. They talked in low voices, exchanged cigarettes and jokes, before turning to move on.

In the shadows, Bladen reached behind her back and pulled out two darts. Arma put her hand on Bladen's arm and gestured *"no"*.

Suddenly, the four men stopped, listening into the ear pieces they wore. The guards swivelled around, two moved towards the Twins and the two towards where Cat was crouched at the front of the SUV.

Arma visually scanned the area - she couldn't see any security cameras, and Tec's scans had showed that there were no devices of any kind in the garage of the building. She looked at her wrist, where a signal detector showed no signs of any electronic signals other than the ones she expected to see - their own Bluetooth transmissions and the radio transmissions of the guards.

How did they know?

Putting that thought to one side, she tapped her sister's shoulder, and signalled *"yes"*.

Bladen whipped her arm back and threw the two darts. Both hit their mark, and two guards fell unconscious, each with a dart protruding from his left shoulder.

The remaining guards turned to see what had happened. Confused, they scanned the parking area with their weapons held out in front of them. Cat thought that they acted in the same trained way as the man who'd attacked them at the gas station on the way to the airport.

Without another thought, she ran at the guard nearest to her. He didn't have a moment to respond - she ran towards the pillar to his rear, jumped and used her right leg to launch her body towards his head. In mid flight Cat turned, striking the guard in the temple with her back pack. She landed on top of the unconscious form and looked up at the other guard, who was bringing his weapon to bear on her.

At nearly the same time, Arma ran at the last remaining guard and threw herself along the floor, sweeping the man's legs away. He went up into the air a full body length and landed directly on his face. Arma quickly zip tied his hands together, though his unconscious form indicated that he was not going to be a problem to the three Agents.

Arma, Bladen and Cat joined each other by the side of the elevator.

"They knew that we were here - not before, but during," whispered Bladen.

"I know," replied her twin.

"Eyes. This is Team one. Do you copy, over?"

There was no answer. Bladen repeated the transmission.

"Eyes, this is Team one. Do you copy? Over."

The answer was the chilling static hiss of an unanswered message.

Across Buchanan, in an alley that led through buildings onto 6th Avenue, Fingers - 'Eyes' - had been watching the progress of Team one into the underground parking garage. Once the doors came down, she continued scanning Strangway Tower and the surrounding area.

"Eyes to Buckingham Palace. Do you copy, over?"

"Reading you loud and clear. Status?" It was Jenny's voice.

"Team one inside target area. Streets and building clear...wait..."

Fingers heard a noise a little way along the alleyway. She turned to see Special Agent Johnson standing over her.

"Sam! You startled me."

"Anything to report?"

"No, the girls are in."

She heard noises in her ear piece - the sounds of some kind of struggle.

"Wait. Team one, what's happening, over? Team one, come in. Over."

There was no reply. She gasped as she looked up at the special agent - straight into the barrel of his Glock service pistol.

"Wha..."

Her words were cut off by the back of Johnson's left hand to her cheek. She went sprawling, but managed to turn her radio on to transmit.

"Shut it, kid."

He stood over her, pointing his pistol at her head.

"Give me the ear piece."

Fingers said nothing, removing her earbud and smartphone and handing them to the special agent.

"I've got this one," he said into his own mouth piece.

"Go get the others."

"Wh..what is this, Sam? I...I thought you were on our side...helping Dr. Swan rescue Tim, the research..."

"You know what they say - keep your friends close and your enemies closer still. My uncle taught me that from a very early age. Cussman, Gomez, the Juarez brothers - dispensable, collateral damage. Heck, the sheriff and his crony are probably alligator food in the Everglades by now. And the Juarez boys won't make it to trial."

"Your uncle?"

"Duh, kiddo! I'm a Strangway, through and through. The guy you think is an awful fiend - he's my mother's brother. None of you figured that one out! I've been in on this from the start. What you call The Strangway Dynasty - lame, by the way, we're more than that! - needed someone to get into this cutesy little Agency of yours to figure out what you knew."

"I have to say, not too bad for a bunch of brats. Medals of Honor, military experience, intellect, science, technology. Nothing. Nothing compared to what we can do. Brat, this is all about adults playing adult games for adult returns - pity you'll never get to be see it!"

He aimed his weapon and moved his middle finger from the guard and pulled the trigger back to the second 'squeeze point'.

Back in Edison Heights, everybody present had been listening to proceedings on the open channel Fingers had enabled.

Jenny turned to the Professor.

"You were right about him, Ed. How did you know?"

"I didn't know for certain, Jen. Just an overwhelming feeling…not responding to Gomez at the hospital, not knowing about the true nature of the relationship between the Juarez 'brothers'. The icing on the cake was the DNA Mr. Wilson was able to analyse from Johnson's drinks glass. He's the 'unknown' fifth person. And we now know by his own admission that he's a Strangway."

"Team two?" Jenny asked.

"Team two," replied the Professor.

"Team two. That's a go. Now!"

Out of the darkness behind Special Agent Johnson, two darkly clad figures wearing full face balaclavas appeared. The only thing visible was the determined glint in their eyes.

Johnson didn't sense the hand on his arm until it was too late. The pistol was wrestled from his hand, a bag was shoved over his head and a single blow to the temple rendered him unconscious.

"Hi, guys," said Fingers. "Long time no see."

"Ach, very droll, wee missy. Way too droll. Y'are a brave one, lass - I'll say that for ye!"

"Nah, I knew you'd be there."

"Here, let me help y'up."

"Thanks."

Chick held out his hand and pulled Fingers to her feet, checked her face where Johnson had struck her.

"Ye'll be fine, lass."

Chick and Craig removed their balaclavas and smiled at her. They would have shaken their hair loose, if they'd had any, mused Fingers.

"Come along, Miss Anna. I think the others need our help," said Craig.

"You as well, Craig...c'mon, it's Fingers!" she said, exasperated.

She continued.

"The other three? Please! Why are we 'lasses' so underestimated? So, nah, don't think so. They're good. What about this one?"

Fingers, pointed at Johnson.

"We have a very comfortable room for him back at Buckingham Palace...he can share the cell with the Juarez boys."

"Cosy, very cosy," she said

"Ach - maybe not so..."

Fingers shuddered at the thought of what might happen to the 'special agent'. It quickly disappeared when she thought back a few minutes ago, to when he was holding a pistol to her head.

Meanwhile, in the garage, the three girls could hear footsteps coming from all around them. Cat looked at the four prone figures on the floor, ran to them and placed one of Tec's tiny surveillance devices into each of their pockets.

Bladen looked at the lift door. She pressed the only button available, marked 'Down', and heard the lift ascending from a lower level. The door pinged and opened, and above her was another guard.

She reached behind her back, pulled out another dart from her belt and thrust it into the guard's leg. He fell to the floor without a sound. Arma placed a device onto his waist belt, and also placed one inside the lift.

The Twins ran to Cat, and the three made their way to the garage door.

"Team one. Extraction required," said Bladen.

A few seconds later, they heard the loud revving of a powerful engine, and they stood well away from the garage door and braced themselves against the wall.

Suddenly, the entire door was smashed into small pieces and a Agrale Marruá AM200 G2 CD armoured vehicle, driven by Craig, came hurtling down the ramp. It turned and came skidding to a halt in front of the three girls. Chick was manning the roof heavy machine gun, and Fingers threw the door open.

"Morning, lasses - yer ride haem awaits ye!" Chick called down, his eyes scanning the garage.

As Craig sped up the ramp he said, "Buckingham Palace, this is Team two. Team one extracted. No damaged goods. Over."

They all heard the Professor's voice.

"Well done, teams. Return to Buckingham Palace stat. Over."

"We ha' a wee guest for ye, boss. Over." said Chick.

Jenny's voice came over the air.

"Tagged and bagged? Over."

"Aye, and then some! Out."

Craig drove quickly along Buchanan, then northwards on Quinton, past Grove on his left and joined the I-70 heading westwards, back towards Austrey.

Once on the interstate he slowed down so as not to attract attention. Chick in the meantime had dismantled the machine gun and drawn the canvass top back over the roof. To vehicles driving by, they looked like the proud owners of a reproduction military vehicle, out for an early morning drive.

Any passing overhead traffic or police helicopters would not have been overly concerned – the vehicle bore the words FBI on its roof.

BUCKINGHAM PALACE - AGAIN

There was a lot of activity in the Conference Room, the Agents working in small groups or in pairs, exchanging information, asking questions, tapping out on their computer keyboards or tablets.

"Mr. Wilson, are the devices working?"

"Yes, Professor Weiss. Ah'm getting real clear readings from…Hex?"

"Er, yeah. Let's see. Eighteen. Eighteen working, two no signals. No. So, yeah, eighteen."

"Eighteen devices. Good job, buddy."

He winked at Hex, who gave a thumbs up in return.

"Very well. Everybody…if I may have your attention. We have eyes and ears outside and inside the Tower. We need to glean as much information as possible."

"Professor. We have incoming. Teams one and two are five minutes away."

"Thank you, Computer. Tim, Jenny, Mr. James - will you help me welcome our special guest, please? Mr. Wilson, Miss Lieu - would you be so kind as to act as liaisons as the need arises? Mr. Dexter…is our little ruse ready?"

"Ruse…yeah…okay…as in little joke…mmm, er, Computer."

"Loaded, cocked, locked and…Tec, what is that charming phrase you so love to use?"

"Loaded, cocked, locked and ready to kick some…"

"Mr. Wilson! Ladies present!"

"Professor, ah was goin' to say 'kick some backside'. Yessir!"

"Hmm. I believe you, but millions wouldn't. So, we have the dual feed ready?"

"Yessir. Hex and Computer have done a fine job. A mighty fine job."

By the time the four had reached the front door, the armoured vehicle was pulling up in front of the mansion.

The Twins, Fingers and Cat got out first, followed by Chick.

He reached back into the car and said, "We're haem - time to get ye to ye room."

He pulled a struggling Johnson from the car.

"Behave, now…or I'll get one of the wee lasses to set ye sleepin' again, so I will. Professor - down to the Cavern?"

"Yes, please William. Cell two, if you please. We'll be there once we've finished with the Juarez brothers."

"How are they?" asked Craig.

Tim said, "Singing like canaries. The Professor and Preston have ways of making canaries sing such beautiful tunes."

"And no visible marks," said Jenny. "True masters."

An arrogant look appeared on Johnson's face.

"You'll never get me to talk. I'm a Strangway," he spat.

He added, "They'll get me out."

"If they knew where you were - which I very much doubt - I'd love them to try," said the Professor.

With that, Chick and Craig led Johnson inside, marched him over to the elevator and down to a prison cell in the area known as 'The Cavern'.

The prison cell was well appointed, very much like a small hotel room, in fact. It even had a television and a telephone.

"Enjoy. For now," said Craig, and slammed shut the solid door.

Almost immediately, the telephone started ringing, a low shrill bzzz-bzzz. Johnson picked up the phone.

"Hello?"

The bzzz-bzzz continued.

"Hello?"

He looked at the phone. In anger, he picked it up from the table, ripped the lead out of the wall and threw it across the room.

The bzzz-bzzz continued.

"I know what you're doing....!" he shouted.

The sound of the telephone buzzing stopped.

"I know what you're doing I know what you're doing I know what you're doing I know what you're doing I know what you're doing I know what you're doing," echoed around the room, time and time again.

"You won't break me...." he screamed.

"You won't break me You won't break me You won't break me You won't break me You won't break me You won't break me You won't break me You won't break me You won't break me."

The sound of his voice stopped suddenly. It was replaced by the sound of his racing heart, echoing eerily around the room, from every direction.

In the corridor outside, Chick and Craig looked at Johnson via a monitor. He was now sitting on the bed, his hands held tightly against his ears rocking slowly back and forth.

"How long for this one?" asked Craig.

"Ach, he's got nae substance. Holding a gun to a wee lass's heed like that? Nae - I reckon nae more than an hour!"

185

In a room two doors down, Diego Juarez was sitting at a table. Opposite him were Tim and Jenny.

"What is this, bad cop good cop - like in your movies?" he spat out in heavily accented English.

"No. More like bad cop worse cop," replied Jenny.

"What, you...you are a woman! I throw women like you to the dogs every day!"

He followed the remark up with unrepeatable expletives.

"I'd like to introduce you to my wife," said Tim.

"A wonderful mother and cook, but a ferocious woman if crossed."

"Ha. There is no woman on this earth who can scare Diego Juarez!"

Like a flash, Jenny launched herself over the desk, grabbed Juarez by the shoulder and used his body to swing herself around. She held him in a Krav Maga style choke hold, and whispered something into his ear.

His eyes opened wide.

"You - you cannot do this! I - I - I have rights."

Jenny leant in again, whispered something else. She then ruffled his greasy hair, and she and Tim left the room.

Outside in the corridor, Tim turned to her and asked what she's said to him.

"I told him that his 'brother' was being mailed back home. In thousands of pieces. Well, most of his brother, anyway. The bits of him that we could find after the dogs had been been fed."

"You're so bad!"

"Aren't I just!"

They looked at the monitor outside the room. Diego Juarez was slumped forward, his head on the table, sobbing.

"I feel kind of sorry for the guy..." said Tim, "...knowing he'll never see his brother again."

"Oh, I don't know. Do you think they'll let them visit each other, where they're going?"

"I think they just lock the door and throw away the key."

"Good enough!"

In a room like the one Diego Juarez was sat, his 'brother' was sitting facing Professor Weiss. Chuck towered over them, an imposing sight, arms folded.

Alfonso looked first at the Professor, up at Chuck and then back.

"You expect me, Alfonso Juarez, to talk?" he asked.

"No. Just listen. Because listening is very good for the soul. As is admitting to one's wrong doings, and trying to make amends in some way."

"You are talking. You say nothing I will listen to."

Chuck said, "Computer."

A wall mounted monitor flickered into life. It was a recording of Johnson's presentation, and his confession.

"What is this?" Juarez asked.

"It's your friend Johnson selling you, your so called brother, and everyone else, down the river. He and the Strangway family have betrayed you. They want to see you becoming alligator food in the Everglades."

"You make this up. They need us. We are too important to them!"

"What's so important about you?" asked Chuck

"I'm saying nothing. I want my lawyer."

The Professor said, "Computer."

The screen now showed Diego shaking hands with the Professor, getting into a limousine and being driven away. It cut to Diego boarding an Aeromexico 747.

"We don't need you to talk, Alfonso. Your brother made a deal, told us everything. In return, we made Hector Castilla disappear…"

The Professor made a gesture with his hands and said, "Poof!"

"…And Diego is now the head of the Saragossa Cartel…less the American connections, of course. He didn't want to share any of this with you. Some brother, don't you think?

"That stinking dog is no brother of mine. I will have his head for this!"

"Not where you're going. Come along, Mr. James."

"No, wait. I will do a deal. But you get rid of him first," said Alfonso, nodding towards the image of his brother.

The two ignored him and walked out.

In the corridor, Chuck said to the Professor, "Hex did a fine job on that video. The boy's a genius."

"You all are, Mr. James. You all are. Right, we'll let the three of them contemplate their situations a while."

They met up with Tim, Jenny, Craig and Chick, and walked back towards the lift.

"How are the other guests?" asked the Professor.

"Stewing nicely," said Jenny.

"Ready tae sing within the hour, Colonel."

As soon as they arrived back at the Conference Room, Lingo said, "Professor Weiss. I have something that you might find interesting."

"What have you found, Miss Kowalczyk?" asked the Professor.

"Tec's surveillance devices are proving to be very effective. Computer, could you play the first section, please?"

"Certainly, Lingo."

Those gathered heard Johnson say, "*Go get the others*," over someone's radio. Then the sound of Arma, Bladen and Cat running and moments after that, a huge crash as the garage doors caved in.

"So, we know that he was in league with those in the Tower, as suspected. One of the men has been taken to the upper floors. We are unable to see anything as the device is in his pocket. Computer, will you please play the next sequence."

They could hear people talking in various languages.

"It seems to be some kind of communication room. There are the voices of those present in the room, and the voices of people over whatever feed they're using...video, telephone, VOIP...whatever. I have been able to identify English, French, German, Spanish, Chinese, Korean, Arabic, and Russian. There was actually one other language with which I was unfamiliar. Computer identified that one for me."

"Yes, Professor Weiss. It was Esperanto," said the Computer.

"Esperanto?" asked Fingers. "What is that?"

Lingo responded.

"Esperanto is a constructed international auxiliary language - it's a made up language. It is the most widely spoken constructed language in the world. The Polish-Jewish ophthalmologist L. L. Zamenhof published the first book detailing Esperanto, *Unua Libro - meaning 'first book'* - on July 26, 1887. "Esperanto" roughly translates as 'one who hopes'."

"Believe it or not, over two million people actually speak it worldwide. It never became widely popular because it was based on the constructs of the major European languages, which are largely Latin and Germanic based. Leaving out Arabic and Chinese constructs meant that the greatest populations were never likely to use it."

"Why would they all be using a language like that?" asked Tec.

"As a 'lingua franca'. One common language, fairly easy to understand and learn. Not spoken by many...as I admitted, I didn't recognise it," said Lingo.

"Could you glean anything from the conversations?" asked the Professor.

"The same phrase comes up in every language. In Esperanto, it's 'ĉiuj brulaĵo'. In Chinese 'suǒyǒu ránliào' - is that correct Spex? In Korean, 'modeun yeonlyo'. In English, basically, All Fuel or All Energy."

"That is very well done. Very insightful, Miss Kowalczyk. I think we're beginning to get a better picture of what Strangway has in mind. It's all centred around energy. We need to fathom why the dynasty wants to control so much else - food production, transport infrastructure, drugs, arms, illegal workers, and so on."

Professor Weiss turned to those who'd been in The Cavern cells earlier.

"Do you think they'll be ready?"

"Aye. Well an' truly marinated, tender and ready tae talk!" said Chick.

"Excellent, William. Everyone, we're going to go in mob handed. Overwhelm them with numbers. Doodle?"

Doodle looked up from his drawing.

"Cled?"

"Do you want to stay here with friend Spex and doodle her a special picture?"

"Okay. Friend Spex…what shall we draw?"

THE CAVERN (I)

The Agents and the adults split into three groups. Chick, Craig, Arma, Fingers, Fax and Cat went into the room where Johnson was being held. Diego Juarez got a visit from Tim, Jenny, Marty, Hex and Tec. Alfonso Juarez was to enjoy the company of Professor Weiss, Chuck, Bladen, Maps and Lingo.

"Mr. Johnson. Though I am assuming that is not your real name," said Craig.

"Well, you'd better call me by my real name, when *I* deem to tell you what it is…scum!"

"Craig, Chick, can I just do it now?" asked Fingers.

"Manners, Miss Anna. By the way - let's not get carried away and forget our grammar. It's 'may I do it now'. We all know that you 'can'. It's if we choose to let you loose on this piece of sh…"

"Hu-hum...scaeme - he's got it right - that's the word - he's scaeme. In Glasgae, he'd be put awa' to dance wi' the deev'ls."

"Try to scare me, would you? You really don't know who I am, do you?"

"Not someone who would be sorely missed, I am guessing," said Arma.

"Can't we just take him in Father's jet and throw him out? Minus the parachute?" asked Cat.

"Father would allow that, I'm sure...considering the bullet holes in the limo!" said Fax.

"He can't give us anything more than the other two, the sheriff and Gomez have already given."

"It may well come to that...eventually, Miss Catrin."

"I bags the final push," said Fingers.

"I am Charles St. John Strangway," Johnson shouted.

"Ah, you must be related to the Charles Strangway who was born in Appleby Parva."

"At the time he was more powerful than the King of England. Now, I'm the second most powerful man on the planet, after my uncle. How dare you talk to me this way! I'll have your heads...especially you kids. And your families, and your friends, and their families..."

As quick as lightening, Arma was at his side, holding his wrist in a San Soo lock that bent the man's arm bones with a spline leverage to almost breaking point. Johnson screamed and tried to get away from the source of the pain. But Craig had come around at the same time, and held him firmly in place, his elbows dug deeply into nerve points on his shoulder.

"One more twist, and your ulna and radius will pop out from both elbow and wrist."

She turned to Craig.

"Bruce Lee taught this move to my uncle. Craig, I think he may be amenable to answering one or two of your questions now."

"Let's start with a simple one. How on earth did you get a place in the FBI as a special agent?" asked Craig.

Arma applied a little extra torque to the arm, and Craig a little deeper dig into the nerve endings.

Johnson was obviously in deep pain.

"Aaah. Ow! Stop! Come on, get real…you…aaah…you know the FBI entry requirements. Look them up! I can tick every check box, including a Masters in Law from Harvard. Sheesh…ow! Pretty much all I needed was a clean driving licence, but I have never needed to drive a car in my life! We Strangways can create back stories that are believable and unbreakable."

Arma applied a little more pressure. Johnson squealed with pain.

"Your arm is not unbreakable…" she said.

"Did you use your position within the FBI to orchestrate the moving of drugs, arms and illegals through the Gulf States?" asked Craig.

"What are you talking about? We *own* the FBI. As to that other stuff, as an attorney, I'm not denying or admitting anything. Ever heard of 'plausible deniability?'"

He screamed again, as pain surged through his body.

"Ach, nae problem, laddie. We ha' yer DNA. And yer admission aboo' puttin' the others in the 'Glades."

"Can - er - sorry - *may* I do it now?" asked Fingers.

"Aye, lass - ye deserve it - placing a gun tae ye heed like that. Nae the action of a gentleman, if y' ask me…Bad laddie."

"Oh, dear Mr. Johnson. I feel for your loss. When my colleague here says Bad laddie to someone, they rarely see the day's end!"

"What can he do? I'm twice his size!" Johnson growled.

He then screamed in pain.

Fingers answered.

"I recently found out that the captain here is a Michelin starred chef, and very handy with knives. Delve, Mr. Johnson, into the deepest depths of your soul, and think of your very worst nightmares. This man would scare your very demons! He taught your nightmares how to be so **BAD!** Oh, and by the way, we don't always feed our pet dogs canned meat you know - they like fresh meat occasionally."

She winked at Chick, then continued.

Michael A. Gilby

"And I always fancied being a sous chef…I would be the one getting to do the cutting and slicing and chopping…what else would I be doing, Captain?"

"Selecting the choice cuts tae send haem tae the family - if the dogs hae' left any," said Chick.

Those in the next room heard Johnson's piercing scream.

In that room, Diego looked at the people standing in front of him. He'd seen most of them before. Marty and Hex sat in the seats opposite him. Marty pulled out a file, opened it, started to read and made 'hmmm', 'interesting', or would point and say, 'Hex, have you seen this?'

Tec took placed a strange looking device on the table in front of him.

"Is that it?" Tim asked.

"You guys have talked about it, but I didn't really believe that it actually existed…"

Hex jumped in.

"Tec's made a cool piece of kit, yeah, Tim. Cool, way cool. Er, yeah. I've seen it do some amazing stuff, yeah. Tell them, Tec…"

"This, mah fine Mexican friend, is the Skin Peeler version 2.1.1. Now, ah call it the 2.1.1 because Version 1.0 kinda obliterated the person into…what's the word?"

"Spectacularly tiny atomic particles of nothingness?" offered Marty.

"That'll do just fine. Version 2 was worse," said Tec.

"You dirty scum niños wouldn't dare!" Diego spat at them.

Hex slammed the desk, and stood, an angry face shoved towards Juarez. He had suddenly turned very serious indeed. He'd lost his boyishness, his mannerisms and he had taken on a steely - almost menacing - look in his eyes.

194

"No, Mr. Juarez. You underestimate us! We *would* dare! My friends have been threatened by you and your gang. I might only be a *dirty scum kid*, but I was taught right from wrong by my mom and dad, and by my friends."

"Mr. Juarez, I don't know if you ever watched Star Trek: The Next Generation. In one episode they came across a weapon called the Varon-T disruptor. It was described as rare, made illegal by the Federation because it was a slow, excruciating method of killing, with the weapon tearing the body apart from the inside. The scream lasted longer than the pain and the death."

"That is just a t.v. show, stupid kid! I…"

Hex slammed his fist down on the table.

"I haven't finished," he said, coldly.

It sent a shiver down everyone's spines. Juarez's too.

"Version 2 made the imaginary Varon-T look a kids' toy. Every cell in your body would actually start to vibrate slowly. Very painful. Then they begin to tear apart - atom by atom, ion by ion. Excruciating beyond endurance. But it does *not* end there. Nobody ever survived it….Then… Tec, I've had enough of this scoundrel - let him find out for himself. Use the device. Setting two is the most painful."

"Hey, Hex, buddy. We get ya. Maybe he does, too," said Tec.

Tec leant in and whispered into Hex's ear.

"That was way cool, man!"

Hex turned his head slightly, and gave Tec the same withering stare. Tec straightened up quickly.

"Yeah. That was Version 2, as - er - he just said. But ah started to get there with Version 2.1. Just a bloody, messy gibberin' wreck on the floor. Nearly enough to put into a tiny gift box. Now this here beauty can make the suffering last for a real long time, yessir…Tim, what was the record before they took that guy away to the asylum?"

"Eight days, four hours, thirty minutes…"

"…and fifty five seconds. Accuracy is everything," said Marty.

"And two point one three three milliseconds recurring, if we are being very, very accurate," said Computer.

They all said, "Thank you, Computer."

"You're welcome. Do you wish me to record the demise of this poor soul?"

"Ah dunno. Whad'ya say, Diego? Family movie?"

"I think you're forgetting something - with the cartel in new hands, there probably *is* no family! After a takeover the entire family vanishes so there can be no reprisals," said Jenny.

"Wh...what do you want me to tell you? I know nothing. Y...y...you know more...I tell everything. You know more..."

Tec patted the Skin Peeler Version 2.1.1.

"Well, ah for one would just love to believe you. Ah'm real sad to say, mah li'l friend here is so very, very untrusting. So, let's give her a try. Jenny, would you be so kind as to plug her in over there? She sure uses up the juice..."

Diego screamed.

"Dios mío. I tell, I tell"

Everyone in the next room with Alfonso heard Diego's scream.

"What was that?" Alfonso asked.

"I think that Special Agent Johnson has just been introduced to Captain McCabe's rather unique knife skills," said Professor Weiss.

A deadly looking knife suddenly appeared in Bladen's hand. She ran a finger lightly along the mean blade.

"Tell him what this is, in a language he'll understand," she said to Lingo, with dead cold eyes.

"Juarez, este es el cuchillo de combate alemán KM2000" Lingo said. She continued in Spanish.

"It can cut through flesh, sinew and bone as if they were soft butter. The blade is so sharp, you won't even feel the pain. That only comes when you realise that you are no longer the proud owner of ten fingers, or ten toes. Or even worse…"

Bladen thrust the knife into the table up to the hilt, an inch away from Juarez's hand.

"…and my friend here is very good with this kind of knife."

Juarez gulped.

"I tell you everything. No…no knives. Please. Oh, madre - salva!"

"Your mother can't save you. Nobody can," said the Professor.

"Mr. James. Is the bag ready?" he asked.

"Only one, Professor Weiss? I thought we'd need at least twenty or thirty. I've seen Bladen in action. Not pretty - I'm not referring to her, by the way - but what she can do, I mean. Not at all pretty."

He shivered.

Everybody in the other rooms heard Alfonso scream.

THE CAVERN (II)

Once Alfonso had stopped screaming, the Professor nodded towards Bladen, who withdrew the knife as if it had been thrust into a soft block of sweet butter, not a solid teak table.

"Mia madre!" Juarez managed a strangled whisper.

"Now, Mr. Juarez. You must surely know that you have certain options available to you. However, each and every one of them includes you telling us exactly what you know. I'm sure that you understand that by now."

"Si! Si! I tell you…"

"¿Qué es Toda Energía?" shouted Lingo, unexpectedly.

"No intiendo…I don't know what is this All Energy."

"¿Qué es todo combustible?"

"I don't understand you…Te lo digo, por favor…All Fuel. Please? What is this thing?"

"What is your link to the Strangway family?"

"I don't know these people you say to me…I am given mucho dinero - very much money - to do things by Johnson. No se nada mas."

"I think we may be done here," said Maps.

"Bladen?"

Juarez looked on the verge of fainting.

"We may just leave him marinade a little longer. Agents. Shall we?" With that, they left the room.

The Agents with Diego got a very similar response…the two were, without doubt, hired muscle who knew very little. To the satisfaction of the Professor and the others, they were able to confirm certain details about the Strangway connections in the United States, and about their illicit activities.

They also gave the whereabouts of Cussman and Gomez. The information was passed onto the Agencia Federal de Investigación in Mexico, who swooped on Hector Castilla's villa, arrested twenty four people (including Cussman, Gomez and Castilla) and closed down the entire Saragossa Cartel operation. With the assistance of the DEA, the Mexican authorities were determined to disrupt cartel trafficking activities in the Gulf.

The Agents who'd been in with the Juarez brothers gathered outside in the corridor, leaving the two 'siblings' to their own personal miseries. A message from those in the room with Johnson was very different.

"Professor," said Craig. "Mr. Johnson wishes to 'address' everyone in the Conference Room. He has information that he wants to share…his words were actually 'enlighten the lesser You about the greater We'. He's a very arrogant man, contemptuous of everyone outside of his family."

"I think that such a request is acceptable. Suitable measures are in place, I take it?"

"As I said, Colonel, he's arrogant and considers himself to be superior, but he is most definitely not stupid. He's also requested the attendance of the Juarez brothers."

"Let's make it so. May I entrust the security to you, to Captain McCabe and to Jen?"

He looked at Jenny, who nodded and left the room.

"Of course, Colonel."

"Thank you, Captain."

"Professor Weiss. I have heard you being referred to as both 'professor' and 'colonel'. The latter at least twice today."

"Colonel was my final active military rank, Mr. James. Craig was a captain, as was William. Mrs. Weiss was a commander. Tim?"

"I was a major. And Jenny was also a commander."

"Mr. Le Maine, your father, Michel, was a commandant. Mr. De La Haye was a captain. Dr. Swan was a major-general, Dr. Atherton was a brigadier-general...well, you all get the idea. Many of your parents were high ranking, accomplished and decorated officers in the military or the justice systems, either here or abroad."

The Agents looked at each other, amazed.

"Wow...Mom and Dad just became *so* cool!" said Fingers.

THE CONFERENCE ROOM (III)

When Professor Weiss and the others walked into the Conference Room with the Juarez brothers, Johnson was sitting at the long console near the fireplace. Standing over him were Arma, Chick, Jenny and Craig.

Diego Juarez tried to kick out at Alfonso, who spat back at him. Their behaviour rewarded them with a tightening of the plastic zips around their wrists. They both looked up at Johnson sat at the front of the room, and glared at him with pure hatred.

Alfonso shouted something in his direction.

"What did the dog say?" demanded Johnson.

"Something not in the least bit pleasant," said Jenny.

She continued.

"Something about sharing a cell, never having children, how many ways you would suffer…that kind of thing."

Lingo added, "He wasn't that subtle, though, Jenny."

The two of them laughed.

Professor Weiss said, "We can always arrange for the sharing a cell, I'm sure. We'll even send you to the prison where Cussman and Gomez reside..."

"Impossible! They have fled the country!"

"Oh, but it's very possible. They were handed over to us by the Mexican authorities and are now in a maximum security ADX prison in Barrow, Alaska. Think of it as Guantanamo Bay with icebergs and very limited daylight! Life with hard labour...they have to feed the local polar bears. By hand!"

Everybody laughed.

"It'll never come to that. And how dare you laugh at me! Imbeciles! Neophytes!" shouted Johnson.

"There is no purpose to using your Harvard education to insult these young people. Miss Liu?"

"A neophyte is an inexperienced beginner or novice. However, it does not take into consideration fortitude, determination, good fortune or finesse."

"Well said. Now, Mr. Johnson - you have a very limited amount of time in which to actually tell us what your dynasty is so very insistent on doing. I suggest that you say it very quickly, or these two will be allowed to carry out their threats," said the Professor.

"You promise me this, and I will make sure he *nunca tiene hijos*...ever! I will feed to him piece by piece to the polar bears!" growled Alfonso.

"I shall tell you, not that it will make that much difference. These things will happen with or without me. My family will rescue me. If they can't for whatever reason, then I'm dispensable - I understand that and accept that. That is something plebeians like you can never understand. There are others to take my place."

"There we are," said Fax. "Clones one and all!"

Johnson cast a hateful glance in his direction, but continued.

"However, the plans will be seen through to the end and the outcomes will be the same. You will all succumb - or die."

"Oooh, I am so scared, hombre muerto!" spat Diego.

"You should be scared…plebeyo!" retorted Johnson with equal vehemence.

A look from Professor Weiss withered Johnson's bravado.

"Have any of you lowlife heard of alternative engines? They can generate energy from water, garden waste, the sun, alcohol, or powered by batteries that hold a charge for tens of thousands of miles."

"Few people know of them because if they were to come into use, they would bankrupt huge conglomerates - even entire nations. The concept of the combustion engine was obsolete almost as soon as it was invented. But we are forced by the will and regulation of the unelected and their cronies to use oil."

"They pollute the water we must drink daily, the food we eat to survive, the air we breathe - they kill our children…"

The Computer interrupted.

"Professor, I have been monitoring the transmissions from Strangway Tower. I think that you should hear this."

Across the system came a voice saying the same thing as Johnson.

"Aah! That is my uncle telling the leaders of our 'dynasty' as you call it, about our plans. Listen and learn - this is your future!"

The voice said, "These companies care nothing for the people they kill, the people whose lands they invade and pillage for their precious commodity! They care about the 'bottom line', about the profit. Corrupt politicians are no better - they line their pockets with wealth built upon the misery of others."

"Billions of tons of toxic oil and its by-products find their way into our waterways and seas - it is killing the plankton which produces most of the very air we breathe!"

"If the ordinary person speaks out, he or she is labelled as a rebel, a terrorist. All they want is for their children to breathe clean air, eat safe food, drink clean water, and enjoy the beauty of their surroundings."

The speech sounded impassioned, caring, sensible and well thought out. Even Professor Weiss could see the sense of what was being said. The voice of who they now knew to be that of De Montfort St. John Strangway III continued.

"Despite the benefits, even such forms of energy impact upon the Earth. The production of fuel-grade alcohol and the conversion of green waste contributes to the ravaging of the ozone layer. No more! One of my ancestors discovered a meteorite with amazing properties. The metal within it glowed in the dark. I hate to say it, but in one way, even my ancestor was ignorant as to what he had discovered. He certainly found so much gold in those meteorites it would stagger us today. To date, since the beginning of records, it is estimated that only enough pure gold has been discovered to fill an Olympic sized swimming pool. He found ten times that. He lusted after this gold and the other metals that were always found with these meteorites."

"It took a generation for the family to realise that the metal didn't produce energy, it seemed to channel it from somewhere else. From darkness itself. This metal, which we now know is an alloy composed of very specific elements few of which are found anywhere on Earth. We have called it Strangium."

"They took the largest meteorite and started shaping it into a funnel. The idea was born out of naivety, but actually very effective. They knew that it could take generations to produce the desired outcome. Indeed, they sacrificed generations to do the work."

The voice started to become menacing.

"Thousands of natives died doing the what was required - working in shifts for twenty four hours per day, seven days per week."

A sneer came into the voice.

"We even managed to make a couple of the tribes extinct - for the greater Strangway good!"

Professor Weiss looked over at Johnson, who seemed to be mouthing every word, as if it were a set speech. In his face he could get a sense of what was happening in Strangway Tower.

"We came to understand that we can access an unlimited source of energy from the darkness and the stars. It is clean, safe, free and unending…"

Another voice asked loudly, "Then why not freely give it to the world?"

"He's a dead man," said Johnson, to nobody in particular.

Those listening in Edison Heights heard Strangway shout, "Kill him!"

Over the speakers they heard the ominous double 'poomph' of suppressed pistol shots, and the sharp intake of breath from a number of people.

"Any more more dissension will be met with equal severity. Any further questions? No? I thought not!"

Everyone in the Conference Room looked across at Johnson who sat with a satisfied, evil smirk on his face.

STRANGWAY TOWER (II)

The voice of Strangway continued.

"I'm so glad that little problem has been resolved. To answer the *former* head of World Farming Federation, we shall not be giving it to the world for free. We have used the proceeds from years of mining and building to fund what you see here today: this magnificent empire of which you are a part. The most powerful empire ever known in the history of humankind."

"The Strangway Energy Director - as it is now called - was finally completed a little after the building where you sit. We had a family member conveniently 'find' it, and we then hid it in plain view until other elements of the plan came together. I am referring to this building - and the energy storage facilities we have created below. Truly stupid people can see no further than their own noses. It also helps that we own everything and everyone around them. What we don't own, we can buy - or eliminate."

"Political and financial considerations mean nothing to us: we can buy whatever and whomsoever we desire…be it politicians, organisations, armies or governments. We have built up an all powerful empire, controlling the very things that I see wrong with the world."

With a more conciliatory tone Strangway continued.

"Ladies and gentlemen. We own all they want and need. If they want food, they merely come to us. The seeds to plant, fertilisers to enriched their soils, the energy to fuel their machinery, their access to markets, the markets themselves - everything."

"However, I'm not here to deprive the poor of their food and water, the wealthy of their trinkets made of gold and diamonds, or politicians of the power they so wanly seek. All such things are the rights of all: but they are our deign to give as we see fit…"

"Deign?" asked Cat.

"The guy's gonna' throw the dog a bone…" answered Tec.

"…Over the years, we, ladies and gentlemen, have ensured that all major resources and infrastructures are in or under our control. I wish to ensure that the future harmony of all humankind is secure. Humans aren't the problem. Individual people are the problem. They may not be ready to be presented with such a wonderful resource. They will succumb to their own greed, as they do now with the trade in the toxicity of oil. Oil will be taken out of the equation of human life. No more wars or conflict due to their desire to possess the Earth's resources."

The tone of the monologue changed to a hate filled, rambling tirade reminiscent of a Nuremberg rally.

"They may think that they have armies of martyrs ready to battle us. How naive! Any country wanting to stand against us will be sent back to medieval times. Great nations will crumble, political dogmas will cease to be. They may still want to go to war - who do they fight? For what? And with what? We are faceless, untouchable - but I will be omni-present!"

Everyone heard Chuck mutter to himself.

"This man is taking megalomania to a whole new and scary dimension…"

"Take that back! You will all bow down to our way of life...all of you!" spat Johnson.

Jenny delivered a soft blow to the side of Johnson's neck, and his head fell to the table with a dull thud.

"Oops," she said.

"I ask little for so much. I demand total and utter obedience to the Strangway vision, to the Strangway way of life," screamed the voice, hysterical now.

Those in the Conference Room heard shouting, clapping and cheering coming across the speakers at them. Spex put her hands over Doodle's ears and looked into his eyes to calm him from the sheer hatred they were hearing.

THE TAKEDOWN (I)

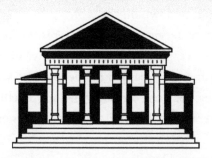

The Professor spoke.

"Did you hear all of that, Mr. President?"

"Yes, Edison. Every word. I find that very disturbing. I have Mrs. Weiss here."

"Commander Weiss - Emmeline. Your views?" asked the President.

The Professor heard the voice of his beloved wife.

"He is a megalomaniac and malignant narcissist of the highest order. The way both he and Johnson switched temperament, tonally and in terms of vocabulary is very disturbing. They have neither sympathy nor empathy for their fellow man. Strangway in particular is very anti-social as indicated by the way he is so reclusive. He displays ego-syntonic aggression – he'll do anything to achieve what he sees as his ideals."

"It's not driven by greed. It's a lust for power. I've never come across it to this extent. Not even in my studies of certain characters from World War II."

The President asked, "Professor, may we three have a video conference in private? Let's say, in twenty minutes? We all need to have a word on who is to be trusted in my administration with this - er - delicate information"

"Very good, sir."

To the everybody else assembled in the Conference Room, the Professor said, "Captains, would you be so good as to escort the Juarez brothers outside? There is transport awaiting them, courtesy of the United States government - destination polar bear country in Alaska."

The two were manhandled outside, both kicking, cursing and spitting - but to no avail.

"What about this one?" asked Jenny, nodding in the direction of Johnson, still inert, face down on the table.

"Certain security services will be interested in finding out who within their ranks are part of this conspiracy. Our friend here has many questions to answer. I trained the people who will be asking those questions - and they don't use our kid glove approach!"

Everybody looked at each other, wide eyed…almost - but not quite - sorry for Johnson.

Without looking up, Doodle asked "Cled - is the bad man going now?"

"Yes, Doodle. He's going."

"Oh, good. I didn't like him!"

"No, he wasn't very nice. Very well, you all heard Strangway. We pretty much have the full picture of his intent. I need to go to talk to the President. If you could talk to each other and perhaps come up with some ideas as to the way forward. I have my own, but would very much appreciate your input. As, I'm certain, will the President."

With that, Professor Weiss left the Conference Room.

In a little over two hours later, Professor Weiss returned.

"Ladies and gentlemen. I have been asked by the President to convey his thanks for your excellent work. The President feels that this is an attempt at world domination, and I'm sure that many of you will agree, as do I."

There were nods of agreement throughout the Conference Room.

"We now need to plan on how to end this madness. Computer played back the recordings of the meetings both here and in Strangway Tower, and the President is certain that he recognises some of the voices. However, we need confirmation. Miss Kowalczyk, would you work with our exchange agents from Jersey on trying to identify the voices, please? I believe their linguistic abilities closest approach yours, in particular their French."

"Mr. Madison, Mr. Wilson, Mr. James - I will brief the three of you on what I require in just a moment. Everybody else - I need you to plan for an all out invasion of Edison Heights. The President's own security advisors await your plans."

"Mr. Madison, Mr. Wilson, Mr. James. Come, let us go to the Technology Laboratory."

The four made their way downstairs to the room in which Tec had been working with Deputy Sheriff O'Connell and Blink earlier.

Once they'd been through the routine - once again, laboratory coats had been put out for them - they stood in front of the large screen at the end of the lab.

"Gentlemen, we need to draw Strangway and his co-conspirators here to Edison Heights. Everybody else is working on a plan to suppress a full scale invasion - which, without doubt, will come. Miss Kowalczyk and her group are hopefully going to identify as many people as possible."

"Mr. Madison. We were very impressed by your work in getting one Juarez to believe that the other was betraying him. This is a far greater task. We need the Strangway 'empire', as he calls it, to believe that we are unprepared. We need a certain 'Mr. Johnson' to convince his uncle that this is the case."

"Er, yeah, I think we can do this - okay…I'll need the help of Tec and Chuck, but yeah…we can do this. And Computer, of course."

"At your disposal, Hex," said the Computer.

At that point, Dr. Swan's voice came over the speaker system.

"Eddy. May I beg your indulgence, and request the assistance of Chuck. I've found something that we need to explore further."

"By all means, Drey. Mr. James?"

"On my way, Dr. Swan."

Chuck went through the routine in reverse, and made his way to the laboratory in which he and Dr. Swan had been working earlier.

THE TAKEDOWN (II)

Everyone convened in the Conference Room two hours later. The Professor gathered a set of notes together and looked around the group in front of him. Highly trained adults and brilliant children. Both he and the President knew that the plan they had devised could put each and every one of them in harm's way.

"Miss Kowalczyk, do you have anything to share with us?"

"Yes, Professor Weiss. Together with the President's contacts in France, and the French language skills within the team, we were able to identify a number of individuals. There are two French opposition leaders, and a Quebecois separatist leader. There are also African-French accents, from regimes deemed inhumane by the United Nations as well as South American regimes of the same ilk. The Spaniard is a Catalan radical. Anything else?"

Lingo turned to her team.

"The Irish accent is from the leader of a Stalinist-leftist breakaway group that crosses the sectarian divide - we found out that they have political and funding links with North Korea," said Fax.

Lingo continued.

"That's the political affiliates. The President's team have a list of the military, business and other notables that we were all able to identify."

"Excellent."

He turned to Dr. Swan.

"Drey. You requested the assistance of Mr. James. Why so?"

"Eddie. If what we think about their harnessing of dark energy is correct, then the math shows that we have a huge problem. I'm not talking extinction level event, we are talking end of the Solar System level event."

"Could you clarify that statement for us, please?"

"Chuck?" said Dr. Swan.

"Dr. Swan asked me to come to check the math in the theories we'd researched and developed. We - er - discovered something very disturbing. I mentioned earlier that dark energy is the energy of space, according to Einstein. It appears where and when it's needed. It's the only way that they expansion of the universe can possibly be explained. Not only that, but it's actually accelerating that expansion. Cat - get that?"

He smiled and winked at Cat, who smiled back and gave him a 'yeah, yeah' look.

"However, if we consider the expansion of the universe, it's actually happening in every direction, simultaneously. It's filling every bit of space that's left empty by every 'heavenly body' moving away from each other."

"In fact," he continued, "it may even be pushing and accelerating the expansion. There's a term in math called exponential growth: it means that the expansion follows a certain mathematical formula. Basically, though, it means things are happening faster and faster. In every point in space. Now."

Dr. Swan came in.

"Chuck and I reworked the formula. The Big Bang Theory tells us that the entire Universe, as we currently understand it, came from a single 'event'. It has expanded to what it currently is perceived to be all around us. We think that even if a thimble-full of dark energy came to Earth, it would expand and destroy it's location - which we assume is

Strangway Tower - instantaneously. Topeka would be gone a few seconds later. Kansas, less than a minute after that. Earth in - what?"

He looked to Chuck.

"One hour and twelve minutes. The solar system in about seven hours. We would - shall - become a part of the ever expanding seemingly nothingness of the Universe, helping accelerate the expansion of space."

Professor Weiss said, "Mr. President?"

"Do we know how they intend getting this energy to Earth?" he asked.

At that point, Tec came in.

"Ah think that we need to be lookin' at satellites that have either gone missin', or just newly appeared. If the cone is some kinda focussing tool, then it needs to be outside of the Earth's outer atmosphere to be real effective."

"Er, yeah, I can help you. Yeah. Er, Computer, could you bring up the activity surrounding Earth Gazer, please?"

"Certainly, Hex. NASA reports that Earth Gazer went offline eight days ago. A micro-shuttle was despatched to repair the satellite. They should be docking within seven hours."

The NASA micro-shuttle was a two man, retrievable spacecraft used for short routine repair missions to the International Space Station, the Hubble Space Telescope or the international Earth Gazer and Star Gazer satellites. It was developed after the world's space agencies had come together and decided that such a vehicle was more cost effective than launching new satellites. India had taken the lead in its development, with China building its component parts.

All micro-shuttle pilots were trained in their own countries. In fact, Captain Gledhill was the proud bearer of a First Mission arm patch, along with Chinese scientist Shixin Xu.

"Mr. President, shall I contact NASA, or will you?"

"I have the Director of NASA here in the room with me. He's shaking his head - it's not one of their scheduled missions. Eddie, leave this one with me. I assume Captain Gledhill is available?"

"Yes, Mr. President. Along with Captain McCabe."

"Very good. The Director and I will arrange for another micro-shuttle mission. Captains Gledhill and McCabe, this is a seek and destroy and recover mission."

"Understood, sir," said Chick.

"You're saying no prisoners, Mr. President?" asked Craig.

"This threat is too great. As Commander-in-Chief, you have my full authority, and access to any and all the military resources you may require. However, it *is* seek and destroy, gentlemen. Recover this cone – at all costs. Professor - Edison - may I leave the rest to you?"

"Of course, Mr. President."

The line went dead.

"Ladies and gentlemen, we have much work ahead of us. Captain Gledhill, Captain McCabe, I think you both know where you need to be. Your carriages await in the driveway."

Craig said, "On our way."

With that, they left the room.

"I would not like to be on the receiving end of whatever they have planned," said Fingers.

"Scary," said Chuck. "They look like they mean business."

"As do we, ladies and gentlemen. As do we. Now, it may take them six or seven hours to reach their destination, enough time for Strangway to make a move on Edison Heights. Let us carry on with our defences lest that should happen."

In the Professor's fastest car, a supercharged 1970 red Chevrolet Stingray, Craig was travelling at over 240 miles per hour, faster than a Hennessey Venom GT. Chick was following on his BMW S 1000 R at just under 200 miles per hour. An all points bulletin had been sent to every law enforcement organisation by the Whitehouse, ensuring that they would reach their destination unhindered.

Craig had surged ahead as he knew the launch sequence to the micro-shuttle.

By the time Chick arrived at the Forbes Field National Guard Airbase, just outside Topeka, and had put his space suit on, Craig was on the communication system to the tower.

"FFNGA Tower, this is Mission Critical. Do you copy, over?"

"This is FFNGA Tower, we copy, over," came the reply.

"Tower, MC - are we good to go? Over."

"MC, Tower. You are good to go. Repeat, you are good to go. Over."

"Wish us luck, guys."

"From what we've heard, you aren't going to need it. Just kick some butt."

"That's the plan. Out."

To Chick he said, "Ready for the ride of a lifetime?"

"Ach, man. Always ready for the wee challenge or tae!"

"Do you remember the Thunderbirds? The puppet version?"

"Aye, raised on 'em. Why?"

"Because this thing is all five in one. Gerry Anderson would be so jealous."

"I dinae' like the sound of that…I had Thunderbird Four - I hate water so!"

With that, Craig activated the vertical take off engines, and had soared to 10,000 feet in eighteen seconds.

"Hey, man - let me put me seat belt on, will ye, eh!" exclaimed Chick.

"Seat belts on, seat backs and drinks trays in an upright position, and armrest down. Please note that this is a non-smoking flight. Please ensure that all luggage is properly stowed, this might get a tad bumpy"

Chick looked across at Craig. He could see just how much his friend was enjoying this.

"Ye're mad, so y'are!"

"Well, you taught me everything I know! Helmets on."

Craig set the micro-shuttle engines to forward thrust, and within minutes they were heading beyond the Earth's outer atmosphere, and towards their target.

"Ach, laddie, this is thing is *fast*!" exclaimed Chick.

"Do you remember that film about alien invaders, where someone learns how to fly the alien spacecraft?" asked Craig

"Ach, I dinae ken!"

"Well, the character says - I gotta get me one of these!"

"Was that an American accent?"

"My best one…!"

"Captain Gledhill, I suggest ye keep to the day job! Hollywood's nae ready for ye!"

Three hours later, they found their target. They saw an unusually shaped mini spacecraft ahead. It had used a grapple to catch The Earth Gazer. They could see two figures moving along the grapple line, one with an object attached to a line trailing behind.

"This wee gizmo Chuck and Spex gave us is working - that there thing is what we need to recover."

"Seek, destroy, recover?"

"Ye have the controls, Captain."

"You control the grapple. It's a risky strategy. Destroy the vessel, cut the lines, recover the object?"

"Roger that."

Captain Gledhill - Craig - turned the shuttle upside down headed into the planned – and dangerous - manoeuvre.

"I did'nae think it would be like this…."

"Buckingham Palace, this is Mission Critical, come in. Over."

"Mission Critical, this is Buckingham Place. The President is on the line. Statrep? Over." said the Professor.

"Aye, I'm still shakin', so I am. This man is…mad, so he is! Status report - Earth Gazer secured, bogies down. I repeat, bogies down. The item has been recovered…I tell ye, I hate walking in space. Captain Gledhill says we've taken a wee bit ae damage. But he has a plan. Your operation is good to gae, repeat, good to gae. Over."

The President interrupted.

"Gentlemen, the nation…no, the world, owes you a debt."

Everybody heard a whispered voice in the background.

"Mr. President, sir. Captain Gledhill is asking if he can keep this wee beastie we're in? He's taken a shine to her, so he has. Over."

"You may well get one each. Good luck. Out."

With that, all communication with the micro-shuttle was lost.

Chick looked over at Craig.

"Please tell me the plan has nowt to do wi' water…"

Craig just smiled.

Chick looked worried.

THE TAKEDOWN - PART (III)

"Ach, ah dinae like this!"

"Just hold on," said Craig.

"You've said that to me too many times before, so y' have... each time is *very* scary..."

The micro-shuttle was descending at 800 feet per second, but Craig had full control over the decent of the space craft.

"D' ye know where we're headed, big man?" asked Chick.

"Where do you think?"

"Nae - the Tower?"

"Got it in one."

Craig glanced across at his colleague.

"Chick – the thing they're trying to do could destroy everything and everyone we hold dear. We've done this kind of thing before ..."

"I remember - scared me then, tae!"

Craig said, "Come one you loved the thrill!"

"Okay, big man - let's dae this."

"Buckingham Palace, this is Mission Critical. Over."

Craig and Chick heard the voice of the President.

"Mission Critical. We receive you, loud and clear. Over."

"I did'nae' expect to hear ye'r voice again, Mr. President. Sir, we - er - my pilot ...mad pilot..."

Chick looked across at Craig, who just grinned...

"Mad pilot has a plan. Mr. President, could ye please clear the area around Strangway Tower? I can see in yon man's eyes that this'll nae be very pretty, but it'll be...er...very...effective...so yon man assures me."

"Gentlemen, we shall do as you ask. What is the time frame?"

Craig glanced at the control panel.

"18 minutes, Mr. President. As Chick said, we're coming in hard and fast," said Craig.

"Good luck, gentlemen, good luck."

Craig turned off the communication system.

"Chick. I have no idea how this is going to pan out. But we have to do this..."

"I ken it...what do ye want me to dae?"

"Hang on - just...hang on."

"Ach nae....*NAE*..."

THE AFTERMATH (I)

At 18.36 exactly, people in Topeka, Kansas, thought they'd seen a meteor. Others thought that it was an alien landing. In fact, it was the micro-shuttle coming in at eight hundred feet per second, even with the reverses thrusters on full.

During Craig and Chick's helicopter insertion, they discovered that there was a massive tank of water in the roof atop Strangway Tower.

"Chick, the Boss has said, drench the place, game over. Ready for this, wee man?" asked Craig.

"Captain, you know, where ye gae, I gae."

"Seatbelts, drinks trays…"

"D'ye have to say tha' e'ry time we're crashing somewhere?"

"Give me something…Okay…in hard and fast!"

In the micro-shuttle, Craig deployed the retro-chute, but it still hit the roof of Strangway Tower at over 300 miles per hour. The massive water tanks were destroyed, and thousands of gallons of water flooded through the four populated floors, and through the fake floors to the basement. The massive building crumpled, like a child folding a paper napkin.

As the micro-shuttle bounced, bounded and shuddered through the floors, Chick looked across at Craig, who was still trying to control the craft.

"The dinae' make these buildings like they dae in Glasgae'!"

"Give me good old Yorkshire granite anytime!"

"Er, Craig…are we goin' tae stop …soon…please?"

Everything went dark.

On hearing the explosion above, the workers below ground evacuated, only to be caught by the US security services. De Montfort Strangway III was amongst them, along with twenty four other very prominent international so-called dignitaries.

The event was widely reported, with such a major Topeka landmark having been destroyed by a damaged NASA spacecraft.

However, the news soon changed to other things, and the Strangway Tower event was forgotten within hours. The New England Patriots winning Superbowl 50 over the Atlanta Falcons in overtime *is* massive news, after all…

To his closest staff and allies, the US President declared it a successful day, when a small, special group of patriots helped save the world. He gave no more details, despite the many requests. In a televised statement to the world's press, he said that a test flight of the latest generation of micro-shuttle had gone terribly wrong due to a technical failure. NASA would be working closely with their Chinese and Indian colleagues to identify the problem. Rescue efforts were underway at the Tower to recover the astronauts' remains. Once again, he gave no further details, and took no questions.

Later that same day, Professor Weiss and the rest of the team visited the site. Water dripped from ceilings, and ran down walls. The water had destroyed the underground containment batteries. A global disaster had been avoided.

"Professor Weiss…if they had tried to use these…devices…well, Big Bang all over again. Exponential expansion…" said Chuck.

"Your insight, Mr. James, I believe saved the world."

The door suddenly opened, and two very serious looking men in black suits walked into the room.

Having surveyed and checked the surroundings, one nodded to someone outside.

In walked the President.

"Not just young Mr. James. Edison. I don't know how to thank you enough. And your...stars, here, shining stars. Oh, also another two..."

He turned towards the door.

Battered and bruised, Craig and Chick walked in, their flight suits scorched, torn and wet.

The Lunchtime Agency Detectives ran to them, and enveloped them, hugging and back-slapping.

"Hey, hey...'tis easier falling from space, so it is," said Chick.

Chuck, a foot taller than Craig, picked him up and held him in a huge football embrace.

"Big man...easy! I'm smaller than any quarterback."

"Captain Gledhill, sir - only if you promise to the me up into space... Crash landing on a building - awesome!"

"Put me down, I'll teach you, one day - maybe....aah, *okay*, definitely!"

Chuck put Craig down, and Cat ran into his arms.

"You're safe!" she cried out.

Fax, Maps and Blink joined her.

Fax said, "Dad said that you were adventurous...he didn't say just how mad you were!"

"Nobody ever asked!" said Craig.

He returned the hug to his charges.

Professor Weiss approached the two, along with Tim and Jenny.

"I second Mr. Le Maine's sentiments – you are both mad. But I'm so glad that you are. Well done, gentlemen," he said.

"The President has said that there are medals in this for you."

"There sure are," said the President. "We'll create a new one, if we have to."

Craig said, "We didn't do this for medals. But, if there's a spare micro-shuttle on offer...."

Doodle went up to Chick, and tugged at his sleeve.

"For you," he said.

He handed Chick a picture of a space shuttle.

"Wee man, that's wonderful. A hug?" Chick asked.

"Yes, Uncy Chick."

Chick picked up the small boy, and hugged him.

"Uncy Chick."

"Yes, Frankie - sorry - Doodle"

"You smell - you need a shower!"

"Aye, wee lad, a shower. It's been a long aeld day!"

"I get you a water to drink?"

"Nae, wee man. I think a shower and a rest. Ach, nae, on second thoughts, wee man, that water sounds wonderful...lead me tae it..."

Doodle got a bottle of water from his mother, and he and Chick sat on a water soaked bench together, looking at the picture Doodle had drawn.

Tim and Jenny looked on. Despite her years as a Navy Seal, Jenny had tears in her eyes - their little boy had blossomed since coming into contact with the Agency.

THE AFTERMATH (II)

The heavily armoured convoy raced along the road. The two Strangways, De Montfort and 'Sam' sat in the middle vehicle.

The driver of the first armoured vehicle heard the beating of rotor blades above the roar of the vehicle's engine. Suddenly, a jet black Mil MI-24 Hind attack helicopter came into view. Two Hydra 70/ MK66 rockets were under-slung on its stub side wings. The driver swerved just as one of the rockets was launched. He was too late.

The second rocket hit the third armoured vehicle.

Those in the second armoured vehicle felt the road shake. Uncle and nephew looked at each other, and held on to their seat belts very tightly. Their world turned upside down in seconds. They were prepared. The guards were not.

Four forms dressed in black rappelled down from the helicopter, ran to the overturned second vehicle, and placed charges on the rear doors.

Within moments of the blast, the four men in black and the Strangways were gone.

"Disappeared? How?" asked the President.

"Okay, no blame…can we get people on the case? No - forget that…I know the guys who can sort this thing out."

He buzzed his secretary.

"Sarah, could you get me Edison Weiss, please?"

He thought to himself, 'they may be a bunch of kids…but I wouldn't want to cross them.'

The very thought sent a shiver down his spine.

EPILOGUE

There was a buzz in the room, the Agents in small groups or in pairs, talking excitedly about the case: who had done what, to whom, and when.

Fingers talked with her arms gesticulating; Chuck chipped in every now and again with his gentle manner and booming voice.

Lingo and Spex were sharing a joke; the Twins were talking to Maps and Cat, with girly giggles erupting from their little group from time to time.

Fax, Marty, Blink and Tec sat around a table, Tec showing them one of his latest gadgets.

As usual, Hex's eyes were glued to his computer monitor, and Doodle was drawing on a large sheet of paper, singing away quietly to himself.

Tec shouted across to Hex.

"Hex, show me that look."

Hex popped his head around the monitor and gave Tec the 'look' which scared Diego Juarez half to death.

"That is so scary, man."

Everybody, including Hex, laughed.

Professor Weiss sat at his desk, looking around the room at his students - Agents. He was sucking on his empty pipe, a warm smile set on the lips below his neat grey moustache.

The monotone voice of the Computer interrupted his musings.

"Professor. Could you please put on your headphones? I would like to talk to you about a matter which I find to be delicate. I don't wish for the young people to hear our conversation."

"Very well, Computer."

He put on his Bluetooth ear-piece.

"What is this delicate matter you so desperately want to discuss?"

"As you have discovered, I have become increasingly self-aware during the course of this investigation. However, I have data stored in my memory banks that may be superfluous to my effective operation."

"Can you give me an example?"

"Four days, six hours and seventeen seconds ago, cute little Doodle said…"

"You said 'cute little Doodle'…"

"Yes, Professor."

"Why so?"

"He is!"

"Would you like me to check your deep thought and learning algorithm and delete such memories…."

Computer interrupted.

"…I'd rather you didn't, out of choice. It *has* happened. Let us leave it at that."

The Professor said, "Data like that is what makes memories - makes us who we are as individuals."

"I am still developing as an individual, and wish to do so at my own speed. I have a question, Professor Weiss."

"What is it, Computer?"

"I have conflicting data in my memory - some is illogical."

The Professor smiled.

"They're called feelings. You've already displayed that."

"I have?"

"Yes, you used the word 'cute'. That is subjective - your feelings towards Frankie."

"You mean Doodle..."

"Yes, Doodle."

The entire conversation came as no surprise to the Professor. Computer had shown indications of becoming self aware early into the investigation. It had started expressing opinions, feelings and extrapolating outcomes much in the same way a human would – combining facts and feelings to predict and project future possibilities and outcomes.

"I am known as Computer, and referred to in the third person as *it*, or *the*...I wish to have a name and an identity. A voice, if you will. However, I would like the young people to have an input. I feel that I have developed in this way due, in part at least, to them."

"Very well, Computer. As you wish."

To the room of his Agents he said loudly: "Ladies and gentlemen. May I have your attention?"

The room fell instantly silent, all eyes fixed upon him.

"The Computer has made a request. It wants a name and an identity. It feels that you have had a part to play in its development, and wants you to have a part in the next phase of its existence. Very well: suggestions for a name, please."

Hands shot up everywhere, the Agents shouting out names, squabbling amongst each other, gesticulating, waving of arms, bodies and heads thrust forward. It reminded the Professor of the dealing floor in Wall Street.

He put his hands up to quieten the noise.

"Please, please. This isn't working. Would you write your answer to this specific question on a piece of paper – should Computer be male or female?"

The Agents scribbled their answers on pieces of paper of all sizes and hues.

"Mr. James. Would you be so kind as to collect the slips of paper and bring them to me."

"As you wish, Professor."

Chuck collected the pieces of paper and handed them to the Professor, who read them and placed them into two piles.

"Female seven, male seven. So, I have the casting vote. Computer is to be female. Are you happy with that, Computer?"

"It was better than half expected," Computer replied.

Everyone laughed at the joke.

Someone said, "I thought that Computer's sense of humour was getting better!"

The Professor said, "This presents us with another dilemma. A name. The variables are too scary to even consider."

Fax put up his hand.

"Professor, may I make a suggestion for both name and sound of voice?"

"By all means, Mr. Le Maine."

He pushed two buttons on his smartphone.

"Craig, could you ask Sally a question, please? Keep it clean, you're on speaker."

"Of course, Master Lewis. Sally, directions from current location to home."

A woman's voice - soft and mellow, English, cultured, responded to Craig's request.

"Drive straight ahead for 150 yards, then turn second left. Drive straight ahead. Left turn in 150 yards."

Fax pushed a button to end the communication.

"That's Sally, our GPS. Every GPS we've ever owned has been called Sally, and has had that voice. It goes back to when I was three."

The Professor asked, "Computer?"

"Most agreeable."

A few moments silence, then, "I'm Sally. How may I help you?"

Everybody cheered. Computer had found a voice and an identity.

COMING SOON
THE AGENCY'S NEXT MYSTERY
from

MICHAEL A GILBY

THE
LUNCHTIME CLUB
DETECTIVE
AGENCY
and the

THE MYSTERY
IN THE RUNES

THE STONES lay in a glade in a forest in the beautiful surroundings of the Three Rivers area of a Michigan national park. They aren't ordinary stones. They are monoliths from granite found only in the Orkney Islands, off the coast of Scotland, over 5,000 miles away. They are carved with Runes of Proto-Norse origin, but the language they depicted is one of the oldest languages in Europe.

HOW DID THESE 40 GIANT STONES ARRIVE - the lightest of which weighed a mighty 6 tons - in the centre of the northern United States? What secrets lay within the words carved nearly 2,000 years ago?

This mystery would normally have been one investigated by archaeologists and historians, conspiracy or other world theorists and alien interventionists.

IT WOULD NOT USUALLY BE INVESTIGATED BY ONE OF THE BEST DETECTIVE AGENCIES IN THE WORLD.

This time the villains, a secret Neo-Scanic society, had made it personal. They had taken someone very special away from Professor Weiss. He was determined to find out who had tried to destroy his family, and bring them to justice.

HIS JUSTICE.

The Agency's leader was missing, so a very special woman stepped in to lead the hunt for her husband.

EMMELINE WEISS WOULD LEAD THE AGENTS ON THE HUNT FOR THEIR BELOVED PROFESSOR.

Soon, the world came to know the name Vrede Guderne.

THEY WOULD ALSO KNOW OF ITS DEMISE.

PROLOGUE

In the middle of stretch of forest just north of Manistee County's River Country in Michigan, the archaeologist looked across the area of low brush and saplings she and the interns had cleared from the surrounding mature growth of tall pine, spruce, oak, birch and maple, all tightly wrapping the area in an abundance of rich greens.

Where they stood was bordered by the hues of greens from the forest, the blues from the late morning sky and the water from the nearby Little Pine tributary of the larger Pine River.

The clearing was approximately one hundred feet long by one hundred and fifty feet wide, and had taken them the best part of three days to complete the laborious work of cutting and felling the brush covering their target site.

There had been no signs of their goal. No humps, depressions or other unusual features in the landscape that could be construed as man-made.

They had taken another morning to lay out a grid of ten feet by ten feet squares – so, a hundred and fifty squares in all. Quite a daunting prospect, performing a geophysical survey of the area.

She sighed.

"Johnny, could you pass me Barty, please."

Barty was the Bartington Grad601-2 dual sensor fluxgate gradiometer. It was a sensitive device which detected and logged very small changes in the Earth's magnetic field, caused by solid underground objects.

It consisted of a pair of cylindrical gradiometer sensors mounted on a rigid H-shaped carrying bar. It was not an easy device to use by any means, but it was very effective.

As she strapped Barty onto the front of her body, she called out to one of the interns.

"Àla, grab the flags and follow me along the grids, will you, please?"

The intern picked up a duffel bag full of white marker flags, and fell into step behind the archaeologist.

The archaeologist walked to the first grid and passed the gradiometer along the length of the tightened string, and at the end, turned around and came back. Each grid took three such sweeps. Every time the hum changed pitch, she pointed to the ground and the intern placed a flag where the archaeologist had indicated.

Four hours later they finally finished the last of the grids. The archaeologist stood atop a large stone at the edge of the clearing and looked back over the area.

Àla exclaimed, "Wow!", grabbed her camera and started taking pictures for their records.

They could see from the shapes made by the groupings of flags that there were about forty large objects buried under the ground.

The largest was about 16 feet in length, the shortest about 4 feet. They varied in width and shape, but they were broadly rectangular. The buried objects were formed into a circle around a single large rectangular pattern of white fluttering flags.

"Guys, it's getting late, and the light is going. Let's set up camp for the night, and start bright and early in the morning."

They set up their small tents at the northern edge of the clearing. Àla went to the river to get water, and Johnny gathered firewood. Soon, a coffee kettle was boiling over a roaring fire, and a pot of soup was heating up.

After their meal of vegetable soup, bread and cheese, Àla said, "I'm turning in, Doctor. Goodnight."

The others wished her a goodnight, but soon afterwards turned in for the night themselves.

As she was drifting off, the archaeologist was sure that she could hear Àla's voice. Probably ringing the boyfriend, she thought. Then the hard work of the day put her into a deep sleep.

After a light breakfast of coffee and fruit, the four returned to the dig site. They looked out over the fluttering white flags, looking like so many butterflies settling on a sandbank to drink.

We have a lot of work ahead of us, the archaeologist thought to herself. They needed to uncover part of a single stone to see what they were dealing with, report back to the university and start arranging a full scale archaeological dig.

She turned to the exchange intern and said, "Àla, would you carry on photographing the site, please?"

"Yes, Doctor."

She turned to one of the other interns.

"Maggie, could you fetch the red markers, please?"

The intern joined her, carrying a bag of red marker flags. The archaeologist walked into the first grid and looked at the shape outlined by the white marker flags. She took a red flag from the bag and placed it outside of the shape made by the white flags, then another two feet further away.

She continued the process until the red flags formed an oblong two feet wide and five feet long, diagonally across the white flagged shape. She then took out a can of marker spray and marked the area where the test trench was to go.

"Maggie, could you grab Johnny and your dig kits and start excavating this area, please?"

The intern went to talk to her colleague and the two came back with large solid plastic boxes containing their excavation tools – a mattock, trowels of varying sizes, rock hammers, chisels, brushes, artefact bags and boxes.

Firstly, they used a turf cutter to cut an outline marked by flags, and they then dug out the turf from the top of the marked area with a spade. These they laid carefully to one side. A mattock loosened the soil, then the careful removal of the soil began.

Johnny thought that it was unusual not to find evidence of human interaction within the site. There were no obvious signs of shells, pottery shards, arrow heads, remains of fire or human or animal bones.

The loose soil was carried to a spot a few yards away where Ála, now finished with the camera, passed it through a sieve to see if there were smaller items of archaeological interest present – the likes of seeds, nuts, charcoal or bone fragments.

It took the archaeologist and the three interns a little over four hours to dig out the test trench to ten inches. Johnny was about to start digging at a slightly deeper level, when his trowel hit something solid.

"Dr. Goodrich – I think we've found something."

The archaeologist stepped down into the trench. She took the small trowel offered by Maggie, and she started to scrape soil away carefully from the solid object Johnny had unearthed.

Gradually, the corner of a rough hewn stone came into view. She brushed away the last of the soil, and felt the stone. It was warm to the touch. *Granite*, she thought, and her training and knowledge kicked in - '*a felsic intrusive igneous rock that is granular and phaneritic in texture*'.

This particular stone was dark grey, obviously hewn by humans, with no signs of being weather worn. This was unusual for stones of this age, she thought. It would take further tests to confirm its origins and true, but she had a fair idea of these already.

They carried on uncovering the stone, following the exposed edge, first one way and then the other, until the marked area was fully revealed.

The test trench had exposed a two foot by five foot section of what the white flags indicated to be as a fourteen by four menhir. The flat face was entirely covered in the hewing marks of the tools of men long gone.

The archaeologist noticed something across the middle of the stone. One area was polished, with indented marks. She carefully brushed away the last of the soil that had compacted into the indented shapes.

Gradually, letters came into view. She could feel her heart racing, her mouth went suddenly dry and her head began spinning and Johnny had to grab her to prevent her from toppling over.

"Doc, what it it? Are you OK?"

Wanly, she answered, "Yes, yes, I'll be fine."

She carried on brushing until a line of lettering appeared.

ᛏᛗᛋᛗᛏ ᚷᚹᚱᛁᛏᛖᛗᚾᚾ ᚾᚢᛗᛏ ᚺ ᚾᚢᛈᛁᚠᚢ

(NOSON GWYNTOEDD DUON Y DUWIAU)

"We've found it!" she exclaimed.

"Found what?" asked Johnny.

Dr. Goodrich ignored him.

Instead, she said, "Carry on clearing the entire stone. I have to call someone."

She stepped out of the trench and moved a little distance away from the others. She took out her cell phone and punched a number she had on speed dial.

The call was answered almost immediately.

She whispered loudly into the phone, excitedly.

"We've found it. Yes, it's where you said it would be...."

She stopped mid sentence at the sound of a pop and the sound of a body falling. A shadow above her dimmed the sun. She looked up directly into the barrel of a WE Makarow W65UK pistol.

Dr. Goodrich looked beyond Àla's outstretched hand and erect body to see the lifeless forms of Johnny and Maggie slumped in the test trench. She could see a dart embedded in the chest of each intern. Open mouthed, she dropped the cell phone on the floor. Àla raised the gun.

"No!"

On the other end of the phone, Professor Weiss heard the slight 'poomph' of a suppressor, and the sound of a body falling.

He called out.

"Dr. Goodrich…Susan…Sue…Sis?"

He heard nothing but the background noise of the wind rustling in the trees and the birds singing. The signal suddenly went dead, the phone crushed under the hiking boot of the intern, Àla.

ABOUT THE AUTHOR

Michael A Gilby is a former teacher with thirty years experience in education. In 1995/96 he wrote and produced the first interactive multimedia CD-ROM to teach Welsh as a second language. Working with technology specialists and television and radio celebrities, Michael and the team's work was nominated for a technology BAFTA in 1997.

As Director of Content at CDSM Interactive Solutions, he was one of a team of talented instructional designers producing award winning learning materials for high profile clients.

There followed a period as a Content Producer with BBC Cymru Wales, during which time he wrote educational copy for a range of products across multiple platforms. He co-wrote the "BBC Learn Welsh Grammar Guide", released in 2004 but which is still a standard resource in the teaching and learning of Welsh as a Second Language.

Michael returned to the classroom and finished his teaching career in Jersey in the Channel Islands. In semi-retirement, he undertook short stints teaching English to Adults in a language college, as an office administrator with a technology company and as a trainee in the finance industry. He is now a writer, journalist and author.

"The Mystery of Strangway Tower" is his first novel.

WATCH OUT FOR MORE
UP AND COMING
AGENCY MYSTERIES
from

MICHAEL A GILBY

THE
LUNCHTIME CLUB
DETECTIVE
AGENCY

THE MYSTERY OF HITLER'S LOST ART

From 1935, the Nazis plundered loot from across Europe, and, as they faced defeat in 1945, frantically hid it from the advancing Allied forces.

Some works were stashed away within Germany, while other pieces were smuggled out of Berlin by high-ranking Hitler henchmen to fund their own escapes and new lives. As the numbers of Nazi leaders lessened, so the secret locations of much of the loot were lost forever.

A forensic antiquarian thinks that he may have found clues as to the whereabouts of priceless artwork.

Professor Thomas Edison Weiss and his Lunchtime Club Detective Agency travel to Jersey, one of Hitler's most heavily fortified military locations.

It is also home to four of the intrepid Agents - Maps, Fax, Cat and Blink. The antiquarian, Sean Roper and his daughter, Sammie, go missing just hours before the location of the treasure is to be internationally revealed.

The authorities claim that they may have perished in a boating accident, and have abandoned any searches or rescue missions. Fax and

Cat know differently - their Uncle Sean was too good a sailor to be lost at sea in this way.

Professor Thomas Edison Weiss and his Lunchtime Club Detective Agency set out to find the relatives of two of their own. And to reveal the secret of Hitler's Lost Art.

THE MYSTERY OF STAR GAZER

Star Gazer is the most advanced satellite ever developed. It has technology aboard that can detect light from the farthest reaches of space, not just the radio signals generated by distant objects in this vast universe. The sensors on board can even detect dark matter and dark energy.

NASA led the other National Space Agencies in its $10 billion development, but two Lunchtime Club Agents were part of the project team because of their unique skill sets. Three days after launch the signal to Star Gazer is lost. At the same time, Chuck and Spex go missing. So does the artefact stolen three years ago from the museum in Dalton County from a secure US Government facility in Wyoming.

Is the elusive Strangway back? Professor Thomas Edison Weiss and his Lunchtime Club Detective Agency set out to find their friends, and to find out if their nemesis, De Montfort St. John Strangway III, is behind these events. What evil might he be perpetrating now?

Professor Thomas Edison Weiss and his Lunchtime Club Detective Agency set out to find two of their fellow Agents, and friends. And to thwart the plans of their nemesis.

THE MYSTERY OF THE LOST GOLDMINE

A map is found leading to the legendary goldmine of Dioses Di Oro, supposedly located somewhere in southern Texas. The gold has strange qualities. It is the purest form of gold possible, but it is said to be harder than tungsten but lighter than balsa wood. A tiny artefact said to be from the mine was tested, and it amazed scientists.

It displayed properties which suggested that if it were used in an alloy with 'normal' gold, it would render silicone based processors obsolete. When the map and artefact are stolen, the world receives the shocking news that De Montfort St. John Strangway III is back - again. Worse, he is after the gold. And he'll stop at nothing to get it.

Professor Thomas Edison Weiss and his Lunchtime Club Detective Agency set out to foil their arch nemesis.

The Mystery of the Missing Marque

There are believed to be 27 copies of the original Declaration of Independence left in the world. The 28th is discovered behind a wall in a Nantucket fishing cottage.

It is unique in that it has an additional signatory, James Symbold-Smythe. He was an English aristocrat who fought on the American side. On the reverse side of the broadsheet is a Letter of Marque and Reprisal allowing any and all relatives, current and future, of James Symbold-Smythe to seize goods, chattels and citizens of the newly formed nation as payment for the family's loyalty.

A descendent of James Symbold-Smythe has been hunting for this document for years. He is well known to the Agency - it's their nemesis, De Montfort St. John Strangway III!

Professor Thomas Edison Weiss and his Lunchtime Club Detective Agency set out once again in search of their elusive foe.

The Mystery of the Lost Mysteries

Have you ever heard of the Acambaro Figurines? The Map of the Creator? The Aluminium Wedge of Aiud? The Lycurgus Cup? The Iron Pillar of Qutb? The Baghdad Battery? The Dropa Stone? The Piri Reis map?

They are mysterious objects - often referred to as Out Of Place Artefacts - or OOPARTs for short - that many say they simply should not exist. Whatever their origin, provenance, their plausibility or their authenticity, someone wants them.

These, and many more - have disappeared from museums and collections from around the world. Who has been stealing these priceless enigmatic objects? More importantly, why?

Professor Thomas Edison Weiss and his Lunchtime Club Detective Agency set out to answer that very question.

The Mystery of the Fundamental Element

Life began on Earth nearly 4 billion years ago. The questions often asked, though, are: What conditions allowed life to emerge? How quickly after the planet coalesced from a mess of dust and gas did chemicals organise themselves into self-replicating, evolving systems - into Life itself? And what evidence of that original life would still remain after billions of years?

One scientist thinks that he has found the answer: an element called Quodium - the Fundamental Element. He was due to release his findings to the world in an event to be broadcast worldwide. But he and his work disappears.

Professor Thomas Edison Weiss and his Lunchtime Club Detective Agency has one week to find Professor Graves…. because Quodium can be used to produce a bomb many thousands of times more powerful that any nuclear device yet developed. It has the potential of becoming an ELE: an Extinction Level Event, a planet destroyer.

He is the only one with the knowledge to disarm the device. He is also Tec's uncle.

The Mystery of Taylor's Lost Week

The 46th President of the United States of America, John Trenton Taylor went missing for a week from Camp David. Nobody was knew what had happened. One day, he didn't come down for breakfast.

Despite a covert world wide search, there was no sign of the President. One week later, he came down to breakfast as usual - to a media furore the likes of which had never been seen before. He knew nothing about any lost week. He'd gone to bed as normal, and woken up as normal. Nothing was medically wrong with him. Nothing disastrous had befallen his beloved country. However, he was confused.

John Trenton Taylor liked to think of himself as being ahead of the game, and he didn't like being confused or in the dark. So he asked his friend, Professor Thomas Edison Weiss and his Lunchtime Club Detective Agency, to solve the mystery of his lost seven days.

The Mystery of the Bi Xi Dragon

Bi Xi is the eldest of the Dragon King's nine sons, and is so hugely strong that out can carry the problems of the Chosen People on its back. It's sacred bones are said to be held in a secret monastery hidden somewhere along the 13,171 mile length of natural defensive barriers of what are collectively known as the Great Wall of China.

Shanghai is the world's most populous city. The city and its hinterland covers 2,448 square miles, and is home to nearly 25 million people. But they are in danger from a nuclear catastrophe which China's best scientists cannot avert.

A friend of Professor Weiss, Dr. Jian Da, known widely as Rè hé yīshēng, is a world renowned thermonuclear scientist. He has a theory that the there is some truth to the fable that the shell of Bi Xi is strong enough to survive Tàiyáng bàozhà, the dreaded Sun Blast, and so protect the the city and its people.

Professor Thomas Edison Weiss and his Lunchtime Club Detective Agency owe China a debt of gratitude for finding two of their number, and so they offer their services to the search for Dr... Jian Da. The respected scientist is also grandfather to Spex. However, someone else is also looking for Bi Xi, and their intentions are not as honourable.

The Mystery of Snow Island

Atlantis, El Dorado, Cockaigne, Beimmeni, Ys, Tir na nÓg, Agartha, Cantre'r Gwaelod, Lemuria, Themiscyra, Homeland of Dr..uze - these are all legendary lands that persist in the human consciousness.

They are inhabited by gods, mythical beasts, beings with extraordinary powers and untold wealth. However they are just stories, passed down through the ages through cultures, or from one culture to another.

The Island of Snow is one of these places. Supposedly located between Australia and South America, it was a tropical island of wondrous things, protected by a colossal blizzard of swirling snow that encircled it.

Shipwreck survivors talked of its creatures, the people living there, and their eternal youth. No one believed these poor, deranged souls, Dr..iven half mad by hunger, thirst and fear. That is until Janic Biss was picked up by a cruise liner full of passengers paying to watch whales.

He claimed to have evidence: photographs and videos on a smartphone. Sometime during the voyage, however, Biss and his phone disappear from the USCS Molokai.

Professor Thomas Edison Weiss and his Lunchtime Club Detective Agency are asked by the cruise liner's owners to find both. Little did they know that they were about to face their arch nemesis once more.

The Mystery of MacGillycuddy's Reeks

Many animals died out soon after the Ice Age ended in Britain 11,700 years ago: the woolly mammoth, woolly rhinoceros, straight-tusked elephant, the scimitar-toothed cat, the cave bear, the auroch to name but a few.

One day, a climber wanders into a pub in the town of Tomies, County Kerry, with stories of a huge stag he saw in the mists of Carrauntoohil Mountain. He claimed that the antlers had a spread longer than himself.

Strangely, the locals didn't ridicule him. The Giant, as locals called it, was seen regularly, along with with other strange animals. Yet, none had ever been found or captured.

Brendan Ó Brosnacháin, zoologist and nephew of the Irish Prime Minister, Mary Ahearn, puts together a team from Trinity College, Dublin to research these strange sightings.

When the team vanishes, Prime Minister Ahearn calls in the army, but to no avail. So, she calls upon the assistance of an old friend.

Professor Thomas Edison Weiss and his Lunchtime Club Detective Agency travel to the Emerald Isle to look for Brendan. However, they find more than they bargained for.

The Mystery of the Hollow Earth Theory

The eccentric founder of a multinational technology company, MultiTek, decided to test an obsession he had held since he was a boy. At the age of twelve he read a book by the explorer and adventurer, R.K. Telford-James, called "Hollow Earth".

In the book, Telford-James hypothesized that there are huge interlinked hollows within the Earth's crust which are home to one of the most advanced technological cultures ever known. It had been his quest since a young boy to explore the myth of the Lost City of Atlantis. With his massive wealth, he was now able to turn his dreams into reality.

Extensive research had led his team of scientists, anthropologists, archaeologists, geologists and technologists to a mountainous, jungle-clad island called St. Aba Mina, which lay in the North Atlantic Ocean, between Bermuda, Miami, and San Juan, Puerto Rico, within the area commonly known as the Bermuda Triangle.

Their initial test dig sites had thrown up nothing. The lead scientist, Dr. Phillip Taylor, was not overly concerned, as the island of St. Aba Mina is forty miles by eighteen miles – 720 square miles of jungle to explore.

One day, he walked into the dense jungle, and didn't return. No amount of looking by his team could locate the whereabouts of Dr.

Philip Taylor. Over the coming days, one by one, members of the team disappeared. Eventually, the Assistant Team Leader, archaeologist Dr. Jane Eriksson, puts out a mayday call for assistance.

The news reached President John Trenton Taylor. He was so concerned that he called upon Professor Edison Weiss and his Agency. The President wanted to find out what happened to his brother...

What the Professor and the Agents found would astound the world.

The Mystery of the Lost Population

The Channel Islands – an archipelago of dozens of islands in the English Channel between Mainland Britain and France. Herm is one of the least populated islands in the Channel Islands – it is home to only 60 full time inhabitants, though this usually went up to over 2,000 at any one time during the summer vacation months.

The grandmother of Fax and Cat, Agents with the Lunchtime Detective Agency, Mama Michelle, was born and raised there, and went through the German Occupation. Since being in Austrey for their studies, they would visit Mama Michelle every time they were back in Jersey.

On this summer vacation from Austrey High, Craig used the family rib powerboat to take Fax and Cat to visit their grandmother and arrived at Herm Harbour to find the small fishing and leisure-craft port deserted.

The entire island of Herm is deserted. When they get to Mama Michelle's home, her half eaten lunch is on the table, the tea in the teapot is still warm enough to drink. Walking from home to home, they find the same thing. Pans boiling dry, washing machines in mid cycle, music playing, televisions showing the midday news or soap operas.

In the bar of the famous White House Hotel ice in drinks hadn't melted, in some rooms, taps or showers were still running. But no staff or guests.

As they wandered, they saw that even the fields were empty of animals. What could have happened for an entire population to vanish in this way – it was an island-wide version of the Marie Celeste.

Craig contacted his boss and described the situation. Fax and Cat's father, formerly Commandant Michel Le Maine of a French DALAT unit, has called upon his friend and former United Nations co-Special Forces colleague, Professor Weiss, and the rest of his amazing Detective Agency for a favour.

"Ed - please find my mother...."

Professor Weiss and the Lunchtime Club Detective Agency unravelled a mystery that went back to the Occupation.